BEWARE OF DOGS

BEWARE OF DOGS

ELIZABETH FLANN

HarperCollins*Publishers*

HarperCollins*Publishers*
Australia • Brazil • Canada • France • Germany • Holland • Hungary
India • Italy • Japan • Mexico • New Zealand • Poland • Spain • Sweden
Switzerland • United Kingdom • United States of America

First published in Australia in 2021
by HarperCollins*Publishers* Australia Pty Limited
Level 13, 201 Elizabeth Street, Sydney NSW 2000
ABN 36 009 913 517
harpercollins.com.au

A catalogue record for this book is available from the National Library of Australia.

ISBN 978 1 4607 5903 5 (paperback)
ISBN 978 1 4607 1274 0 (ebook)
ISBN 978 1 4607 8440 2 (audiobook)

Cover design by HarperCollins Design Studio
Cover images by shutterstock.com
Map illustration by Dr Steve Sinclair
Typeset in Berthold Baskerville by Kirby Jones
Printed and bound in Australia by McPherson's Printing Group
The papers used by HarperCollins in the manufacture of this book are a natural, recyclable
product made from wood grown in sustainable plantation forests. The fibre source and
manufacturing processes meet recognised international environmental standards, and carry
certification.

In Memoriam

I would like to dedicate this book to Judith Rodriguez who gave me unstinting help and encouragement throughout its early development, but sadly did not live to see the final result.

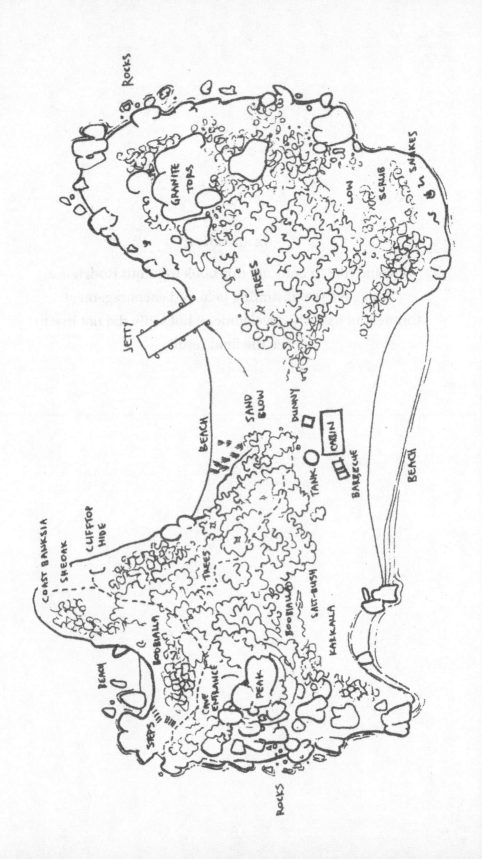

CHAPTER ONE

Karkalla *(Carpobrotus rossii)*

Also known as Pigface, these plants are found in dry, rocky and sandy locations. The flowers are pink or purple and the horned, fleshy fruits are purplish-red. Every part of them is edible or can be used for medicinal purposes. The fleshy leaves can be eaten raw or cooked, and the fruits have been described as tasting like salty strawberries, fresh figs or kiwifruit. With the fruits I find it best to peel off the outer skin and suck out the soft pulpy seed mass. Karkalla leaves are also salty enough to use for seasoning cooked meats if no salt is available.

Professor Atkinson's *Guide to
Bushcraft for Geology Students*

FIELD DIARY - Friday 13 April

Not much daylight left now. So why waste it on writing a diary no-one is going to read? But as my heart stops pounding and my pulse begins to slow I find myself falling into old habits: organise shelter for the night; write up field diary. Perhaps in some future time surveyors with theodolites will come to turn this island into desirable real estate. 'Sought-after location, split-level design, ocean views'. They will stumble across my mouldering remains and read my diary to find out what happened. What will it tell them? How can I find the words? I can't even begin to make sense of how I got to this place, so perhaps I should start by describing my surroundings.

My refuge is not a true cavern. It could best be described as a shallow rock shelter gouged progressively by pounding waves in primeval days when the sea level was much higher. It has a narrow slanted entrance, clean dry air quality, and a half-circle of small ceiling holes letting in a surprising amount of daylight. Although not large, it has a number of advantages. I noticed some of these when I first explored it, but in my new and different circumstances I was afraid that it might turn out to be dank and fetid or, worse, too small for occupation. It's fortunate that I'm not claustrophobic because, particularly with the tree masking the entrance, it's a pretty close fit. Still, there's not much chance I'll be putting on any weight.

Taking stock, I have between me and starvation a 100 gram bag of sultanas, a 100 gram bag of peanuts, six stems of fruiting karkalla (about nine fruits), and two honey menthol lozenges (found in the pocket of my anorak). In the morning I will use

the tiny specimen bags I always keep stuffed into the
pockets of my pack to divide the nuts and sultanas
into daily rations. This will be a nice quiet activity.
Since I cannot risk going out in daylight, I'll need
to find things to do. I hear my father's voice, like a
phantom echo: *The Devil finds work for idle hands.* I
wish I had some music, though as I think this I know
that even with earphones it would be dangerous.
They could be right outside and I'd be too busy
jamming along to hear.

Suddenly, as if I've conjured it, a sound, a sharp
crack, shatters the silence. It's coming from the
seaward side and, pen in hand, I freeze. There's no
way they could have gone up there without my
hearing them. Although I know it must be a natural
occurrence – a falling branch perhaps or a fruit stone
dropped from a bird's beak – the desire to look is
almost overwhelming. I take some time to hug my
arms around my legs and rock myself calm, until
I gradually manage to muffle my rasping breaths.
What if I'm wrong? What if they are out there, taking
up position, ready? I have my weapons out, my knife
unsheathed, but in my heart I know there's no-one
there. Now that my breathing is back to normal I will
get back to describing the cave.

Just to the right and out of sight of the entrance
is an area a little above my height but without much
room for movement. Beyond this is a wider area with

a sandy floor, too low for me to stand. Sitting cross-legged, I can quite comfortably unpack and arrange my supplies, but I can't find any way of lying down, and getting up from this position is quite difficult. How am I going to sleep? I'll take my newly emptied pack and see if I can use it as a cushion to form some kind of sleeping space.

Keeping very quiet, *just in case*, I next sort out the contents of my pack. The water bottle, still full, I place in the far corner where there's no danger of knocking it over, covering it with my hat to keep out dust. The small plastic specimen bags go next to it, with their tangle of rubber bands, topped with the pack of much larger kitchen tidy bags I managed to scrounge this morning. They are weighted with the jagged rock I collected on the beach in case the time came to bash someone's head in, ensuring that it will be within easy reach when darkness comes. At first I don't know what to do with the food. What if something comes in, scavenging? (I don't want to think about this, but I must.) Are there goannas here? In the end I decide to wrap all the edible supplies in my anorak, twist it into a kind of sling and hang it by the sleeves from a tree root that snakes through the cave's roof.

But exhaustion makes me clumsy and the entire parcel crashes to the floor. Too tired and demoralised to care and drained by the effects of the tension of the past twenty-four hours, for some time all I can do is sit, cross-legged, head bowed, the cave so silent I can hear the seconds ticking by on my heavy-duty waterproof sports watch. When I finally open my eyes, it's appreciably darker, but the relief at finding the food bags unbroken gives me new energy and the second throw allows me to knot the sleeves into a functional swinging larder. Not much time left, but not much more to do.

My rock hammer and torch I line up on a small rock platform near the back of the cave, making sure the hammer, too, is within easy reach. I empty my pockets of compass, waterproof matches, pencils and pens and line them up on the floor. (Now, finally, I am reaping my reward for being prepared for most eventualities.) The only thing I keep with me is the scout knife that was a gift from my brother.

Then clothes. From inner pockets I extract socks, spare underwear and handkerchiefs. In the backpack are a long Amnesty International T-shirt, a tiny red pouch containing a bright-red emergency rain slicker (a gift from Kathryn) and a spare hat. I am still wearing the two T-shirts I had on when I left the cabin. The cave is not cold and I suspect I am overdressed, but I have no energy left to go through the contortions that would be required for taking my clothes off.

With the light fading fast, I fold all the unneeded clothes as flat as possible into the backpack and then squash it to form some semblance of a cushion. I take my water bottle, drink one mouthful of water and carefully pour another mouthful into the cup that functions as an extra lid, placing the cup close to where I plan to sleep. The bottle I reseal and put back in its spot at the rear of the cave, so I can't risk trying to drink in the dark and spilling the rest of my supply.

Then, sitting cross-legged again, with the pack between me and the wall as a very inadequate kind of pillow, in the last of the light I set the alarm on my watch for five a.m. Even at that hour, I can't risk sound, and set it to vibration mode. I don't think I'll have any trouble waking. *If* I manage to sleep. With the water beside me, handkerchief up my sleeve and knife in my hand, I wait for darkness. The time is 5.57 p.m. on Friday the 13th of April.

* * *

Now the cave is in total darkness. I can't see to write but my mind is spinning like a crazy wheel. All I can do is close my eyes and listen to my thoughts …

I had forgotten the thick dead blackness of the inside of a cave, even a shallow cave like this one. As soon as the light goes I begin hearing things – rustlings, patterings, *slitherings*. This could be any kind of creature's lair. I rack my brain for likely contenders. Bats? I don't mind bats, but

I don't think so. Anyway, they're nocturnal. I would have seen them asleep, hanging like velvety black corrugations from the roof. Not bats. Spiders? There's been no sign of spiders or webs, and most cave spiders are harmless, as far as I know. This is not much comfort as my skin rehearses the experience of fat hairy bodies using me as a ladder, or a sleeping platform. I shudder, feeling tiny feet creeping across my face. I brush my face frantically, to no avail, there's nothing there, and try to force my thoughts away from creeping, slimy, slithering creatures. Especially slithering ...

Dreams. Of someone (Dave?) locking me in a dungeon, where I fall down a chute into black, black water. I'm choking, drowning, losing consciousness ...

... and wake into a state of instant paralysing terror. The darkness feels soft and thick, like the wings of a moth. I pull back my sleeve and the luminous dial of my watch glows eerily, its hands showing 2.16 a.m. I've slept. I do a quick calculation. An amazing eight hours. My back is cricked and aching and without thinking I go to stand up. *Crack.* My skull hits rock and there's an acrid taste of blood. The pain is excruciating, but I'm afraid to move. I can't remember the configuration of the cave, where I am, what's around me. I can't see a thing, and have to force myself not to panic.

The longing for light becomes obsessive. I know my torch is nearby, but I also know I can't risk using it in case the beam shows through the roof holes. Torchlight looks like nothing in nature. Can I risk lighting a match? Slowly, with every muscle screaming, I lean in what I think is the direction of my supplies, hand closing on something metallic. Pen. Reach to the right. Pencils. Which side are the matches on? I struggle to remember. Other side of the pen. Finally I find them and with much fumbling succeed in striking a light. Overwhelmed by the utterness of the darkness, it flickers feebly and goes out, after illuminating nothing beyond my hand, corpse-white in the surrounding blackness. I hear whimpering, and go cold until I realise it is coming from me. *Kop op!* I tell myself, just as I used to do as a child. *Get a grip on yourself, Alix. Deep, deep breaths. Calm down.* It can only be two and a half hours at most until daylight.

I sit back, and my parched throat lets me know I'm thirsty. Slowly, carefully, I feel along the rock floor for the water cup, trying to make my movements as gentle as a butterfly's wing, terrified of knocking it over. My finger touches plastic and I manage to close my hand around the cup without spilling anything. When I sip the water tastes dusty, but comforting. I eke it out, taking an extraordinary pleasure in each sip, wetting my lips with my tongue. I realise also that I'm hungry, haven't eaten since lunchtime yesterday. I decide to apportion my food into two meals a day, one at eight a.m. and a lighter one at noon. Just making a decision makes me feel irrationally better.

What can you do to fill up hours when you can't move and can't see? My neck is killing me, my head still throbs and my knees tell me I'm getting too old for this kind of game. I try counting the minutes, but thoughts get in the way. I begin to wonder when someone will notice I'm missing, and a terrible realisation hits me. *Will* anyone notice? So independent, so in control of my life, I might just as well not exist. Work thinks I'm on holiday. Kathryn thinks I've floated off into the sunset with a potential Mr Right. For at least another week, possibly two, there's only the remotest possibility that anyone will wonder where I am.

I'm very aware that I have flouted Professor Atkinson's Golden Rule for Survival, which he hammered into our heads at the beginning of every class, shouting in his eagerness to be heard: 'I cannot stress too strongly that, whatever else you may disregard, do not neglect the first and most important rule: Always leave information about where you are going with a responsible person.'

I can picture the professor wagging a remonstrative finger if he could see me now. I wish I had the little pocket book the university printed out to go with his lectures, but here I find my photographic memory, which has served me so well in fast-tracking my academic career, is proving its value again. I can remember quite a lot of it pretty much word-for-word, especially the descriptions of bush food, which had particularly interested me. But some of the even more crucial things that hadn't seemed so important at the time I cannot remember at all, like many of the bush methods for obtaining water.

For someone who is normally absolutely meticulous in letting the right people know, in packing for all exigencies, in being prepared, I've been shockingly careless. The problem is that although I'm so steeped in the lore of bushcraft, this time, this one time, I had no idea I would be going into the bush. Mainly because Dave made sure that I had no idea.

It's no excuse. No excuse at all.

And if anyone does miss me, no one knew where I was going. Except Dave. Who's not going to tell. Did I leave any clues? How could I have when *I* didn't know where I was going? I try to recall the last time I saw Kathryn. *If it wasn't for Kathryn I wouldn't be here.* I hear this thought in the back of my mind but I know it is not the whole truth. This is not her fault or mine. No sane person could have foreseen the situation I am now in.

Kathryn knew I was going away for the Easter weekend with Dave. But did she know his other name? I don't think so. Did I tell her where he lives, still in the same old place? I might have. *He isn't there, though, is he? He's here.* I still don't know Matt's other name or anything about him really, except that he's a psychopath. Even if Kathryn did track him down he'd easily manage to hide that little fact from her. She likes to think well of men.

Lana might be another matter, but since I hadn't met Lana before we got on the boat, I could hardly have mentioned her.

I was pleased with myself, I remember that. 'I might be going away after all,' I told Kathryn. 'With a blast from the past.'

'I didn't think you had that kind of a past. You've always said Jonathan was your one and only.'

'Dave's not "that kind",' I remember telling her, already slightly annoyed. 'He lived next door to Jonathan and me. That's all.'

That probably didn't register with Kathryn. She had just met her latest Mr Right and could barely spare any time to spend with me, so she was probably feeling a bit guilty about not being available when I finally needed her. I think she was trying to ease her conscience by making sure I had somewhere to go.

'At least you might meet someone there. No-one has parties any more, but they're a great way to mingle.'

Although I'm younger than Kathryn, she constantly points out that my chances of meeting 'the right man' are equally slim. I used to find this amusing. Having failed so horrendously in my first relationship, I wasn't at all sure I wanted to try again. But now that almost everyone I know from work, university, and recently even rock-climbing, has married and dropped out of normal life, Kathryn is pretty much my only social contact. It has become an issue, with her requests for me to join her on what she calls 'double dates' becoming more and more intrusive. And even though Kathryn's brief conquests usually seem more unexciting than dangerous, I guess I'm a bit warier of strangers than she is.

My boss had been blunt when I resisted the idea of taking leave. 'Use it or lose it, Alix. I see here you haven't had any leave at all since you started.' I continued to argue, about projects that needed me, about wanting more time to make travel plans, but he was adamant. 'Use it or lose it.' I didn't want to lose it so I gave in.

'You could enjoy yourself, Alix. People do that on holidays. Go to Noosa, go horseback riding, see some movies.'

I didn't want to go to Noosa. I didn't want to go horseback riding. And all the Easter films seemed to be aimed at children under five. There wasn't even any climbing to be had. Everyone I knew was spending Easter with their family – or Mr or Ms Right.

I managed to fill up the first few days by getting my teeth checked, my eyes checked, even making an appointment with my local clinic for a general physical checkup. They were able to tell me what I already knew, that I was in very good condition. This would have been welcome news if I'd been planning some extreme rock-climbing, but at least I had enough sense not to try that on my own.

By the time the fourth day came around I was thoroughly bored. On my kitchen wall was an invitation to a photographic exhibition in my old stamping ground, St Kilda, a few doors from where I used to live with Jonathan. The cover was a stunning picture of sun rays reflecting off a rocky cliff. I looked at it and thought, well, I am on holiday, I'd better do something at least slightly festive.

And I found, to my profound relief, that St Kilda held no ghosts any more. When I emerged, energised by the extraordinary scenes of mountains and rocks, I decided to extend the experience by treating myself to a drink at a familiar and lively bar next to the local backpackers.

As I struggled through the throng in search of a vacant bar stool, I suddenly found myself face to face with David Grogan, very much, as I told Kathryn, a blast from the past. And yet someone I found myself not particularly pleased to see, for reasons I couldn't put my finger on at the time. Dave was certainly pleased to see me. 'Alix!' he said. 'Alix Verhoeven! Long time!' And he grinned, a strangely familiar I'm-just-the-boy-next-door grin and I can remember thinking, *Oh well. He may be irritating, but at least he's not dangerous.*

And soon I had a drink in my hand and found myself being introduced to 'my boss and co-conspirator. This is Matt.' Something about Matt made me uneasy. Perhaps it was the slight flash of pain when he shook my hand just a little too hard. More likely it was the way he launched straight into very personal questions.

'Do I detect a slight accent there? Where in the world do you come from, Alix?' Although he was good-looking in a clean-cut, Bondi lifesaver sort of way, there was something about the unblinking stare from those piercingly blue eyes that was just a little bit creepy.

Compared with this, Dave looked even more ordinary than usual. Nondescript hair, mid-brown eyes, shorter and stockier in build, he looked like the lesser version, the sidekick to the Golden Boy. For no obvious reason, I felt uncomfortable in their presence and found myself backing away, trying to find a gap in the conversation so that I could leave, but somehow, somewhere along the line, with all their relentless questioning they found out that I was on three weeks' holiday, and didn't have anywhere to go for Easter.

Dave was delighted, bouncing like an excited puppy. 'This is perfect, Alix. Matt's having a house party for Easter. You've got to come. Can't have you all on your little lonesome, can we?' He turned to Matt and they exchanged a look that I couldn't interpret. 'How about that? Poor Alix doesn't have any family or anything. She's absolutely on her own.'

Matt took his time. I had the impression he was the kind of person who pauses before speaking to ensure that everyone is giving him their full attention. 'I think you're right. Alix could be perfect.' I didn't register at the time what an odd response that was.

'I don't think so. I've got things to do.' That's me. Ms Cautious. But not, in the end, cautious enough. 'But thanks for the invitation.'

'Oh, come on, Alix. You'd love the place. Very outdoorsy. Cliffs and beaches. Just your kind of thing.'

And Matt said, turning those unblinking ice-blue eyes on me, 'And we're a bit low on females, aren't we, Dave?' You'd think that would have alerted me, but no.

When I told Kathryn about this, what did I tell her? What did I know? I didn't accept it at the time. In fact

I didn't think any more about it. But Dave called me up the next day to make arrangements. He found my phone number and *tracked me down*. Why didn't I realise how sinister that was? I'm very careful about online security, and I'm not on social media. 'How did you find me?' I asked him, and he laughed.

'You can find anyone if you know where to look. How many Verhoevens do you think there are in Melbourne?' (Twelve. I checked. And I don't know any of them.) He tracked me down and sweet-talked me. And here I am.

'Matt has a house party every year … Cliffs and beaches.' He didn't mention the boat. Or the island. So the most Kathryn could possibly remember was that I was going to the beach with someone called Dave. That should narrow it down.

I run the afternoon's events over and over in my mind, but can't come up with anything new. And I'm so tired …

Dreams. Of Dave saying 'I always knew I'd get you in the end.' Of running, falling into a hole, and black creatures hovering over me, pressing closer and closer.

They press on my face and I begin to scream …

I wake with a cry to find light creeping in through the holes in the cave roof. For a moment relief floods me as my surroundings begin to take shape and form. Then new fears set in. What if my cry has been heard? I don't think there's much likelihood of their coming in the dark, but it means I cannot risk sleeping at all during the day. How am I going to fill twelve hours of daylight in a space where

I can barely turn around? My bladder reminds me that sometime soon I am going to have to leave my shelter. The very thought terrifies me, but the alternative is too horrible to consider.

It would take them at least half an hour to get to this place from the cabin, so I estimate that I can allow twenty minutes to find a suitable toilet spot and stretch my stiff and aching legs. Torn between the longing to move and the knowledge that when I do the pain will be terrible, I remain in my cramped position. If it wasn't for the urgent message from my bladder, I don't think I'd be able to move at all, but somehow I force myself to crawl slowly to the entrance of the cave, where I try to stand up. My body is so knotted that for a moment I don't think I'll be able to do it, and then when I do the pain is so intense I almost pass out. Slowly, every muscle screaming at me to stop, I inch my way to the entrance. Shaking, heart pounding, I move aside the tree I set to block the entrance, and am temporarily blinded by the full force of the sunlight.

CHAPTER TWO

In an emergency situation, as a guide to prioritising
and planning, bushcraft should take into account
the 'rule of three', which states that a human being
can survive:

- **3 minutes** without air
- **3 hours** without shelter in extreme circumstances
- **3 days** without water
- **3 weeks** without food

Atkinson's Guide

FIELD DIARY - Saturday 14 April

It's now almost three o'clock as I prepare for my
second night in the cave. I have done everything
that can reasonably be done to make this a better
night than the previous one, but I'm not very
hopeful. In some ways the day was worse than the
night, and just as terrifying, but I'm confident I can
survive, at least until the food runs out. Now that
I've discovered the best and the worst about my
shelter, I find myself longing for the kind of cave

depicted in the children's books left behind by the British missionaries. (These books were far more influential on me than the more formal texts used by my mother for improving our English. I was deeply disappointed when I first arrived in England to find that their jolly descriptions of ginger beer, crystal-clear mountain streams and friendly smiling people were cruelly false.)

The caves in those stories were always light and roomy and bedded with soft white sand. While sitting immobile in my not-so-perfect cave waiting for time to pass, I have visualised my own ideal cave in loving detail. It has a natural ledge for sitting on, a stone basin that collects cool, clean rainwater and a hidden spyhole from which to survey the surrounding terrain. The entrance is naturally concealed behind a clump of living bush and, this is the best bit, there is a secret tunnel to the beach, making it possible to steal out at dawn and wash myself and my clothes (not that the English children ever did this). Close to the cave are banks of heather that can be harvested to make a comfortable, fragrant, springy bed.

My cave is nothing like this. It is narrow and cramped, the floor is rocky, and the two natural ledges are too high or too low for seating. There is no water in the cave (although this is also one of its advantages), and no way to see out, or to reach the beach. I don't know which I hanker after more, the possibility of being able to see what's going on outside, or the possibility of having a wash. No, that's not true. Of course my greatest wish is to be able to see what's coming. But it is also this lack of viewpoint that makes the cave so secure, and although no trees naturally grow over the entrance, I uprooted one when I found the cave yesterday morning and stuffed it across the narrow slit in the cliff. Even if it dies, it should provide an effective screen if anyone comes, unless their search is exceptionally thorough. It wouldn't fool a ranger or an experienced bushwhacker, but I don't think Dave or Matt would know a dead tree from a live one, especially in this terrain.

My Australian friends would be panicking about the lack of bathroom facilities. Not that I wouldn't enjoy a shower right now, but it's not looming in my mind the way the food problem looms. Kathryn would be in trouble. When we leave to go anywhere, even just for a coffee, she walks right up close and whispers, 'Sniff me, Alix. Do I smell?' She has an almost pathological horror of what she calls 'crotch-stink', although any natural smell emanating from her body would be so totally masked by the heavy perfume she wears it would be quite unrecognisable. I wonder if she performs this sniffing ritual with men. It might explain why she has so much trouble finding a lasting partner.

Although I'm dreading another night, the day, apart from my fear of discovery, went slightly better than expected. In fact if it hadn't been for the constant worrying it wouldn't have been too bad at all. The early morning toilet run was far and away the worst part. By the time I'd unknotted my muscles enough to make a few shaky steps, it was already fully light. Hobbling out from the shelter of the cave into the blinding glare was the most terrifying moment. My sight didn't clear for a good thirty seconds, and even when I could see, I could barely move. If Dave or Matt had been there I'd have had no chance.

My body was screaming at me to take things slowly, but I knew I had no time to spare. The branches I'd used to cover my footprints on the journey to the cave were still where I'd left them in the undergrowth, and I took a couple of branches with me as I searched for a suitable spot to relieve myself. About thirty metres from the cave entrance I found a circle of dense shrubs with a shallow dip in the middle and a thick ground covering of leaf litter. There were some old animal scats, mammalian by the look of them, which worried me a little, but I couldn't imagine anything that could pose a danger to me. Having decided that this would be the place for my toilet, I then had to find a way to do the deed. At such moments I would give anything for a penis, although I don't think this is quite the kind of envy Freud had in mind.

I had carried a weapon in each hand (knife and rock), so I carefully placed them out of range on the ground, and cleared a wide circle in the leaf litter. With some considerable pain because of the stiffness in my arms, I pulled down my jeans and underpants, and tried to squat down, straddling my legs at the same time. Any woman who has ever been in this predicament, fully dressed in jeans and boots, will know what a challenge it presents. The pain in my legs was a great deal more acute than in my arms, and I was afraid they wouldn't hold out. I didn't want to fall flat on my face before I'd even finished. It was no use wishing for toilet paper, because apart from being an environmental hazard, it's also a stark giveaway of human presence. It was all I could do to pull everything up and then stand up myself. Next time it would make sense to choose a spot closer to a tree, and use the trunk as a pulley. The urge to wash my hands was ridiculously strong, even though I hadn't touched anything beyond waistbands. *It's all in your mind, Alix.*

Once I'd buried the evidence and also covered any tracks that led to the spot I allowed myself a few minutes to stretch my legs and explore a bit. A little to the right of my original track there was a small hollow wooded with what looked like boobialla and coast banksia. I didn't have time to check it out at that moment but I decided to make it my goal for the following morning. The area I knew nothing at all about was the cliff beyond the cave. It was also out of sight of the approach and I would hear anyone coming before they saw me. Or so I hoped.

Ten nervous but productive minutes later I had a very much clearer picture of my environment. The cave is at the far north-west of the island, which reaches a low rocky peak of which the cave forms part of the base. Seen from this direction it was, as I had suspected, not a true cave at all, but a gap formed by the slippage of several large granite rocks one against the other, probably the result of a fairly major landslide, and then gouged out further by the tides. I didn't have time to climb to the clifftop, and anyway it would be too risky without ropes. I couldn't afford to fall. Not that there seemed to be much up there, but I'd have liked to check out the provenance of the roof holes.

Instead I walked carefully (trying to step on rock where possible) to the end of a flat natural path that led to a conglomeration of boulders. When I reached the end of it I found, to my great excitement, that a kind of rough rocky staircase led down to a tiny sand and pebble beach, at the edge of which I could see a scatter of green and pinky-red. *Karkalla*. No time to explore further, but it raised my spirits. I calmed down enough though to erase any footprints with my leafy branch, which I took back into the cave with me, pulling the tree carefully across to cover the entrance as thoroughly as possible.

One other thing I noticed on my expedition was a flat weathered rock a little to the north-east of the rocky path to the sea, through which I thought I could see daylight. I made a mental note to check it out and see if it might not make a better toilet than the one in the bushes, which will quickly become uninhabitable. It's also closer, which would enable me to nick out and back in a minute or so if necessary. At least the lack of food has brought an accompanying constipation, but I'm a bit worried about the sultanas that will be making up half my diet from now on. One thing my line of work is good for is training the bladder, so I was able to last the whole day without discomfort, but I will have to go out night and morning.

As soon as I came back in, before sorting out the food, I made out a Day Survival Plan. (If I can think of any way of making a Night Survival Plan, I'll do that as well, but I don't think there's a lot of scope there.) I followed my plan religiously today, and found that it helped to break up the time. There were plenty of stretches of monotony, when I began to feel I couldn't stand it any longer, but just knowing there was an activity to come helped to a surprising extent. The plan also includes regular changes of position, plus the small number of exercises that are possible in this restricted space, and certainly I was not as uncomfortable at the end of today as I was after last night. This is how the plan went today.

Daybreak: Go outside for exercise and toilet.
Maximum twenty minutes from first light.
Nothing to add here really, except that I didn't realise how terrified I'd been until I was back inside and it took another twenty minutes for my heart rate and pulse to subside.

6.00–8.00 a.m.: Housekeeping. Organise food and supplies. Change clothes if necessary.
This was the busiest time. I worked out the clothing situation first, taking off my dirty T-shirt and putting it in the back pocket of my backpack, away from the clean clothes. I've decided to wear my knickers until they become uncomfortable and then hang them up to air near the roof of the cave. With two spare pairs, they should last about nine days, nearly as long as the food. I've got three pairs of socks in total so plan to change them also every few days. That will definitely give me something to look forward to.

Organising the food took a satisfyingly long time. I had to work out some way of decanting the contents of the food bags so I could count the nuts and sultanas out into smaller rations. I had thought I'd use my anorak as a tray but it was too dusty, so I tried a plastic bag, but they rolled around too much and I was afraid of losing some. I ended up having to retrieve the dirty T-shirt I'd just taken off, and it was fortunate I didn't use a clean one because it was even dirtier when I'd finished. The nuts left a patina of grease on the cotton surface, and then the sultanas, when I followed the same procedure with them, turned the grease into a sticky mess. I can't imagine when I'll be able to wash the shirt, so please God I won't need to wear it. I fervently hope it won't attract ants, and with this in mind have shoved it into a kitchen tidy bag and hung it from the tree root.

It's amazing how much you can spin out a job when you know there is absolutely nothing else to do. There were 196 peanuts in the 100 gram bag. My plan was to allow rations for ten days, an optimistic plan in some ways (thinking I'd survive for ten days) and a pessimistic one in others (thinking I'd have to). This meant I'd have twenty nuts a day for nine days, and sixteen for the tenth day. Sultanas must be a bit smaller because there were 220 in the 100 gram bag, dividing neatly into twenty-two per day. By the time I had very carefully counted out twenty nuts at a time, bagged them into specimen bags and sealed them with a rubber band, leaving the final sixteen in the original bag, and then done the same with the sultanas, it was 7.30 a.m. already. The two cough lozenges I bagged and put away for the future. I'm worried that they might make me thirsty, so I'll keep them as emergency rations. Thirst is becoming a problem and I could barely wait for food time, when I could finally have a drink. I must stick to the plan though, because once my water supply has gone I'm going to be in trouble. I haven't seen a sign of any other source of fresh water, and the bush methods of water-gathering I've been able to remember would be dangerously visible, putting them out of the question.

The karkalla plants were a welcome distraction from dreams of water and I took them from their bag and examined them carefully. The nine fruits I counted last night were all still clinging to the stem, but clearly would not keep for much longer, so I decided to have five of them as a snack in the middle of the day, and keep the other four for tomorrow. I think they'll make it that far. I spent the remaining time devising plans for getting down to the little rocky beach to harvest some more.

8.00–9.00 a.m.: First meal. Ration of nuts and sultanas. Small cup of water.
At eight o'clock precisely I poured a small cup of water and very slowly sipped until it was half gone. I'll have the rest just before nine. I managed to

extend this time by counting to thirty after each
sip, a trick I learned from a field hand when I was
working out at Norseman, but I still finished far too
quickly. I was worried that the food would make me
thirsty again, and very glad the nuts were not salted.
By then I was desperately hungry, and I counted
out ten from the twenty in the bag and crammed a
handful recklessly into my mouth. The remaining ten
I managed to eat in two lots, but it didn't make much
difference. With the sultanas, I was able to show
enough restraint to pick them out one at a time and
savour each one. I don't normally like sultanas, which
is why I pack them as emergency food. Nuts always
seem to burn a hole in my pack and I tend to declare
a state of emergency on any kind of pretext and eat
handfuls of them until they're gone, but sultanas
often remain to take the journey home with me.

These sultanas tasted sublime. By the time I got
to the last two I waited a full five minutes between
each one, and then sat enjoying the aftertaste, and
voluptuously running my tongue around my teeth for
any remnants. To my amazement this meagre repast
had taken over half an hour, and once I'd licked my
teeth over again it was almost time to drink the rest
of my water. There must have been sufficient fluid in
the sultanas to offset the sugar, because when nine
o'clock came my thirst was more comfortable than
raging, and I was able to stretch the experience out

for almost fifteen minutes, taking a sip, savouring it, thinking about it, then taking another. Mealtimes are definitely going to be the best part of the day.

10.00 a.m.–12.00 p.m.: Stand in entrance space.
Do any exercises possible in the space.
The next stage was the most uncomfortable. I had been sitting in the low space to do the sorting and to eat my rations. Now I had to force myself to get up and move to the standing space near the entrance to keep the blood flowing so my muscles wouldn't seize up.

This was quite a procedure. First, I did what exercises I could in the sitting position – neck rolls, hand rolls, ankle rolls, rocking from side to side. Unfortunately, there was not enough room for full arm rolls, but I tried to keep changing the position of my legs, from sitting cross-legged, changing from one foot to the other, to semi-kneeling (a position I couldn't keep up for very long). Then, and this has proved to be the most painful bit, I manoeuvred myself forward into a crawling position and half-crawled to the space near the entrance, when, still painfully, I slowly stood up.

There's a small stone ledge on the east wall of this space and I'd decided to try leaning against that to see if it was more comfortable. It wasn't exactly more comfortable, but it was less uncomfortable, and I found that there was enough room to do some leg-flexing exercises and to pump my lower arms in and out which, combined with the sitting exercises, might help alleviate the stiffness if I do them often enough. In fact since there's nothing I can do to distract me when in this standing position, regular sets of exercises are a welcome diversion.

12.00–1.00 p.m.: Return to sitting. Fruit snack if available. No water.
After a standing break, returning to the sitting position was much less painful, and I briefly wondered if it mightn't be a good idea to try to spend some of the night standing up. Then I remembered that the contortions necessary would be pretty much impossible to achieve in complete darkness, so I've abandoned that idea.

However, there's no doubt that any change of position helps, and I must be rigorous in sticking to the plan. To this end, I repeated the sitting exercises, and only when they were completed did I allow myself to pull out the karkalla and pick off one of the fruits.

I'm grateful that I took Professor Atkinson's summer school course to get to know the Australian flora. Not only do I know that karkalla is edible, but I have actually eaten it. Well, not the fruit, which wasn't available at the time, but the leaves, boiled up in a billy, bush-style. We also tried the leaves raw, so I know not to try them now. Apart from the saltiness, uncooked they have a sharp, rasping quality that leaves your mouth sore and parched, the last thing I need at the moment. I don't think they're actually poisonous, so if I reach a really low ebb I might have to try eating them, but for now I'll stick to the fruits, which are supposed to taste like strawberries.

These fruits tasted like no strawberry I've ever had, but they were certainly edible. A bit sweetish, rather watery, more like a fig or a kiwifruit, but not as nice. However, I had no trouble eating my five allotted fruits, (skins and all, despite Professor A's suggestions), and found them watery enough not to need a drink. This was fortunate, because only two small drinks a day are permitted in the plan, and even on this regime, I'll run out of water in just a few days.

While I know it's illegal to forage for native vegetation, I don't feel nearly as bad about it as I probably should. I'm counting on two things here: the first is that I'm on a privately-owned island so the rules may not apply; the second is that even if they do still apply, this pales into insignificance compared to the risk of dying of starvation. I'm usually not a rule-breaker, but in this case I feel my behaviour is perfectly justifiable.

1.00–3.00 p.m.: Write up diary.
This has turned out to be another enjoyable part of
the day. I managed to extend the time by reading
yesterday's entry over again, and now writing it up
gives me time to analyse how well my timetable
is working, and to fine-tune it if necessary. Once
housekeeping has been dealt with, the time between
one and three o'clock is going to be very difficult to
fill. I find myself tempted to make lists or doodle, but
I don't want to run out of paper, so I'll only indulge
myself with one list on the inside cover of my diary.

Things I most wish I had with me:
- Pillow
- Rescue beacon
- Rope
- Mobile phone

The pillow is self-explanatory, as is the rescue beacon.
Of course even if I had a beacon I could only use it
if I knew for sure that no-one else was on the island,
and then I'd have to time it very carefully to avoid the
bi-weekly boat run, since I fear I cannot trust the Duffy
brothers. At present it would be no use at all. Rope
I regret the most. It would enable me to hang things
much more easily, enable me to climb up and down
the cliff safely and (to me the most compelling reason)
if I did manage to catch any of my hunters before they

caught me, it would enable me to tie them up securely. The mobile phone I know is silly. Dave said mobiles don't work here, and even though I now know he is not to be trusted, common sense tells me he's right about this, but somehow, irrationally, just having my phone beside me would make me feel safer.

One other thing I do regret is that I didn't bring my Atkinson's Guide. Professor A is a legend in the geology department, with a history of daring, usually successful, forays into inhospitable and remote areas in search of rare minerals. He's also a keen botanist and bush survivalist, and completely crazy. His guide contains the kind of common-sense advice everyone should give you, though normally no-one does. He's retired now, but still comes in each year to do his summer school and he's always the first to arrive at parties, where he brings bizarre bush tucker offerings and ends up standing on the table reciting 'The Man from Snowy River' and 'The Man from Ironbark', his special party pieces.

Fortunately, with my neurotically retentive memory I can recall quite a lot of his advice, but despite that just having the guide would have helped to evoke his larger-than-life presence and given me a bit of company in my own survival story, as well as something to read.

Now I've run out of things to do. I hadn't planned to move to the standing space because I'll have to go out later anyway, but I think I'll add a new item to the list just to break things up a bit. I'll bring my diary so I can meditate about any possible substitutes for my wish list.

3.00–4.00 p.m.: Stand in entrance space. Exercises.
The only alternative to a mobile that I could think of is telepathy, so I guess I can abandon that particular dream. I can't think of any alternative cushioning material either except cushion bush, and I don't think there'll be any on this side of the island, as its preferred habitat is on sheltered sandy beaches. However, the idea gives me a goal, something to search for, and I realise that is important because it makes the concept of a future seem somehow much more real. Rope. Not much chance of that. Then I think of the karkalla stem. Not strong enough for rock-work but it might make a functional tie. Would it be strong enough to tie a person? I doubt it, but even the possibility is exciting.

Feeling pleased with myself for finding such an excellent way of passing the time, I am just about to turn my mind to rescue beacons when there is a loud crack and a crash. *What was that?* But of course I know what it is. Now that it has finally happened, I recognise only too clearly the unmistakable sound of a human being crashing through bush. Hand over mouth, I crouch and wait ...

Sunset.

What I've been dreading has finally happened, and
the experience has been both far worse and less
bad than I had been able to imagine. I'm still alive,
that's the good part, but so sick with fear that it is
only with great difficulty I can force myself to take
a tiny drink of water. Even though I'd thought it,
even written it, somehow I don't think I had really
believed they'd come this far. I should have known.
Dave tracked me down once, now he's tracking me
again. And that's the worst of it. I'm beginning to feel
that, whatever it is he's wanting from me, he'll never
give up. In the back of my mind I'd been counting on
the boat coming back on Monday and picking them
up, but now I'm faced with the possibility that Dave
won't leave until I do. The others may go, probably
will. But he'll stay. And while he does I'm trapped
here.

Which makes it doubly important to stick to
the timetable, but the shock has left me craving
sweetness. Crawling back to my food store, I permit
myself to eat two of the remaining karkalla fruits.
However, I do not allow myself even a tiny sip of
water, yet still my bladder tells me: *I have to go out.*
I know this, but don't think I can do it. However, two
positive things have come out of this manifestation
of my greatest fears. *I heard him coming, and I heard
him going away.* Which means I have covered my

tracks well enough that he didn't find me. Of course there's the possibility that the going away was a feint, and that Dave is hiding out there, waiting for me to show myself. But I don't think so. I have a real sense that I'm alone in this part of the island now. Not that this makes me any more eager to leave my shelter.

I make a deal with myself. I'll just nick out quickly, no exploring, and I'll head for that flat rock and use it as a toilet no matter how suitable or unsuitable it proves. I know this is a good plan because if someone is there, I'll be more experienced on rocks than he will, and if they've gone away and then return I'll be out of sight of their path.

Quick toilet run. Exercises if possible. Prepare for sleep. Finish diary.

Well, I've done it, and, obviously, lived to tell the tale. I crouched under the light from the largest ceiling hole for a full minute to help adjust my sight, then slowly crawled to the entrance, stood up and, heart in mouth, pulled the tree aside. I stood like this until my vision cleared. Nothing moved. No-one came. As fast as I could with my slowly unstiffening limbs I made it round the point, all the time scuffing out my prints with a branch. When I reached the flat rock, it was even better than I'd thought. A shallow depression in the centre dipped into a hole about five centimetres across, and beneath this hole was a deep chasm.

Unfortunately balance was even more difficult than this morning, but eventually I managed to do what I had to do, relieved in every way as I heard the evidence trickling onto the rocks below and out of sight. I even took a moment to take in the view and gulp some deep draughts of bracing salt air. It would have been beautiful if not so fraught with danger, and in fact it was beautiful, the rocks disappearing at this point straight into the blue-black depths of the sea. *Aqua profondo.* Not Homer's wine-dark sea this. A clear poisonous cobalt blue. But dark, certainly dark. And deep.

It took a bit of time to pull my jeans back up, and by then the light was fading fast. I peered round the rocks, no sign of movement anywhere, then picked up my branch and made my way back as quickly as possible, still taking care to cover my tracks. It was the work of less than a minute, but I couldn't breathe easily again until I threw my branch into the bushes, darted into the cave, and pulled the tree carefully across the entrance. Then I stood, stock still, listening.

Nothing. I needed to move fast now, because while standing on that rocky outcrop an idea had come to me, and I wanted to try it out before my limbs stiffened up again. I've had my jeans on from the moment I decided to leave the cabin. Not only were they now becoming quite uncomfortable, but they also made my toilet dashes both difficult and dangerous. What I wanted to do was take them off and use them, folded, as a ground cushion overnight, and then leave them hanging to air while I made my morning dash, wearing only my long T-shirt, socks and boots.

This involved a very complicated procedure. I needed to crawl to the interior sitting position in order to take off my boots, then crawl back to the standing position where, with enormous difficulty, I peeled off my jeans. There was a terrible moment when I thought I was going to be stuck, jeans round my ankles, unable to move, but finally desperation took over, and I managed to drag them off. I felt naked and vulnerable as I folded the jeans and stuck them awkwardly under my arm. The crawl back into the cave was painful, with sand and rock grazing my knees, but there was nothing sharp enough to draw blood and I brushed the sand off using the jeans as a duster, before placing them as a cushion between me and the cold ground. The light was almost gone by then, but I forced myself to pull the Amnesty T-shirt out of my backpack and put it on, plus the pair of long socks I'd left stuffed in the bottom of the pack.

I just have time to drink my overdue water ration, fold the backpack, now skinny and totally inadequate

for its role of cushion, and place it behind my head,
finish writing up my diary and prepare for sleep,
knife in hand, rock and hammer nearby.

The time is 5.58 p.m. on Saturday the 14th of April.

* * *

Reluctantly I put my diary away as darkness descends, leaving me once again with only my thoughts for distraction ...

As blackness envelops the cave, I begin to feel almost safe. Having spent one night in this space, I know that nothing lives here but me, and I'm also confident I have nothing to fear from Dave or Matt after dark. Their bush skills are limited enough by day, and I've seen no sign of any equipment that would enable them to patrol the island by night. In fact, I think it was my superior bush skills that enabled me to escape so easily, and their collective ignorance that enabled me to hide my intentions. The people I usually hang out with wouldn't have been fooled for a minute.

That first morning I had made the decision to behave as if everything was completely normal. I'd heard enough the night before to know that I had to get away from the cabin area some time that day and find somewhere to hide where I could work out an escape plan. They were all pretty seedy when they finally emerged late on Friday morning. I had made myself a large breakfast and offered to cook something for Dave. He groaned and took some black coffee.

'I'm going exploring,' I said, as bright and breezy as a pixie. 'Coming?' I knew he wouldn't, and set out in a way I hoped would allay any doubts about my intentions. I was lightly dressed, carrying nothing but a large water bottle and a small backpack.

There were paths on the island, perhaps forged by Matt's ancestors, and though overgrown in places, they seemed to have been maintained to some extent. After a number of false starts, I found the route up to the north-west point. And I found the cave. Then I scuffed out all trace of my footprints, except for those along the beach, made sure I was back in time for lunch, ate as much as I could, and waited until my moment came.

I waited most of the afternoon, while Matt and Dave drank steadily and became nastier and nastier, first to each other, and then Matt changed tack and turned on me.

'I hear you're quite the athlete, Alix. When are you going to give us a demo? Some nude wrestling, maybe?' He squinted and looked at me narrowly, as if sizing me up. 'Dave says we're in for a treat. Can't wait.' I had a bad feeling that I couldn't wait much longer either, and that Dave tended to say a lot of things that bore no relationship to the truth.

It was not until Dave parked at the jetty that I learned we were going to an island.

I'd never have accepted the invitation if I'd known there was a boat trip involved. Did Dave know that? I wonder. What he did know was that I had no real way out because we'd come in his car. I'd wanted to drive myself, but he'd insisted that it didn't make sense, that sharing would save on petrol and parking problems.

He'd also convinced me to leave my phone locked in the glovebox of his car. 'Matt's place doesn't have any reception,' he'd assured me. 'It's not really worth the risk of losing it if you can't even use it, is it?' He'd made a great show of leaving his own phone as well, which made me inclined to believe him.

But as I looked around in consternation at the tiny mussel-encrusted jetty, one alarmingly small boat, six people, and a car park the size of a football field containing just two cars and a beat-up old truck, he grinned.

'Dave, you said ...'

'I lied. Path of least resistance.' He was still grinning, obviously finding my alarm extremely funny.

'Calm down, Alix. I'll introduce you to Lana.'

Just one glance at Lana told me I wasn't going to fit in with this group. She was wearing white from head to toe. Expensive white. Italian sandals, linen skirt, some kind of artfully low-necked designer shirt, cute yachting cap. She was also wearing heavy makeup, and her hair was styled in a creative disarray that must have been set in concrete. Not a curl out of place. 'Hi, Alice,' she said in a lisping Marilyn Monroe voice that sounded weirdly artificial.

'It's Alix, not Alice,' said Matt lazily. 'And she's an exotic import a bit like you, aren't you, Alix?' It appeared that Matt and Dave had been talking about me.

I was feeling more and more out of my depth, almost disoriented. Perhaps I should have protested then and there, but what could I have done? No car, no phone, no real idea of where we were, and the fleeting idea of appealing to the two men on the boat to take me back to town died the moment I got a good look at them.

Although both Matt and Dave were for the most part all charm on the boat, it was there I felt the first stirrings of unease (apart from the overwhelming unease of actually being on a boat), and that was mainly because of the Duffy brothers. Matt really should keep them in better check.

'We better get going. Tides won't last for fuckin' ever.' This was the older, bulkier one who looked like your archetypal axe murderer. The other one, with a mean, pinched angry face, was moving around the boat, unfurling ropes. They were introduced to me as Mick and Kel Duffy. The Dodgy brothers. A glance at their truck made me shiver and take a step back. It was guarded by four Rottweilers on very long chains that would have enabled them to deal with any potential thieves without any trouble at all. When I looked their way they growled and strained at their ties, just raring to get at me. No help there.

'Right. All aboard. Got your stuff?' Matt was organising us, throwing our bags onto the deck, herding us along the jetty. He offered his arm to help me onto the boat, but I balked. 'I can't.' I could hear the hysteria in my voice. I'm sure they could too. I realise now how much at least four of them must have enjoyed it.

Dave was the first to jump down into the boat. 'Come on, Verhoeven. I'll catch you!'

But I stood there frozen, just repeating, 'I can't.' Dave tried a new approach. Softly, softly. 'Alix, this is not like you. It's quite safe.' He reached down and pulled something up. 'See. Lifejackets.'

But I couldn't move. I was utterly frozen. All I could see when I looked at that boat were broken timbers and bodies churning in grey water. It was Lana who broke the spell, jumping gracefully onto the deck and saying in that same little-girl voice: 'I can do it. See. It's easy.' And then Matt was behind me, his voice rough, 'And so can Alix.' He was guiding me firmly towards the boat, his fingers gripping me like a vice, when suddenly he lifted me up and turned as if to throw me into the water. I experienced a moment of sheer terror looking into black and weed-filled depths. Then, without a word, he turned again and pushed me onto the deck.

If Dave or Lana saw they made no sign.

Unlike the others, I did put a lifejacket on, but it didn't make me feel any better. The whole journey, which took almost an hour, passed in a daze of nausea, one part sea-sickness, three parts nameless fear, as the others laughed and joked around me. Whether they were laughing at me I didn't know and didn't care, but occasional impressions reached me. Of Dave trying to tell the loudest jokes to impress Matt, of Lana fetching and carrying at Matt's command, and of the louring presence of the Duffy brothers, who now and then looked at me as if somehow I wasn't what they had expected, although I couldn't see how it could matter to them.

Once I vomited over the side, and I could see Lana make a little moue of distaste. 'Eeeww,' she said. But Dave was surprisingly nice about it, bringing me tissues and cups of water.

And then the next shock, when we got there. All along, despite all the signs, I had retained the image that had first arisen when Dave talked about Matt's holiday house.

I had pictured an A-line timber cottage, one of a street of similar cottages ranged along the edge of a bay. I had pictured a kiosk, a pier and perhaps a hotel, at the very least a bakery. And people. Lots of people. Families and caravanners, all enjoying their holiday.

But Matt's island was nothing like that.

CHAPTER THREE

Drooping Sheoak (*Allocasuarina verticillata*)

An attractive salt-tolerant tree that often grows in thickets. It has curved drooping branchlets of grey-green needles, likes sunny locations and tends to colonise coastal regions. The sheoak's main claim to fame is that it has separate male and female plants. Male flowers are produced on yellowish to light brown spikes and the female flowers are reddish. The female plants produce the woody cones containing the seeds for germination. An 1889 book suggests that chewing the needles can relieve extreme thirst, so if you're desperate, it might be worth a try.

Atkinson's Guide

FIELD DIARY - Sunday 15 April

Despite a very broken night, interrupted by terrible nightmares, I woke up slightly less stiff than yesterday, and almost refreshed. I must be acclimatising to this new life. The dawn rush to the toilet was so much easier in the long T-shirt and boots that I think I'll leave the jeans off unless I'm exploring or rock-climbing. It's not cold in the cave, so a T-shirt should be quite adequate.

I was still spooked after yesterday, and had to force myself to walk up and down and exercise my legs and arms for a few turns before scuttling back to the safety of my cave. I hope that Dave will have decided that I'm not hiding in this part of the island, but at the back of my mind is the fear that yesterday was simply a reconnaissance, and that today he might return with the others for a thorough search.

The nightmares didn't help either, a strange melange of shark attacks, drowning and, worst of all, waking to find myself trapped in the cave with Dave and Matt. No, not worst of all. *Be honest, Alix.* Thinking back over the boat trip before going to sleep has served to revive old horrors I thought were fully vanquished. Even now, in the light of day, I can't get the picture of the ferry out of my head. *I will not think about it.* I will push it to the back of my mind.

I force myself back to reporting the facts. Today I have stuck rigidly to my timetable.

Daybreak: Go outside for exercise and toilet.
Despite my terror, this part went without incident.

6.00–8.00 a.m.: Housekeeping.

Not much of this today but I managed to fill up the
time fairly successfully, mainly by making an effort
to rearrange and hang my clothes. I spent a good
fifteen minutes working out a system of folding the
jeans inside a kitchen tidy bag to make quite a good
kneepad, so I can manage the kneeling stage of my
plan with less discomfort, then took them out of the
bag, turned them inside out and hung them over the
tree root for a well overdue airing.

8.00–9.00 a.m.: First meal.

I have decided to reduce the water ration to keep
my supply going as long as possible, so used every
possible ritual to stretch the tiny allowance out. I
resisted the temptation to gobble my food, and
ate the nuts as well as the sultanas one at a time,
with a long pause between each morsel. It certainly
enhances appreciation of every nuance of taste, but
this method doesn't seem to alleviate hunger nearly
as well as gulping by the handful.

10.00 a.m.–12.00 p.m.: Stand in entrance space.

This was the worst part. Today, trying to keep from
indulging in morbid introspection, I thought I would
go mad with boredom. I only just managed to force
myself to wait until the dot of twelve before allowing
a change of position.

12.00–1.00 p.m.: Return to sitting position. Snack time.
Even though I had the full ration of nuts, sultanas and
water at eight o'clock, by the time I was scheduled
to eat the two remaining karkalla fruits in the middle
of the day I was ravenous, and thirsty. It's clear that
I will need to find more wild food. The nuts and
sultanas might be sufficient for survival, but without
anything to supplement them my energy will flag
and I can't afford that. I've also got to find some kind
of water source. When I wrote my wish list the main
things on it should have been a camp stove that
could safely be used in the cave to boil leaves and a
machine to desalinate seawater. But I don't have such
a machine and I don't have a stove, so that's that. I
think boobialla fruits are edible, but I don't know what
they look like, or whether they're in season. Tonight
or tomorrow morning I'm going to have to make a
search. Or go down the rock staircase in search of
karkalla.

1.00–3.00 p.m.: Write up diary.
What more can I say, other than that I have
determined to make a thorough search for more
food supplies when I go out at sunset. I'm not sure
what sources of animal food might be available
here. All I can think of are small lizards, which are
unfortunately most active in the middle of the day,
and perhaps insects, which are at least more likely to

be nocturnal, but I haven't seen anything bigger than tiny ants so far, and I'm not desperate enough yet to try eating them. There were shellfish on the eastern beach, but the coastline here doesn't look very crustacean-friendly, and anyway it's too far for me to risk going down the rocks.

One good thing, though, is that the island appears to be free of mosquitoes. I haven't seen one, by day or by night.

Now I think I'll spend my time standing in the entrance trying some yoga breathing as well as the exercises. Maybe it will help me visualise an alternative food source.

Sunset: Prepare for sleep. Finish diary.
Back again in one piece. I have managed to convince myself that evening is likely to be the least risky time for exploration, so I struggled into my jeans and anorak, filled my pockets with plastic bags, hefted my weapons, and set off to check out the small woodland beyond my original toilet area. Again I had a strong sense that no-one was around. I felt brave enough to go a little beyond the wood to where the ground dropped down into the valley. This valley cuts across the centre of the island and leads to the beach on the east side (where the cabin is). It's really the only way to access the north-west point that houses my cave, so I took a good long look for any

signs of activity. No doubt there were small creatures going about their business, but not a sight or sound of anything large or dangerous.

I had calculated that I had twenty minutes of good light, so I set about exploring. There was fruit on the boobiallas, but it looked like the last of the season, and was clearly not going to solve my food problems. However, I gathered a bagful of about two dozen berries for the next few days. They were smaller than the karkalla, and I had no idea what they would taste like, but when you are forced into hunter-gathering, you gather what you can.

What I did find though was something to cushion my sleep. Behind the boobiallas was an overhanging stand of sheoaks, and when I touched their clumps of drooping needles they were as smooth and soft as any English heather. Well, almost. Carefully, so as not to leave obvious destruction in my wake, I pulled off half a dozen branchlets from the base of the bushes and put them in a pile with my bag of fruit. If my mouth got uncomfortably dry with the shortage of water, I'd heard that chewing on sheoak needles could provide a measure of relief, although no actual water. Why, I wasn't sure, but it was an added comfort to know that I'd have a supply near at hand. I now had about five minutes before I needed to head back, so I pushed through the sheoaks to a rough thicket beyond.

This turned out to be a little copse of coast banksias in full flower, and I recalled one of the sources of both moisture and food used by local Aboriginal people in the past. When the banksia flowers are covered with morning dew, they can be squeezed to provide a kind of nectar. It might be too dry here for dew to form, but I was excited enough to plan to set my alarm very early one morning and come and find out.

Suddenly cautious, I took a moment to check the valley again. Still no sign of life. I collected my gatherings and, happily burdened but still careful to scuff out every footprint with a branch, I returned to the cave, where I deposited my treasures and returned outside to peel off my jeans by bracing against the entrance rock. Next, a fast, jeans-free toilet run. Then, cover tree back into place, and just enough time to finish writing my diary and prepare for sleep. The time is 5.57 p.m. on Sunday the 15th of April.

* * *

What can I think about that won't bring back the nightmares?

With sheoak branches tucked behind my head and back and into the gaps between me and the rock wall, I feel comparatively comfortable. In fact, no worse than in many of the camps I've had to endure in the past, particularly in England.

One of the many things I liked about Australians from the outset was their love of comfort, so that even the most remote camps would have high quality sleeping equipment, good food and, usually, excellent beer. Coming from my father's abstemious, self-denying household, then England's wet, cold, masochistic discomfort, how could I fail to be beguiled by the four-wheel-drives and helicopters and seafood dinners?

I think I chose geology initially because of its perversely romantic image of hardship and lonely isolation. Having disappointed my family by turning my back on their beliefs, I could not have adopted merchant banking or advertising copywriting, or even competitive rock-climbing, with their connotations of decadence and wealth, even fame. But the other contributing factor to my decision was, of course, my love of rocks.

Many of my happiest memories involve rocks. The one childhood holiday in Madagascar, spent without my father, scrambling with Abel among the fabulous limestone cliffs of Ankarana, was the beginning of a long love affair with cliffs, rocks and caves. My lonely adolescence in England, which I resentfully regarded as exile, was made endurable by rambling the Yorkshire moors. And as a foreign, and alien, undergraduate at the University of Manchester, all of my leisure time was given over to expeditions to the limestone cave systems of the Pennines. The Pennines excursions, however, were done in company. No matter how foreign and alien you may be, at an English university you can always find a club full of people who are even stranger than you are.

Thinking about that magical family expedition, I wonder now how Moe persuaded my father to let us go on holiday at all. Although done under the most primitive conditions, it would have cost money. We had a tent, stretchers, ropes and boots that must have come from somewhere. And the food. Normally we lived on food the congregation brought us in lieu of paying a stipend. This was not the kind of food you could take to a remote camp, especially as the giver would be back that day or the next to retrieve her pot. My mother preferred to receive cooked food, and until that trip to Ankarana I assumed that Moe didn't know how to cook.

The camping trip revealed more than one hidden talent of my mother's. She used the old curtains from the sleepout, which she had always hated, to make sleeping bags for me and my brother (she herself slept wrapped in her thickest *lamba*), and she unravelled one of my father's unneeded pullovers to knit us socks to go with the two pairs of heavy boots she had found at the back of Ulysses' store.

I went with my mother, full of excitement, on several expeditions to the *Epicerie* at the other end of the village (the name, a reminder of the French-colonial past, proclaimed itself in uneven red letters on a pale-green board hung from the ceiling). Most villages had a store of some kind, many built out of mud like the houses, some just a mat on the ground where goods were displayed anew every morning. Ulysses had been more ambitious and built an edifice of timber offcuts and driftwood, held together by faith and a few nails. The back half was covered with pieces of scrap tin of many colours, and the front with a plastic shower curtain decorated with pink flamingos. Rummaging with Moe in the most remote corners, I felt I was in Aladdin's cave, surrounded by a wild assortment of hats, toys, umbrellas, buckets – and, oh miracle of miracles, boots – with Ulysses scurrying behind us, pointing to one item, pulling out another, eager to give us a full appreciation of the riches on display.

With these supplies, plus ropes and stout sticks, and bright *lambas* wrapped round our heads to keep off the sun, Abel and I felt quite well equipped and professional.

At the time of the caves trip I was about ten and Abel would have been twelve. Because he was habitually given a lot more freedom than I was, we rarely spent time together at home in the village, so it was exciting to set off exploring with my big brother. Except for a guided tour of one of the larger caves, Moe didn't come on these expeditions, but would stay back at the campsite to prepare strange meals out of the limited foods we had been able to bring and, as we discovered one day when we came back unexpectedly early, to read novels, the works of the Devil, a forbidden pastime. (Except, of course, when used in the reputable endeavour of improving our English, but these novels, even we could see, were not of that kind. And more wicked still, they were in Dutch.)

We never told my father. Where she managed to obtain the books I don't know. Perhaps she smuggled them all the way from Home. In fact none of us said anything, but she must have sensed our complicity, because from then on she relaxed quite amazingly, so that mealtimes became a shared game.

'Alix, what will we have for dinner?'

'Rice?'

'We shall have rice.'

'Abel, what will we have with the rice?

'Manioc?'

'It so happens we have some manioc here. We shall have rice and manioc. Now, is there anything we have that would make it edible?' This would precipitate a mad search among the increasingly dwindling supplies for food with any flavour at all. We finished the eggs within the first two days, and the dried fish also disappeared, except for a few eagerly sought scraps. For the last two days we were left with a dilemma: either eat rice and manioc au naturel, which formed a kind of gluggy mess with no flavour at all, or add to it the contents of a small tin of English mock-ham, which was vibrant with flavour (and pink dye), but somehow repellent.

That holiday, including the cooking, still stands in my memory as the best holiday of my life. I wonder if Abel remembers it the same way. I try to recall when I last saw my brother, and realise it must be at least eight years ago. He visited me in Manchester on his way to his seminary in Canada.

When he turned up at my door I didn't recognise him at first. He'd been a doughy sort of boy, somehow unformed, with soft fair hair cut in a basin cut with Moe's sewing scissors. The neat stocky figure who greeted me in the Malagasy way ('*Salama*, Alixi') and handed me a small wrapped parcel was an adult. His face had settled and tightened into maturity and he was no longer soft but solid. Someone you could depend on. Someone you could trust.

Sadly, Abel had not lost his quiet reserve, and I had lost all ability to trust. It was early days for me at the university. I had not yet met Jonathan and his friends, and although I showed Abel around the place, took him to lunch in the student cafeteria, asked about Moe and Vader, there was a formality to the visit neither of us seemed able to break.

But when he talked about his studies at the seminary in Canada my usually taciturn brother was on fire. 'It's not like all that hell and damnation Vader goes on with.' He had already acquired a faint Canadian accent and his English had improved out of sight. 'It's about helping people live their lives. About day-to-day things – work, children, sickness.'

He'd been back to Madagascar for a visit and would be flying on to Canada the next day from London. I could sense that the visit with our parents had not gone well, though he did not say so, and that he would not go again.

I was flattered that my big brother had taken the time to come and see me. But I was seventeen, still absorbed in my own sorrows and grievances. I didn't know how to ask Abel about his feelings – about our parents, about Madagascar, about the future – and he didn't know how to tell me. He could talk at length about his happiness in his vocation, and I'm sure that was real, but if there were any undercurrents, doubts or fears they remained unsaid.

Just before he left, he looked at me searchingly and asked: 'Are you all right, Alixi?'

'Yes,' I said. 'I'm all right.'

And that was that.

When he left, I didn't open his gift. Instead, I found the scarf Moe had sent me for my birthday. It had animals on it, so I hadn't worn it – too un-English. Now I wrapped it round my head and climbed into the cupboard among my hanging clothes. I stayed crouched on the floor, my shoes sticking uncomfortably into my spine, fingering the silky fringes of the scarf, for what must have been hours. When I finally opened the parcel it contained the pocket knife I have with me now.

I haven't really spoken to Abel since then, except ... *So much for taking my mind off things.*

When I last spoke to my brother I was alone in the flat taking the opportunity to get stuck into some serious study when the phone rang. 'Is there somebody there by the name of Verhoeven?' It was the Australian Embassy in Manila, looking for Abel. I asked what they wanted, but they wouldn't say. I didn't know anyone in Manila, so I wasn't worried. I gave them Abel's number in Canada and rang off.

Five minutes later the phone rang again. This time it was Abel, to tell me, without any preamble, that our parents had been in a ferry accident and were feared dead. The embassy wanted him to go to the Philippines and identify two of the bodies, but he felt that didn't make sense. I was closer. I should go. 'Alix? Are you there?'

Abel's reticence could make him seem blunt and insensitive. What kind of pastor he makes I don't know, but as a purveyor of bad news he is severely lacking. I sat down, stunned and shaking, unable to speak as he bellowed down the phone. Finally, I managed to get some words out.

'Are they sure they're dead?'

'Of course they're not sure. They've got some European bodies and Vader and Moeder were on their way to some kind of missionary gathering so they want it to be them. Makes their job easier.'

'They ... they must have some reason.'

But Abel wouldn't hear of it. I guess he didn't want to hear. All his beliefs would be telling him he should rejoice in our parents' glorious reunion with their Lord, when his heart told him he wanted them alive, back in Luang Prabang, behaving like their usual wrongheaded selves.

I couldn't argue with him. I was, indubitably, closer. I had no-one dependent on me and it was university holidays. The embassy would pay the fare. I should go.

It may sound as if Abel is heartless, selfish even, but that would be unfair to him. He is simply very practical. If you look at the geography, it makes more sense to go from Melbourne to Manila than from Toronto to Manila, and as far as my brother was concerned, that was the end of the argument.

I was twenty-one years old when I identified what was left of my parents, in a tiny coastal village near where they died, and now I know the memory will haunt me forever. I'm sure if Abel had known what was in store he would have behaved differently, but he is not an imaginative person. He was probably going by his own pastoral experience of burying people neatly arranged in their coffins. He had no idea.

Neither did I.

Nearly one hundred people had been on that ferry, and the small number who managed to jump into the water were met by packs of sharks. Few survived in one piece. The rest of the passengers and crew were trapped inside and crushed or torn apart in the panic. When I got to the airport at Manila, where I was to be met by the relevant officials, I picked up an abandoned English-language newspaper while I was waiting. On the front page was a picture. 'FERRY CARNAGE!' screamed the headline. The accompanying article described pieces of wreckage, bits of bodies, chairs, sandals, a dead baby, all floating together in a chaotic mass. Around them, grimly visible in the photo as torpedo-shaped shadows, circling before the kill, were the sharks.

The bodies I was asked to identify had been fairly ineffectually surrounded by ice. They were not complete, but I had no doubt that they were the bodies of my father and mother.

I never got to tell Abel what a horrific experience this was for me. Now, I make a decision. If I get out of here, I'll visit my brother in Canada. And this time I will tell him what I saw.

It was a little before the death of my parents that Dave Grogan moved in next door to the flat where Jonathan and I were living and over the next few weeks he always seemed to be at the door, returning an oven dish or wanting to borrow some flour. And he always seemed to have time for a cup of tea or coffee.

While I was in the Philippines Jonathan had been called away to resolve a work problem interstate, so I was not expecting to be met when I and my backpack were flung through the exit doors. But there was neighbour Dave, grinning and waving. He'd written the flight down from the note above the phone and come out to meet me. At the time I was charmed. He was all affable, just-your-friendly neighbour good humour, and in that mode he was sort of appealing. He drove me home, made me a cup of tea and sat me down.

'So. Tell me all about it.' And, unusually for me, I did. It seemed better somehow to unload to a virtual stranger than to poor Jonathan, who would probably be arriving home drained and exhausted. I told Dave how I'd had to stay a few days after the identification to settle my parents' effects; how the embassy would have flown me to Luang Prabang to sort their things. But where could I have put them? How in the end I arranged for their effects to be packed and shipped to Canada.

'Without even knowing what they were?'

'They didn't have much stuff.' They were itinerants, my parents, wandering preachers who scorned worldly goods. Although my mother wasn't so scornful of the share market. It later turned out she had made some canny European investments before embarking on their voyage of folly. I wonder if my father knew. I didn't tell Dave this, though. One thing I had noticed from our neighbourly exchanges was that he was rather obsessed with money, always asking how much things had cost and how much people earned. It was slightly creepy.

And he knew all about my horror of boats.

CHAPTER FOUR

Southern Boobialla *(Myoporum insulare)*

Often known as Tucker Bush or Native Juniper, it is
a salt-tolerant plant that can grow as a tree up to
six metres high or take a prostrate form, particularly
on cliffs and rocky headlands. It flourishes on
sand-dunes and in coastal regions. In summer the
small white flowers can have quite a long blooming
season, which is then followed by a crop of smooth
round purple fruits about six millimetres in diameter.
The fruits are inclined to be sourish in taste but
are not unpleasant. Although the fruits of the *M.
insulare* are safe to eat in small quantities, those
of some *Myoporum* species have been found to
be toxic to humans, so identification needs to be
precise.

Atkinson's Guide

FIELD DIARY - Monday 16 April

Daybreak: Go outside for exercise and toilet.
Giving myself permission to think about my parents'
deaths seems to have freed me in some way, and

I spent a night without nightmares, just a strange series of dreams about rock-climbing across water-filled abysses. I even found myself thinking what an interesting place this island would be for climbing, which made me laugh out loud. *You're a prisoner here, for God's sake, Alix! Get a grip.* It's the daymares that really get to me now, my mind constantly filled with images of Dave and Matt, determined to find me before their time is up.

Today's the day when the four of us were booked to return to the mainland on the Dodgy brothers' boat. I can't believe we only arrived last Thursday. Four days. It feels more like four weeks. I don't know what I'll do if they don't get on the boat, and I don't yet know what chances there are of escape from the island if they do. What their departure would give me is an opportunity to seek out all possible ways of attracting attention and do a thorough exploration of what this isolated landmass has to offer.

I'm going to make my toilet break very brief this morning in case they make one last thorough search before they leave. *If* they leave. Then my usual timetable will be completely disrupted because I have a dangerous plan.

6.00–8.00 a.m.: Housekeeping.
Housekeeping today was all about weapons. After an uneventful toilet run, I dressed with considerable

difficulty in clean underpants, jeans, clean socks,
boots, and a used but not too dirty shirt, giving my
trusty Amnesty T-shirt a well-earned airing. Then
I filled my anorak pockets with necessities: the
morning water ration decanted into a specimen bag
and tied securely; eight boobialla fruits likewise; knife
in the easy-to-reach top pocket; rock and hammer in
the wide front pocket. After a bit of thought, I added
matches and a pen. *A pen in the eye always takes
them by surprise.* Sometimes Kathryn's maxims have
a lot of sense to them.

8.00–9.00 a.m.: First meal.
Going without water so I could carry some with
me seemed like a good idea in the planning, but
I'd forgotten how dry my throat gets in the early
morning. I wasn't sure I'd be able to last until midday,
but couldn't afford to increase my water ration. In
fact, I'll have to start reducing it from now on. At any
rate, no matter how frugal I am, the water will run
out before the food.

Of course I know from Atkinson's Guide the
famous 'rule of three', that a person can survive
only three days without water and that the daily
requirement is two litres per person. I have been
dangerously below that limit, but there are other
factors to be taken into account, such as exposure.
Living in the cave should enable me to survive for

longer with less, especially as I am only going out in the cool of the evening and early morning. Food helps too, providing fluid and also salts and minerals. I don't know how safe my regime is, but I can't see any alternative with the resources I have available.

I excused myself from the need to eat my breakfast slowly, on the premise that if they don't leave any supplies in the cabin I would soon run out of food anyway. I grabbed handfuls of nuts and sultanas in succession and stuffed them into my mouth. Despite the fact that it was my own rules I was breaking, I felt wicked and energised. Then I sat like a big fat boa constrictor digesting its prey and paid for my excess by feeling full and uncomfortable.

10.00 a.m.–12.00 p.m.: Write up diary.
I didn't bother to change position, since I'd be going out quite soon, but I did my exercises diligently, and brought my diary up to date. When I ran out of things to do, nervousness hit me and I had to try some yoga breathing, but it didn't help much. And then came the sounds I'd been dreading – the heavy tread of two pairs of boots and Dave's voice yelling: 'Alix! Where are you? The boat's coming today!', and then Matt's voice, not yelling but conversational, addressing Dave but perhaps hoping I'd be able to hear. 'Don't work yourself up, mate. She'll be there when the boat comes.'

'Think so? She's really stubborn.'

'I know so, Dave, because your little friend didn't steal any of our food. She'll be starving by now, so she'll come crawling and grovelling back. I'm looking forward to that.'

He laughed, a jolly little laugh.

'Then what?'

And Matt laughed again. Then suddenly his tone changed. 'Then we'll see.'

One set of footsteps receded and then Dave's voice came again. 'Alix, don't be scared. I won't let him hurt you. I'm your friend.' Now his voice, still calling 'Alix!' also began to recede and I managed with great effort to recover from the shock of their presence, finish my writing, and prepare for what had to be done.

4.00–5.00 p.m.: Meal and water.
It's now four o'clock and I've been out of the cave for what seems like hours. The boat was booked for noon, and I worked on the assumption that no matter what their plans, they'd go to the jetty to meet it, but I still set out with considerable trepidation.

My main problem was that I needed to be able to see the boat arrive and leave without being seen myself. I also needed to reassure myself that they were not still scouting my side of the island. The only way to do that was to go to the edge of the valley and take a look. So, knife in hand, heart in mouth, that's what I did. The food and weapons slowed me down, but I couldn't risk leaving them along the way for searchers to find. The need to wipe out every footprint made the journey even more nerve-wracking. After each step I had to turn my back on my destination in order to ensure that my tea-tree branch scuffed out every tell-tale mark of passage.

The only sign of life was a flock of birds that rose from the underbrush, disturbed by my careful footsteps. I took that as a heartening indication that the area had been undisturbed since Matt and Dave had passed through, but continued to proceed cautiously. Nothing else stirred, and I began gradually to relax a bit and think about where I could find a viewing point.

On the first morning on the island I had tried climbing the height above the sandblow that traverses the island, without success. Thickets of tea-tree and sheoak were so knotted and tangled by the wind that there seemed no way through, so then I turned my attention to a rocky point that jutted out of the western side of the island. This little promontory was well out of view of both jetty and cabin, but I didn't want to be visible to the men on the boat as it arrived. Keeping as much cover as possible in the low-growing scrub, I scouted among the rocks for a possible hiding place. My first foray was unsuccessful, but on the second time round I ventured out towards the edge of the rocks where they formed a finger out over the sea. Feeling very exposed and looking nervously behind me every moment I found, under a ledge of rock, what looked like some kind of burrow.

One of the reasons I chose the north-western end, where my cave is, was what I found on the morning of the first day when I went to explore the south-eastern end, which looked, with its sand dunes and low scrub, far more accessible than the west. It was also closest to the cabin, and I strolled along the flat open sandy area that joined the cabin and the jetty, turned into the sandhills and began a gentle climb. As I wandered further into the dunes I began to notice burrows, and from their size I guessed that this was a mutton-bird rookery. As I realised this I also remembered other creatures that were attracted to rookeries, and went cold. Among the dunes were slender dark objects I had subliminally taken to be washed-up sticks, or ropes. Lots of slender dark objects, one of which then began to move.

So did I. There is a tradition that geologists are unfazed by snakes, but this is definitely not true in my case. I fear them with a dread that goes way beyond the rational. How I got out of there without putting my feet down on the ground I don't know, but I swear I managed it.

The odd thing is that I have only ever once been threatened with this particular danger, and that was not in Australia at all, but in good old safe-as-houses England. I'd been swimming with a group of climbers at the end of a hard day's climb in one of those legendary crystal-clear pools I'd found so hard to discover, when suddenly a moving object brushed my leg underwater. I scrambled out quick-smart and yelled for the others to do the same, and we all watched in fascinated horror as what must have been an adder slid out of the other side of the pool, probably trying to get as far away as possible from us, and disappeared into the undergrowth. I don't know about my companions, but even though it was quite a small and unassuming little creature, and probably far more scared of me than I was of it, I never entered any kind of wild waterway in the UK again.

To be on the safe side, I carefully memorised Professor Atkinson's advice on dealing with snakes and I believe it has helped to prevent any further incidents of this kind. In the bush I always wear above-ankle boots, thick socks and long pants, which is precisely how I am dressed today. I normally wear gloves when collecting firewood and try to keep to marked paths whenever possible. I am also meticulous about stepping over logs the Atkinson way, which involves climbing to the top of the log, looking carefully down and only then stepping off on the other side. And of course I never, ever, put my hand into any kind of hole or crevice.

Faced with entering a burrow and perhaps sheltering in it for hours on end, all my fears returned. It didn't look like the home of either bird or serpent, and it appeared undisturbed as if it had been empty for some time. It was only just large enough to fit one scrunched-up human, and it took some deep breathing and mustering of courage before I could bring myself to crawl in.

Once I did my fears subsided. There were no signs of habitation and, like my own cave, it seemed to be the result of natural forces, and not the work of animal or human. Unlike my cave, it had filled with debris, but apart from this it was fairly clean and well ventilated and afforded a panoramic view of the ocean. No boat could arrive from the mainland without being in full view from this eyrie and I immediately set about making it as invisible as possible to anybody approaching by boat.

Again keeping a wary eye out, I backtracked and found two small tea-tree bushes, about the height of the entrance. I pulled them out by the roots as gently as I could, mentally apologising to them for my necessary vandalism, then spent some time filling in the ground and covering the area with leaf litter.

Next, with considerable difficulty because I still had to cover my tracks with the smaller branches I was carrying, I hefted them onto my back and made my way, keeping to the rocks where possible, back to my new hiding place.

I left the two bushes outside while I settled my belongings in my shelter, then pulled them across the entrance to form a hide, so that I could see out but no-one would be able to see in. Then I waited.

As a special treat and to relieve both the nervousness and the monotony, I allowed myself to eat my snack half an hour early. Perhaps it was the effect of hunger, but the boobialla fruits were a pleasant surprise. They didn't look promising. Pea-sized and an alarming dark purple, they had a worrying resemblance to deadly nightshade berries. I bit into the first one tentatively, and found it tasted like a rather sour and salty plum. As I ate one, then another, the taste grew on me and I enjoyed the aftertaste for some minutes.

I dropped the large central seed-cases into a specimen bag and planned to scatter them when I next collected some fruits. That way I wasn't being a complete environmental vandal by preventing the seeds from germinating. Whether the birds that would normally eat and distribute them would be interested in such thoroughly chewed pits was another matter, but at least I could try to do the right thing. Although what the right thing is does become much less clear-cut when it's a matter of your own survival.

Then all thoughts of food were forgotten. First, the sound of an engine, then the boat, with the unmistakable Mick Duffy at the helm, hove into view. Of Kel there was no sign, which was strange. It had seemed like a two-person boat at least. I didn't know how long they would stop, but I thought I heard voices about twenty minutes later, and soon after that the boat appeared again, heading for the mainland. I craned to see who was on it. A mist had come up over the sea and the figures were no longer recognisable, but I counted three males and recognised Lana by her bright hair that no mist could disguise. My heart thumped with incredulous relief. It seemed I was wrong, and both Dave and Matt had left as they had planned.

I was alone on the island. I still had to find some way of safely attracting attention, but at least no-one was coming after me.

I found myself shaking and unable to move, so great was my surprise. I drank my water ration and scrambled out of the shelter, not bothering to brush away my traces. But somehow I couldn't believe it without checking. I climbed up the ridge to try to find a vantage point from which to see the cabin. Just to be sure.

Eventually finding a gap in the scrub, I peered through and saw ... nothing. The cabin was closed up, the barbecue covered, and the fishing rods were gone. But I still couldn't bring myself to go down there, and anyway I needed to return to the cave to get the rest of my stuff. Still, superstitiously, I kept on covering my tracks this close to enemy territory, even though I felt assured that the enemy had gone, at least for now.

I will stay in the cave for tonight. Just knowing I'm not confined here any more makes me feel quite sentimental towards my shelter, and despite its many discomforts I am almost reluctant to leave it.

Sunset: Second toilet run. Prepare for sleep.
Finish diary.

This could be my second last toilet run. I take the opportunity to sit on the headland, writing my diary, breathing in the sea air, remembering how Jonathan used to call it 'ozone', and that I would always remind him that ozone actually smells more like chlorine. The feeling as I sit here is almost anticlimactic, as I realise I may be leaving my cave for good. I decide that tomorrow morning, before I go anywhere, I will venture down that rock stairway and explore the little beach.

It's almost completely dark by the time I'm settled for the night, and I have to use the torch to write the

final entry in my diary at 5.56 p.m. on Monday the
16th of April.

*   *   *

I'm so stirred up I can't sleep, my brain whirring like a
windmill in a hurricane.

To calm myself down I begin to make plans for my
new, if limited, freedom. Basically I'm exchanging cave
confinement for island confinement, but there's no question
about which is preferable, so I'm nervous but excited. If I
can get into the cabin, I'll have no more food problems, and
even if not, I'll have plenty of water, and can cook bush food
on the outside fireplace, making survival certain instead of,
as it seemed until recently, coming to its time limit.

I'll stick to my plan to go down the rock staircase,
partly out of curiosity, because I've been so longing to do
it, and partly out of caution. If I can't get into the cabin,
and I have to see that as a possibility, I'll need to exploit
all available sources of food. For the same reason I'll stick
to rationing my supplies until I'm sure of replacements, but
I won't need to follow my timetable, and can stay out all
morning if I want and explore this whole area, since I may
not need to come back here again.

I should be at the cabin by lunchtime and if all goes well,
I may be able to have a proper meal to celebrate. Fantasies
of wood-fired stews of shellfish and karkalla leaves finally
let me drift off ...

Dreams. About rock-climbing with Jonathan and Lana. Jonathan is obsessed with the idea that I want to climb with Lana more than with him. He's dangling on a rope, threatening to cut it, saying, 'Choose. It's me or her.'

Which is strange because Lana is about the last person I'd expect to see at the end of a rope. Certainly I didn't ever see her doing anything remotely sporty. She can't even swim. The person I first went climbing with was Jonathan, and all my early Australian climbs were with him and his friends so that makes sense, but why does he still appear in my dreams? I don't like the way dreams are forcing me into introspection. I never used to dream like this. In fact I hardly remember dreaming at all. Now each night I seem to be dragging myself back into the past. I suspect this is what counsellors make you do, which is why I've always resisted the idea of seeing one.

Kathryn believes I have a fear of commitment and she's always having a go at me to see a counsellor so that I can be cured and go out on 'dates' with her. She thinks I haven't got over Jonathan dumping me and that I go rock-climbing in all my spare moments to avoid having to build up a social life of my own.

I suspect that she's right in many ways about this. I also suspect it isn't quite as simple as that, but I have to admit I haven't thought about it all that much. My work is so demanding that in my spare time I like to get away, in company but without intimacy, to drink in the beautiful Australian outdoors and feel the texture of rock under my fingers. It's hard to explain to a non-climber just how much pleasure there can be in rocks, both in enjoying the variety, the colours, the responses to your touch, and in conquering a difficult and challenging climb.

In fact it was rock-climbing that brought Jonathan and me together. After my pathetic reaction to my brother's visit, I was determined to find some kind of social life at university. I couldn't be sure that this would come from other students in the science faculty, who would probably mostly be male. And English. I'd had almost no contact with English men, so I decided to broaden the possibilities by joining a club. After a careful survey of what was on offer during orientation week, the number of contenders dropped quickly. The Young Conservatives Club, the many Christian societies, GROW ('find your inner self by reaching out to others') and Women Who Want to be Women were early casualties, followed by other religious and political groups.

The final choice was out of four: the university's branch of the Pennines Rock-climbing Association, the Chocolate Appreciation Society, an international students' club or a hiking club.

I recognised a girl from Lambton School at the hiking-club table, which was enough to tell me that it was not for me. Face averted, I quickly moved on. The chocolate fanciers were handing out free Mars Bars and seemed quite friendly, so I signed up for that. Then I moved on to the rock-climbing club. A lone figure was sitting there, hair askew, reading a Gerald Durrell paperback. He looked up as I approached. 'You English?'

I wondered if it was a trick question. 'No.'

He leapt from behind the table, and grasped my hand. 'Then please join us. We're nearly up to quota and I'm trying to keep this club a Pom-free zone.'

How could I resist? It turned out that all Jonathan and I had in common was Anglophobia, but it held us together for the three years of my undergraduate degree. And when, just before it was time to graduate and go 'home', I got the letter from my mother telling me that she and my father were moving on to Laos and I realised I had no home, it was Jonathan who urged me to find a postgraduate course in Australia. 'You can just nick over to South-East Asia any time from Oz,' he said. 'It's like our backyard.'

I don't think either of us realised how much being on his home turf would change him. Or had being away from it changed him and he had reverted to his real self? I had somehow thought I wouldn't be so foreign in Australia, but to Jonathan's friends and family, to the people he introduced me to at parties, it was always: 'This is my wife, Alix. She's a Dutchy.'

For some reason this Australian version of Jonathan found my Dutchness highly amusing. If we met his friends at a coffee shop he would turn it into a kind of party trick. 'What's the Dutch for "with cream" Alix?' he'd ask, smirking in anticipation.

'*Met slagroom.*'

'What if we wanted to go to the lolly shop?'

'*Snoepwinkel.*'

Then his favourite. 'I need to go to the hospital, Alix.'

'*Ziekenhuis.*' This would have him almost pissing himself. Even though I felt uncomfortable, it seemed churlish not to play along since Jonathan enjoyed it so much. I hope none of his friends ever needed to use the Dutch words. I only learned them piecemeal and second-hand from my parents, so they were probably hopelessly out of date.

Because my father was determined we would all become fluent in English (the international language and, by extension, the language of God) the only Dutch words my parents used tended to be exclamations of shock, anger or elation, which I would instantly memorise. If a visitor came and used phrases of contemporary Dutch I would store them up and savour them. But not Abel. He regarded English as his ticket out, and I doubt if he would remember more than a few Dutch words.

To the students and staff at my new university things were even more complicated. My application had been full of anomalies. My nationality was Dutch, but my place of residence was Manchester, and my permanent place of residence was Madagascar. When, during the graduation process, my parents moved to Luang Prabang ('Where the fuck's that?' one frustrated clerk queried. 'Sounds like Shangri La.') I began to wonder where exactly, if anywhere, I did belong.

Again, the only people who accepted me without question were the rock-climbers, and I think it was the climbing that kept Jonathan and me going and supplied me with most of my happiest memories of the eighteen months it took me to complete my graduate studies. We travelled all over Australia in our efforts to find the most difficult or most beautiful climbs. So when I told him I'd been offered a senior position at a fat salary, the fact that it was in Western Australia seemed unimportant.

'What?' And then a silence. 'When did you apply for this?'

I was taken by surprise at his reaction. He had quite recently finished his studies, and although he had a job in Melbourne, he talked endlessly about moving 'onwards and upwards'. I had just assumed that he would come with me and make his upward move there. 'You'll get work straight away. There are plenty of jobs in Perth.'

'I've never even been to Perth. I don't have any contacts there.'

There was another silence and I felt a sudden shift in the air as if something between us had suddenly disconnected.

Then he looked at me. I still remember that look – hurt, sad, bemused, but not angry. 'You're going whatever I say, aren't you?'

I found it hard to look at his face. 'It's a great opportunity. I'll be managing all the field work – Broome, the Kimberley, Norseman …'

I wonder now what would have happened if I'd been more tentative, asked him how he felt. But I didn't. I simply presented it as a fait accompli, and took it for granted that he would follow me there, as he would have taken it for granted I would follow him if the circumstances were reversed. What I didn't take into account but now, with all the advantages of hindsight, I can see quite clearly, was that our career paths were beginning to diverge.

I was in a rapidly expanding field where jobs were plentiful and well paid, and where there was a shortage of qualified geologists. For me, the time was ripe. You could go in with very little experience, prove your worth, and cut a swift path to a senior position, even as a recent graduate.

For Jonathan, it was the opposite. The legal workforce moved slowly, along historically defined trajectories, and the path to senior levels was arduous and heavily tainted by nepotism. No wonder Jonathan was afraid of disrupting it.

That evening, however, he arrived home with champagne and roses and cooked a celebratory dinner. I thought everything was going to be all right.

I left for Western Australia about eight months after my journey to the Philippines. Jonathan didn't follow me. I don't think he'd even considered it.

CHAPTER FIVE

Coast Banksia *(Banksia integrifolia)*
A large tree with dark-green leaves that are silver
underneath. It is named after Sir Joseph Banks,
who first collected samples in 1770. The distinctive
pale-yellow flowerheads are made up of pairs of
individual flowers and are followed by the woody
grey cones made infamous for my generation by
the wicked Banksia Men in May Gibbs' *Snugglepot
and Cuddlepie* books. The blossoms are an excellent
source of nectar if soaked in water, but to avoid
natural fermentation do not store the blossoms or
allow plastic bags for gathering both nectar and
dew to become heated by the sun.

Atkinson's Guide

FIELD DIARY - Tuesday 17 April

Daybreak: Go outside for exercise and toilet.
Explore beach.
With my increasingly sparse liquid intake, the
urgency of the daily toilet stops has diminished
markedly, which I'm very much afraid is not a good

sign. Once the necessities were over I returned to
the cave and put on my jeans and boots, which
is becoming quicker and easier as the jeans are
becoming looser. Then, whistling recklessly, I finally
took the rocky staircase down to the beach. It was
still very early, and quite cool, but I was hoping there
might be some way of having a wash in the sea. The
constant dirtiness, which had been so familiar I didn't
even think about it, has become suddenly unbearable
with a possible end in sight.

It was only when I got to the beach that I finally
began to feel a real sense of freedom. Even then, I
was still careful to step on rocks whenever possible
so I wouldn't leave boot prints. Much of the sand on
the little beach was covered in small pebbles and
piles of plant debris, so it wasn't too difficult to avoid
leaving a trail. I told myself it was in case they came
back and searched the area, but in reality it was
more of a kind of obsession, a magical insurance. *If I
allow for the worst, it will prevent it from happening.*

I had built up great hopes for this little beach, so
of course they were bound to be at least partially
dashed. The karkalla was as abundant as I could
have wished, and I picked an armful of long thick
strands, to supply me not only with fruit but with
rope as well. However, my hopes of washing in the
sea were sadly disappointed. The sea was deep and
clean-looking, but almost inaccessible. The beach,

such as it was, was surrounded by a conglomeration of jagged rocks, slippery with seaweed, which I attempted to climb to see if there was any kind of diving platform. I soon realised that it was crazy to try this, particularly now when my prospects were just getting better – hardly the time to go seeking injury. So I gathered my spoils, and set off back up the steps, stopping about halfway up to make a thorough survey of the beach below.

I'd been in such a hurry to get down there I hadn't taken much notice of the lie of the land on my descent but now, viewed from above, I noted a possible launching place if the time ever came when I had to take to the water from this side of the island. I memorised it as best I could, took a good last look around, and then returned to the cave.

Since it was still very early, I decided to make a short trip to the coast banksia scrub, to see if I could obtain some nectar from the flowers. I found some blossoms in the remnants of shade that were still heavy with dew and tried squeezing the nectar into my hand, and then into my mouth. It turned out to have a gentle honeysuckle flavour, not at all overpowering, but sweetly delicious. I wondered if this was what the ambrosia of the gods tasted like.

I managed to fill two small bags, tying them tightly and packing them into one of the remaining kitchen tidy bags. I knew I'd need to store this nectar carefully and keep it cool. I couldn't risk it fermenting. Alcoholic abandon is the last thing I need in my situation.

Again, by force of habit that was now superfluous if not downright superstitious, I brushed away my footprints on the return journey. Then I carefully stowed the nectar in the coolest and darkest corner of the cave until it was time to leave.

6.00–8.00 a.m.: Housekeeping.
I was slightly late with starting, but loading my backpack and clearing the cave took a surprisingly short time. I was determined to leave my shelter as close as possible to its original condition, and by the time I had finished, all that was left to do was to eat my breakfast, make my plan, and then sweep out all reminders of my presence.

8.00–9.00 a.m.: First meal.
It was just after nine o'clock when I sat down to my peanut and sultana feast. I skipped the usual morning drink and decided to strip the karkalla plants and put some of the fruit out in readiness for my midday snack. I packed the rope-like stems, which might yet prove useful.

Then I moved to the entrance space and went over my plan yet again, somehow finding it hard to believe that it was safe to leave my hiding place, even though I was convinced that they had all left, and that now I had the island to myself.

12.00–1.00 p.m.: Fruit snack.

At midday, I got out my allowance of boobialla and karkalla fruits, but I felt sick and apprehensive and had to force myself to eat. Then I checked again that I had packed everything, that nothing was leaking, that everything was right with the world. For once the time seemed to race, and I felt my heart beating, not so much from fear of danger as from, ironically, fear of change. I have become used to my restricted life, and a part of me was reluctant to leave it.

3.00–5.00 p.m.: Prepare to leave cave.

At exactly three o'clock, wearing several layers of clothing, my pack on my back, I found a leafy branch and swept out the cave. As I surveyed it one last time, I was both gratified and chilled that no sign of my presence remained. Placing the tree once more across the entrance, and still carrying a branch to cover my tracks, I set out for the cabin.

Sunset. Prepare for sleep. Finish diary.

My heart's still pounding. I know I'll be awake all night. It's not quite dark yet, so I'll just have time to write up my diary. My journey began very well. I was worried that I would be too weak to carry my pack any distance, but found that although I was very much less fit than usual, I still had enough stamina to carry my already much diminished supplies. In fact, it was such a novelty to be out during the day, without the need for constant fear and vigilance, that I was thoroughly enjoying the scenery, the fresh air and the physical exercise.

I think I might have begun whistling, or even singing, when the path stopped climbing and I reached the much easier terrain in the valley. Still, as I came over the rise, habit impelled me to hold my branch in front of me, so that I was at least partially shielded as I heard a soft crunching sound and instinctively ducked behind a bush.

Heart in mouth, I peered cautiously out, and came almost face to face with Dave. He was looking the other way, down into the valley, perhaps having heard my not so careful approach but unable to locate where the sound had come from.

For a moment time seemed to stop. I froze, overwhelmed with horror, all my reactions suspended, unable to move or think. Dave was still looking around and, just before he had time to turn my way, I somehow forced my body into action, pulling the jagged rock from my pocket and throwing it as far into the valley as I could, praying that he would follow the sound.

With a curse, he turned and hurtled down the path while, still shaking and sick with fear, I retreated as quickly and quietly as I could, still making the time to erase my footprints until I found a place where I could leave the path and push my way through scrub, frantically hoping to reach the cave before he decided to search in that direction. Choking, retching, scarcely able to breathe, I reached the path to the cave, forcing myself to go on erasing every footprint, pulled the bush from the entrance and then replaced it as I half-fell inside, almost fainting with terror. I shook off my pack, took my remaining weapons into my hands and waited, trembling, for the footsteps I was sure would come.

It is now two hours later, and no sound has broken the silence. I have not made a toilet run, too afraid to venture out. If my need becomes desperate, I will use a plastic bag. I have set the alarm on vibration for 5 a.m., first light, and if I can gather enough courage I will go out then to try to squeeze some morning dew from the coast banksia flowers, enough at least for one day. But that means a five-minute walk. Can I risk it? The only way to soothe the nausea and retching as I waited in dread of discovery was to take tiny sips of nectar, and over half of what I collected this morning is gone. Although I have food enough for five more days, in my shocked and weakened state I know I cannot

survive for very long without water. I have made
myself eat some boobialla fruits to add moisture,
but the nausea is still there and my heart is beating
like a jackhammer.

I try to calm down by convincing myself that
Dave was trying to rescue me, that he had stayed
on without Matt because he didn't want to leave me
stranded on the island. But even as I think it, I know
it is not true. In that one brief terrified glance I saw
what Dave had in his hand. A hunting knife, three
times the size of my pocket knife, balanced ready to
plunge into my rapidly beating heart.

No. He stayed on to do a job. He wasn't searching.
He was stalking. Should I just give up and let him find
me? But in this state I'd be no match for Dave. And
I don't know what his plan is. Would he care about
revenge, with Matt not there to watch? *Is it better
to be raped than dead?* This is crazy thinking, Alix.
By now he'll be in such a state of induced rage, he'd
probably try to kill me whatever the plan. I wish I
knew if he had any other weapons or any fighting
skills. And what he is seeking revenge for.

As darkness falls, I sit hunched, clutching my
weapons, without any attempt to make myself
comfortable. The time is 5.54 p.m. on Tuesday the
17th of April.

* * *

I cannot sleep, as adrenalin pumps through me, and my mind stays on red alert.

As on that first night on the island, sickness and fear battle for my attention. That night I did sleep eventually, but only when I was quite sure that Matt and Dave had fallen into their various states of drunken and drugged unconsciousness. It had been a long and frightening day, and an even longer night.

When we left the boat my sickness quickly diminished, but I was so upset by the boat trip and the obvious isolation of the island that I must have continued to look slightly green. Dave was still all attention, carrying my pack for me and offering to get water, but Matt eyed me coldly. 'Thought you were supposed to be the supergirl.'

The Duffy brothers also gave me some strange looks, but I was not in any state to care about what they thought. They took considerable time loading a lot of identical white boxes onto a wheeled cart, while Lana and Dave carried insulated bags of food.

To shield myself until I could work out what was going on, I let myself slump into a kind of haze. On the short walk from the jetty to the cabin I asked no questions. I didn't need to. It was clear enough that Matt's cabin *was* the settlement. No architect-designed A-lines here, just a simple fibro-cement shoebox with an outside tank and what looked like an outside dunny.

Matt must have caught my dismay. 'Feeling all right?'

I made it as half-hearted as I dared. 'OK.'

'Better smarten up. We're here to have a good time.' Though his voice was light, there was a hint of menace in it. It was a warning. He was ahead of the rest of us, carrying a very expensive digital camera, and had the place unlocked by the time we struggled up. 'Welcome to the Island of the Damned. Cocktails on the terrace in ten minutes.' They all looked at me. I made an effort.

'I should have packed my crucifix.' It was pretty lame, but Matt and Dave laughed. The Duffy brothers remained impassive as they drew their cart up to the door and silently unloaded box after box, carrying each load carefully into the cabin.

When that was done they parked the cart around the back and turned towards the sandblow. 'We'll be off then.' Matt followed them and I saw money change hands. The three of them spent some minutes in muttered conversation, then Matt slapped each of them on the palm. 'See you Monday then.'

'Yeah, Monday.'

After a short time I heard the boat start up and had a terrible feeling that I should have gone with them, that even the Dodgy brothers would be better than what was in store for me on this island, although what it was that worried me was hard to pin down. There was a charged atmosphere that seemed to infuse every gesture, every comment the three of them made, and I couldn't help wondering about the camera. Not one of them struck me as having the patience or the artistic temperament to equip them for landscape or wildlife photography.

Matt's expression didn't make me feel any better. 'Well, here we all are.' Since the commencement of the boat trip I'd had a dizzy feeling that I was taking part in a scenario where I alone hadn't read the script. I needed a delaying tactic until I could get my bearings.

'Is there a toilet?' I didn't need to put on the shake in my voice.

Dave was immediately all concern. 'You still sick?'

'A bit.'

He took my bag, pointed out the dunny, even opened the door and checked for spiders, but I could feel ill-will all round me. I shut myself in and sat down, about to sink into despair, when another of Kathryn's useful tips came to me. *If you're stuck at his house and you don't want to fuck him, throw up. Puts them right off.* I tried some heaving noises but they didn't sound convincing, so I did the full bulimia thing and stuck my fingers down my throat. It took a couple of tries to get the hang of it but eventually I managed it. I'm not often sick and when I am I try to be quiet, but this time I went for gross-out.

It worked. When I came out, genuinely green about the gills this time, they all looked pretty green as well. 'I think I need to lie down.'

Matt couldn't even look at me. 'Put her in the bunk room.' Again, Dave did the honours and although I didn't get much chance to look around, I noted a largish living room with a kitchen area and several doors leading off it. The bunk room was small and cramped, but for the moment it was mine. Dave dumped my bag, said to call if I needed anything, and quickly left, shutting the door. *Thank God.* I was so strung out I lay down on the lower bunk and, amazingly, fell into a fitful sort of dozing state. When Dave came back it was beginning to get dark outside. He was also clearly drunk. 'Ya want some food?'

I did. I was starving, but I couldn't let him know that. 'I don't think I can eat anything,' I said, 'but I'll get up. Is there a tap?'

Better still, there was a bathroom. No toilet of course, but a washbasin and shower, fed from the adjacent tank. Perhaps for Lana's benefit, the basin had a large and revealing mirror. I looked like shit. *Good.* I did a very basic clean up and went outside.

I hadn't seen the barbecue when we arrived because it was behind the cabin on the beach side. It was huge, built of brick, with wings on each side to serve both as tables and woodboxes. On one of these tables was a bowl of lettuce, some sliced avocado and tomato, and a pile of plates. On the other was a mixed array of glasses, bottles and debris. Clearly the drinks party had been going for some time, but I was just in time for the food.

'Drink?'

I asked for soda water, and when Matt pressed me, jocularity leaving him as the drink kicked in, to have whisky in it, I said, apologetically, 'I don't want to be sick again.' That shut him up, but it didn't improve his mood. I sensed that my time was coming, but he started in on Lana.

'What are you having, darl? A lettuce leaf? Can I cut you a teeny tiny sliver of meat? Or would that make you too *fat?*' He turned to me. 'Lana says she's a vegetarian, but what she really is, is *anorexic.*' I had no answer for this. Of course she was. How else could she stay so pleasingly thin? 'You're not a vegetarian, are you, Alix?'

Something in his tone stirred an odd feeling of solidarity with Lana. 'I think I'll just try salad. I don't think I could face anything fatty.'

Lana must have picked it up, because she said quite kindly. 'I could cut up some cucumber, if the avocado's too rich.' I thanked her and went to follow her into the cabin, but she brushed me off. 'I can do it.'

I picked up a plate and chose some lettuce and tomato. Somehow I had to eat some meat and, if possible, avocado, if I was to follow the plan already hatching in my mind. While Lana was occupied, I needed to get the men away. A distraction. On rock-climbing trips, all that was needed to galvanise a group of blokes was to ask them to build a fire.

I made a huge effort to make my voice sound normal. 'I would have thought you'd have had a bonfire going here.' I looked around me. 'Plenty of fuel. But maybe you're not allowed to light fires. When's fire-ban season?'

As I'd hoped, Matt immediately leapt into action. 'No rules here. My dad owns the fuckin' island. We can do what we fuckin' like. Burn it to the ground if we want to.

Not going to spread anywhere, is it?' He made a sweeping gesture, taking in the surrounding sea, with no other land to be seen anywhere. 'C'mon Dave. Show her how it's done!'

The effect was instant. Matt used his foot to draw a circle on the sand, well away from the cabin, I noticed. Dave busied himself collecting driftwood and small sticks and then adding logs from the woodpile, while Matt stood to one side, watching. 'A few more on this side, mate. Now, one more log.'

Finally, he was satisfied. 'That'll do.' He turned to me. 'You want to light it?' But years of assiduously obeying 'no lighting fires' laws kicked in, and I couldn't bring myself to strike the match. I shook my head and casually wandered back to where Lana was standing at the barbecue.

Whoosh! It didn't take long before the whole pile was alight and the darkening sky turned red, and Lana moved towards them to watch. The two guys started dancing around it, whooping, hollering and capering like secular dervishes, fuelled by what seemed to me to be more than the effects of alcohol. *Who says modern man is civilised?* But at this moment I didn't care. I quickly grabbed a steak, the leanest I could find, covered it with avocado and took it around the other side of the cabin, eating as quickly as I possibly could without really making myself sick. When I came round the far side of the cabin Lana was putting slices of cucumber on the salad plate. She looked at me oddly. There was a tap attached to the tank, and I ostentatiously washed my hands (and surreptitiously my face), appearing beside her and adding some cucumber to my as-yet-untouched plate of food. 'I knew there'd be a tap somewhere.'

I could see she was puzzled by my behaviour, as we stood silently, nibbling salad and watching the blokes stumbling into the shallow water and then moving further and deeper. They started pushing each other's heads under, first playfully, then, at least on Matt's side, not so playfully. It was unnerving to see how innocent they looked, the firelight reflecting kindly on their country-boy faces, tousled hair and strong white teeth, the kind of young men you would choose to advertise toothpaste or a health spa. *Just as long as you didn't look too closely.* Jumping around in their multi-coloured board shorts, they could have been brothers, with Matt the handsome, blue-eyed elder, and Dave the slightly inferior copy, always trying to keep up.

I turned to Lana. 'How long have you been with Matt?'

She didn't say anything but silently beckoned me to come inside the cabin. 'Stay sick as long as you can,' she whispered, her voice urgent, and somehow different. 'Do not go anywhere alone with Matt.' Just as quietly, she hustled me outside again and got back to cooking the steaks as if nothing had happened.

I don't think anyone said another word to me until I told them I was going to bed and Dave said goodnight, and helped me to my room, even bringing me a glass of water for my bedside.

Why was he bothering to be so nice to me?

CHAPTER SIX

Caves and rock fissures make ideal shelters. However, make sure your chosen shelter is completely dry and above the waterline if close to a river or seashore, and check for signs of inhabitation that might make your stay uncomfortable (for example, by bats, insects or reptiles). Dry caves are generally warm in winter and cool in summer. If necessary, a fire just outside the entrance can deter nocturnal visitors such as dingoes.

Atkinson's Guide

FIELD DIARY - **Wednesday 18 April**

Today will be a day for sticking to my timetable to the letter.

Daybreak: Go outside for exercise and toilet.
A hideous night of feverish nightmares interrupted by wakeful periods trying to stop myself from genuinely throwing up. I thanked the entire pantheon of gods and goddesses when the alarm began to

vibrate, and I knew the long night was over. It was not yet dawn, but I could see enough to get myself ready and the moment a hint of light appeared I put on my boots, grabbed my knife and hurried as much as was humanly possible to get myself outside, looking behind me nervously on the short journey to the holey rock. I had held it in for so long and so successfully that I thought I wasn't going to be able to go at all, despite the pressure on my bladder. Eventually, thinking about waterfalls, massaging my stomach, even making myself cough, I managed to let go, but the resulting stream was worryingly small. I now had only about a quarter of a bottle of nectar water for the day, and then I would have no water at all, but I could not imagine ever daring to go out collecting again.

My body was knotted up from stress and lack of movement, so I did a rapid kind of dance on the rocky headland to try to loosen up, but was so spooked by the possibility of Dave's return that I scuttled back to my cave before I could get any real benefit. It was not even six o'clock yet, and I stood just inside the entrance, peering through the branches of the dead tree, breathing the slightly fresher air.

Finally, when my watch showed six, I managed to haul myself into the interior of the cave to start my day.

6.00–8.00 a.m.: Housekeeping.
Since I changed my clothes yesterday, and have
been too scared to go out searching for nectar,
there wasn't much in the way of housekeeping to
do. Instead I read over my diary and tried to predict
my future. From conversations half-heard on the
boat coming over, I know that the Duffy brothers run
a fishing-tour business, available on Mondays and
Thursdays, when they also run any errands to the
inhabited islands, so there's a remote chance that
a boatload of tourists might stop off on this island
tomorrow. If I could find some way of bypassing
Dave, I could leave with them, because surely even
the Dodgy brothers wouldn't dare do anything to
me in front of onlookers? But how to bypass Dave? If
there was a way down from yesterday's hide I could
stash myself there at dawn and then coolly step out
of the scrub to join the party. But there isn't and no
other plan has presented itself, no matter how much
I scour my mental map of the terrain.

By seven o'clock I was so fed up I ate my ration
of nuts and sultanas and took two tiny sips of the
rapidly diminishing nectar. *To hell with the timetable.*
Unless Dave or I leave the island tomorrow, the
next opportunity would not come for another four
days. By then I will have run out of food as well as
water, unless I can find a way to gather some more.
A thick lump of fear and despair clogged my chest

and throat. I longed for the release of tears, but the ability to cry was beaten out of me many years ago by the flowers of budding English womanhood at Lambton School for Young Ladies.

As a way of improving my spirits I decided to do a complete survey of the cave. First, using the last remaining sharp pencil, I drew an outline, as close to scale as possible (5 centimetres = 1 metre), into the back page of my diary, marking in the compass points at the corners of the page. I know my pack is half a metre long, so I found a long karkalla stem (I knew they'd come in useful!), doubled it over and cut it with my knife to form a rough metre measure. Then, walking, crawling and edging around the cave, I drew in rock outcrops, shelves, holes and crevices until I was satisfied I had an almost complete cross-section map of the walls. I turned over the page and made a rough plan of the ceiling holes. If I ever get a chance to climb the cliff above, I can search for the location of the cave using this map. If I had enough water, I could pour some through the holes as a check. *If. If. If ...*

I didn't want to damage the cave too much, but I collected my hammer and knife and chipped out a sample of the wall, a sample from one of the outcrops and a scraping of fine sand from a crevice in the cave wall. These I placed carefully into plastic kitchen bags. I took a moment to rejoice that I'd had the presence of mind to pocket an entire pack of these useful items that have made my life easier in so many ways.

As I had thought, the cave appeared to be a standard granite rockfall, so I didn't expect to find anything world-shattering in there, but it would be interesting to analyse it, if I ever get the chance. *If.*

Who was I kidding, thinking I was ever going to get out of here? Suddenly, a kind of rage gripped me. I wanted to tear up the pointless map, throw the tools at the walls and scream in frustration. But I didn't. I sat, hugging my pack, bottling up the sounds and the feelings until it was time to put my things away and do some exercise.

10.00 a.m.–12.00 p.m.: Stand in entrance space.
When I finally reached the standing space, instead of doing exercises, I found myself silently punching the rock walls and kicking the floor. In the split second when I heard myself thinking, *Don't draw blood!*, an idea came to me – a way to convince Dave that I really have gone. It would take a lot of planning, and a lot of nerve, but it just might work.

12.00–1.00 p.m.: Return to sitting position. Snack time. Write up diary.
The remaining boobialla fruits were already shrivelling and drying. I knew they wouldn't last

another day, so I ate them all, and again found them surprisingly satisfying and to some extent thirst quenching. But the shock of yesterday has left me weak and in no doubt that my diet, while adequate to sustain life, does not provide enough energy to cope with physical or mental stress. As I stashed the pits away for later disposal in the hope they might grow future new little boobialla trees, I pondered how I could find ways of enhancing my diet that would go beyond fruits and leaves, but without much success.

I have only been so weakened by stress a couple of times before, and then I was fully nourished, and able to sublimate some of the anxiety into bouts of excessive exercise. Now I do what exercises I can, and they make me tired. I know this is a worry, but I don't want to think about it.

I wonder where I'd be now if I wasn't here. I still have about half of my holiday to go. I'd had some vague thoughts of going over to the west, to see a few friends, and perhaps do some climbing. I just somehow never got round to organising it. I'm sure if I had gone the loose network of climbers would have supplied me with partners and opportunities for rock-climbing, but nobody was booking me up in advance. Then Dave's invitation came, and I got charmed (or more accurately, bullied) into that.

I'd worked in the west for eighteen months without forming any important ties. Was this because of some failure on my part? Was it, as Jonathan had implied, because I was 'foreign'? I hadn't wanted to think about this before. The nature of the work meant that people came and went. As field project manager, I'd assemble a team, organise transport and equipment, oversee the work and then disassemble the whole thing and write up a report. Each project was different. Each project lasted two or three months from beginning to end. Of course sometimes people or places overlapped, but basically it was a whole new adventure each time. And I loved it. I'd done it well, so well they'd offered me a promotion back to the head office in Melbourne. Ironically, an office job that didn't seem to require any of those skills.

This was when I started working with Kathryn. We both held senior management positions and that was when we discovered that we made a formidable team. We also gradually found out that we had an unofficial job that must have been intended all along, but which came as a surprise to both of us the first time it happened. This initial joint venture earned us the title of 'The Troubleshooters'. A huge field enterprise had come so unstuck that the team leaders had actually quit, leaving an entire camp set-up and body of workers bereft and rudderless. Kathryn and I were sent on urgent despatch to sort out the mess.

As a field rescue team we quickly found out how complementary our skills were. She is a genius at organising and managing people. My skills are in managing work schedules, equipment and supplies. Together, we are unmatchable.

Oddly enough, in those early days we didn't socialise together much, although we got along really well. When I arrived back in Melbourne, I was still married to Jonathan, and once Kathryn had established that he didn't have any single male friends she left us peacefully alone. Not that this did us any good. By then our marriage was all but over, although I was still blissfully unaware of what was happening.

Now I wonder if I should have gone back to the west and tried to put down some roots there. Maybe I'm a nomad at heart. *I don't like this kind of thinking.* I bring my mind firmly back to the present.

Too much sitting has made me stiffen up. I need to put my diary aside and force myself to do more exercise, knowing I won't be going out again today. I try to move every part of my body, and now I do feel marginally better, but somehow my heart isn't in it. Instead I turn my mind to the problem of food.

The boobialla crop is almost at an end, and harvesting more karkalla from the rocky beach is now out of the question. If I am to survive, then tomorrow I will have to go out very early and try to squeeze out some nectar from the coast banksia flowers. I know this, but I can't believe I will do it.

Sunset.
I have not gone out. The lack of fluid has made the need for a toilet expedition far less pressing than the need to remain hidden, although I have my plastic bag at the ready, along with my weapons, just in case. The time is 5.53 p.m. on Wednesday the 18th of April.

* * *

Surrounded once again by utter blackness, I'm so keyed up I feel I could burst.

As I wait to pass the night confined in the darkness, my body craves the relief of a long fast walk. That was how I dealt with bad times in my before-island life. I find myself wishing I could at least weep, or tear my hair, anything to deflate the pressure, but the traditional outlets for feelings were firmly squashed out of me many years ago.

Despite everything, the worst time of my life was probably the lonely journey into what seemed like exile when I was thirteen years old. The first misery was the ship, an ancient rusting cargo vessel where I was squeezed into a cramped dark cabin with a family of British missionaries who had managed to negotiate a free passage, plane travel to and from Madagascar being both unreliable and highly unsafe, with one of the highest airline fatality rates in Africa. While this seemed to me like a voyage of the damned, the well-meaning guardians briefed to 'keep an eye on me' loomed surreal and terrible above me at intervals, like Dickensian grotesques with their religious fervour and filthy black garments, interrupting the almost continual bouts of stomach-wrenching weeping that were my only comfort.

Then, even more unreal, arrival in cold, grey England, to be greeted by relatives I had never met, who spoke a language quite unlike the English of my schoolbooks, and sent me to school among strangers. Until then, I had never been parted from my family for even one day.

I was so angry and upset I would not say goodbye to my mother, who travelled with me by *camion-brousse* to see me safely onto the ship. It only occurs to me now how great a loss this must have been for her. The time spent with me in 'English lessons' would be hard to fill. A little teaching of the younger boys, the weekly health clinic, ('my Witch Doctor day' she used to call it), when she ministered to minor ailments, and her Tuesday mah jong game were all she had to do. No wonder she was always willing to coach me through *Treasure Island* or *Jane Eyre* and then talk about England, its geography, its history, its lost empire.

She was not happy, my mother. She made her way gravely through the days, and my only memories of her laughter come from the holiday in Ankarana and the one extraordinary time she and I went into the Big Town, Tana, on our own.

Vader, trying to mend the roof from a rickety ladder, had fallen and twisted his ankle and Abel, who hated going into town, offered to stay and look after him while Moe and I set off in search of embrocation and painkilling medicine. Although we said little during the zebu-cart ride, I sensed that this was a momentous occasion, a feeling confirmed when we arrived at the market-square in the lower town. Once the driver had helped us down and gone on his way my mother scooped me up in her arms and danced me around, crying 'Free! Free! Alixi, we will take the whole day!'

However, first we went into the section of the market that sold local medicines, where she bargained and hummed and hawed over medicines for Vader. There were all kinds of liniments and embrocations on display, but the painkilling tablets were brought out from under the counter after a great deal of whispering and haggling. I realise now they must have come through the black market. They certainly cost about six times as many francs as the liniment.

Normally visits to Tana were conducted as quickly as possible, with no time for dawdling or dallying. This time, however, as soon as duty was done I discovered that Moe had plans. Our driver had been dismissed, to return later in the day, but now she engaged a *camion-brousse*, producing a secret purse, quite different from the big black housekeeping purse she had used for the market, and instructed the driver to circle the lake.

'I'm going to show you the sights,' she said to me, and for the next hour we took a scenic tour. First the lake, with jacarandas in full bloom reflected in the black water, then up the hill to the old queen's palace, the *rova*. We stopped at the top to admire the view but didn't go in. Then we circled down and down, seeing a town I had not been aware of, all red clay roofs and hanging pots and more jacarandas, much lovelier than our usual approach through the paddy fields to the markets.

'Here,' she told the driver, as we drove along the Avenue de l'Indépendance, and she had paid, climbed down, lifted me down and waved the driver off before I had time to collect my wits. I looked around and saw shops and street stalls and cafes with little tables outside. To my amazement and delight, Moe led the way to one of these, selected a table and sat down. She ordered coffee for herself, a *citron pressé* for me, and cakes. I couldn't believe what I was hearing. But sure enough, the waiter returned with a tray, from which he took our drinks and placed them in front of us, taking a cloth napkin for each of us and unfolding it on our laps. Then he lifted a silver tower with a domed handle and placed it carefully in the middle of the table, with a pair of silver tongs beside it.

When he had left, Moe turned to me. 'Which one would you like, Alixi?' On the top level of the tower were tiny cakes filled with cream, on the next layer little yellow cakes baked with fruit, and on the bottom layer tiny open pies. I was struck dumb.

'Perhaps we'll start with the savouries,' and Moe picked up the tongs and deftly served us. I don't know how long we sat there, but we managed to finish everything – cakes, pies and another drink for each of us. And while we sat we had a conversation, like ladies at a tea party. That's what I remember most of all.

Moe did most of the talking. She talked of Home, of her family, of her schooldays, of things Leni and she used to do as children. But most of all, she talked of England, a place she had never seen but which seemed to hold for her an endless fascination.

Why was my mother such an Anglophile? Did she feel that her sister, by marrying an English diplomat, peer of the realm and former well-known man-about-town, had made a better choice than hers? It had certainly put Leni into the public eye and the social pages, but would Moe really have enjoyed all that?

Tante Leni and Uncle Raoul had no children. Perhaps Leni was as dismayed as I was when the gangplank was lowered and we faced each other for the first time. She meant to be kind, I know, but she was not tough like my mother and my unremitting sadness wore her down. Jonathan used to say, 'People who have had a hard time always blame other people, but people who have done well congratulate themselves.' Leni was like that, and Raoul even more so. All affability when about his diplomatic duties, at home he seethed with resentment of his older brother Rupert, who inherited the manor house while poor Raoul only got the eight-bedroom cottage. 'I'm the only one who ever had to work for a living,' Raoul was fond of saying, and Leni would quickly join the lament. 'We've worked hard for what we have,' she would say. 'Nothing's been handed to us on a plate.'

But it seemed even to my thirteen-year-old self that it had. For all Leni's stories of an idyllic rural childhood playing in the fields and streams, I remembered my mother's stories of coming home from school to make cheese in the family's dairy, of missing school to mind baby Leni, sick with measles. 'Leni was always the favourite,' she would say, without any trace of envy. Leni was her favourite too. 'Leni was the beautiful one, the clever one.' I know little about their family, but I do know that my mother, a self-taught photographer who had built up her own niche business, paid for beautiful clever Leni to go to pharmacy school, and made the dress Leni wore to the party where she met Raoul. These were stories my mother sometimes told, although Leni seemed to have forgotten them completely.

One thing you could say about my mother. She made her bed and she lay in it, uncomplaining, for the full term of her life. Whereas I, displaced and terrified, lay in the canopied bed in my aunt's house, crying my heart out, until the school term started and all my tears dried up.

I remember almost nothing about Lambton School, at which I was a weekly boarder for four years. The only lessons I learned there were never to show weakness, never to show fear, never to turn your back, and never, ever to shed a tear, even in the dark. *Especially in the dark.*

I couldn't believe that my kindly mother would have sent me to this place, so like a Dickensian prison with its absence of heating, constant threat of punishment by both staff and pupils, and the unrelenting, unforgivable stigma of being an outsider in a place where even being an insider was a sentence to a life of torture.

I suppose Moe, like me, failed to recognise the understory of cruelty and sadness in our English books. When we read *The Secret Garden* what we remembered was the magical garden, allowing us to forget all about the terrible past histories of the children who reclaimed it. These books, now I'm looking back on them, were primarily about stoicism, punishment and independence, only the last of which really has anything to commend it.

I didn't cry after my parents' deaths. I took to roaming around the streets and foreshore, and developed an addiction to fat and grease. I'd pause in my ramblings to lunch on potato cakes or dim sims, and then at nine or ten o'clock I'd grab a pizza or a souvlaki. On weekends, while Jonathan was poring over his law books, I'd take the train to more distant places, to the zoo where I'd sit for hours watching the penguins swim pointlessly around in circles, or prowl the walkway beside Merri Creek, glaring at the graffiti and the snake warning signs and the passers-by, who would detour up onto the grass to avoid me. I was in a permanent daze, barely sleeping, burning up the fast-food kilojoules in manic exercise, unable to study, the words dancing before my eyes like snowflakes.

Jonathan was never very good at dealing with misery, 'I get enough of that at work,' he'd say, and my fellow students, at a loss at how to deal with such naked sorrow, chose to ignore my state. Ironically, it was this state that must have cemented Dave's interest. Perhaps not so ironic. *Damsel in distress*, Kathryn would tell me. *Men love it.*

I already knew Dave, of course, but his attention had seemed quite brotherly until that one afternoon in my life I broke my own rules and confided my feelings to a virtual stranger.

My mistake.

CHAPTER SEVEN

Famadihana *ceremony*

An unusual ceremony in Madagascar is the *famadihana*, meaning 'turning of the bones', carried out by the Merina and Betsileo people. This takes place between four and seven years after the first burial when the remains of the selected relative are removed from the tomb or crypt, rewrapped in a specially woven burial shroud, called a *lamba mena*, with their name rewritten on the new cloth so they will not be forgotten. During this time the corpse is lovingly handled and informed of all the latest village gossip and brought up to date with family events. *Famadihana* is regarded as a time of joy with festivities including drinking, music and dancing, which will often include holding the body aloft and dancing with it as the relatives circle the tomb before replacing the newly enwrapped corpse.

> Alix Verhoeven, 'Life in Madagascar', *Tempora mutantor*, Geology Department student magazine

FIELD DIARY - Thursday 19 April

Today is the Duffy brothers' regular boat trip day.

I had not allowed myself to get up too many hopes, but at the back of my mind was the possibility that Dave would give up, not having found me after his pretence of leaving, and go with the Dodgy brothers to the mainland. I reacted to the shock of seeing Dave on Tuesday by falling to pieces. Today I must gather the pieces back together. I decided to make my preparations for observing the boat after checking for nectar and making a toilet stop. Even without the alarm, I awoke just before light, and knew I must steel myself to go out.

Daybreak: Go outside for exercise and toilet.
After an uneventful visit to the toilet rock, I returned, put on jeans and boots, filled my pockets with plastic bags and ties, and made a fast beeline for the copse of coast banksias. My heart leapt when I found their blossoms not just damp with dew, but heavy with moisture, hanging ready to drop their load. I squeezed four good bagfuls, sealed them carefully, and headed for home, stopping briefly to harvest the few remaining boobialla fruits on the way and scatter my leftover pits for the birds to recycle. I deposited the bags inside the cave, returned outside to remove

my jeans and boots, and then happened to look up.
The sky was black.

6.00–8.00 a.m.: Housekeeping.
It has not rained since I came to the island and I
don't think it had occurred to me that it could. I
had no idea how my cave would be affected. Would
it leak, even flood? I spent some time packing
my damageable belongings into the backpack,
which I placed on the rock ledge to await further
developments. Rain would enable me to capture
at least some drinking water, which made me wish
I had managed to bring more suitable containers.
It could also be an advantage if it deterred Dave
from searching and encouraged him to leave.
Furthermore, it would provide visual cover for me
to go to my hide on the clifftop to watch for the
boat. I've packed my anorak with weapons and a few
boobialla fruits. There won't be any need to carry
water, which can be squeezed directly from the coast
banksias along the way, unless the sun comes out
and dries everything up.

8.00–9.00 a.m.: First meal.
Although the nausea had diminished, for once I
was not really hungry. However, I ate my peanuts
and sultanas, one at a time, forcing myself to finish
them. I have realised how important it will be for

my survival to stick rigidly to the timetable and not
give in to misery or panic. My lapses of yesterday are
already showing an effect, and I can't afford to give
in to such weakness again. I made myself drink a few
sips of the nectar water and carefully decanted the
remainder into my water bottle.

Because I was planning to leave early, I reversed
two items and instead of moving to the entrance
space for exercise I have continued to write up my
diary. I'll get enough exercise walking out to the
hide. I'm guessing the boat will come some time
between eleven and one o'clock, so I plan to set out
shortly. However, as the time nears I become more
and more nervous. What if I run into Dave again? At
least I am forewarned this time, and the path to the
cliff is well overgrown, providing good cover, but the
worst moments are going to be leaving the cave and
crossing the ridge, where the terrain is more open. I
know I have to do this, but I seriously wonder if I will
have the courage.

2.30 p.m.: Write up diary.
I finally forced myself to go out. Despite my head
turning anxiously all the way, I made good time to
the hide and was settled in by just after ten. My heart
sank when I saw the sky from that vantage point.
Black clouds were rolling and building, and I could
see lightning in the distance. The sea was a roiling

mass of grey. By twelve there was no sign of a boat.
Then the rain started, pelting down in torrents, and I
knew they wouldn't come. I waited for a break in the
downpour, then finally realised there wasn't going to
be one. Protected as best as possible by my anorak
and spare kitchen tidy bag, I made the dash back,
not even bothering to cover my tracks, which would
have been obliterated immediately by the sheets of
water turning paths into treacherous streams. I fell a
number of times and feared once I would be carried
down a steep incline, but I finally managed to reach
the path to the cave. There was no sign of Dave.
I crouched behind the cover tree, and with great
difficulty took off every bit of clothing, a task that
took me almost half an hour. I was soaked to the skin
and very cold, but at least I felt clean.

I won't dwell on the naked crawl into the cave,
and the challenge of unpacking my dry clothes from
the backpack while avoiding the small pools of water
that had formed on the floor of the cave wherever
there was a roof hole. I dressed myself in cleanish
half-aired knickers turned inside-out, short-sleeved
T-shirt, and the longest socks I could find, with my
Amnesty sleep T-shirt over the top, and dried my
hair as much as possible with a used and very dirty
T-shirt.

I was still cold. Fortunately most of the cave was
dry, and the temperature seemed to have remained

115

the same as usual, which meant that if I could warm myself up, I would probably stay warm. I took every item of dry clothing out of my backpack, folded the pack up and covered it with the sheoak branchlets I used to soften my sleep. I sat on this cushion of relative warmth, removed the long socks and replaced them with a shorter pair, draped the dirty T-shirt over my dripping hair, the long socks around my neck and the remaining pair of socks on my hands like gloves. I couldn't exercise without dislodging my makeshift comforters, so I just sat there, taking deep diaphragm breaths in the hope that they would stimulate my circulation, feeling like a damp but dignified, well-swaddled Buddha.

4.00–5.00 p.m.: Second meal.
This time I was hungry. I gradually untangled myself from my coverings and found that though not yet warm, I was no longer feeling deathly cold. The food helped, and when I finished eating I shucked the extra clothing and did what exercises I could in the sitting position. The entrance was still full of wet clothes, so I used the energy gained from the food to deal with them. I was able to hang the jeans from the tree root and the socks on the inside of the cover tree. They would only be visible if someone moved the tree, and if they did that, I was in trouble anyway. I also put out my water bottle, wedged upright in a

little depression in a nearby rock. That was risky but at this hour I felt it was a reasonable risk, and in no time at all I was able to bring it inside full to bursting with lovely clear, clean rainwater.

I didn't go out to the toilet. The rain was still coming down in torrents and I knew I could last the night if necessary. Even with the nectar, I'm drinking so little now that one toilet visit a day is enough. My bowels have been totally inactive on the restricted diet. What the health implications are I don't know, but at least I've made it this far in sufficient health to be able to move around and to think relatively clearly. But I'm beginning to worry. I've got enough food for only three more days, and I don't think I can cut my ration any further without endangering mobility.

There is no likelihood of the boat coming back before Monday, which is four days away. Even if Dave leaves then, I don't know how I can manage to get off the island, but at least there'd be access to the water tank and barbecue, and even possibly the cabin if I'm really lucky.

Sunset.
It will be dark soon, but the rain shows no sign of abating. The pools below the roof holes are slowly spreading and I hope they don't reach me in the night. They're not large, and I've put the dirty T-shirt

on the only one that threatens my sleeping space at the moment. I hope I don't end up having to sleep standing up.

On a hunch I crawl through to check out the entrance, and am horrified to see fingers of filthy water beginning to flow in. I have no containers, no towels or rags. All I can do is use my sheoak branches to try to soak up the inflow, dooming myself to an uncomfortable and uneasy night. I line my sleeping area with plastic bags, place my folded backpack under me as a kind of buffer cushion and wait, without much hope, for sleep. The time is 5.10 p.m. on Thursday the 19th of April.

* * *

Darkness falls and in my weakened and exhausted state I dream an oddly comforting dream ... I am back in Madagascar, but not as a child, nor as I am now. I am older, and more like my mother, but I know it is myself. I revisit all the old familiar haunts, and they come back to me in perfectly delineated detail, untouched by time. There are people there, but they are not people I know. They are incredulous when I say I used to live there. 'No, no,' they say. 'No foreigners ever lived here.' I ask for Ulysses' store, but am met with blank incomprehension.

I wake, feeling safe and happy, in spite of the negative reactions of the people in the dream, and then remember where I am and the thought comes to me, sharp as pain, *I want to go home.*

But where is my home? If I went back to Madagascar no-one would welcome me, except perhaps Ulysses, and my dream tells me there's no guarantee of that. Abel told me during his England visit, amused at my surprise, that the Malagasy didn't really like us, and only put up with us out of natural politeness and of course for what we could offer them. He had played with them, studied with them, and I had always thought they were his friends. 'We were in their country, telling them everything they believed was wrong,' he pointed out. 'Why should they like us?'

He'd been happy to leave, had known all along he had no place there, that the boys who played cheerfully with the cricket and football gear left behind by the London Missionary Society, who allowed him to participate in their *famadihana* rituals, to visit their families and join in their meals, would forget him the minute he was gone. They were not friends at all, just a congregation, made up almost exclusively of boys lured by the promise of learning English, my pragmatic father's way of ensuring regular attendance and food supplies. I think he hoped to save some souls and train them for the ministry, and he was regularly hurt and surprised when, armed with their new English skills, they lost interest in the church and got jobs in the fledgling tourist industry or, more commonly, the government.

None of them would remember me. Girls in Malagasy society did not have even the limited freedom their brothers had. Except for the few who came to Moe's Sunday School, who were just as shy as I was, I rarely met any. The London Missionary Society still has a website that coordinates an elaborate network of penpal communication between children of missionaries and children they met at the various stations around the world. The society no longer operates in Madagascar. I'm not surprised. Even my father gave up eventually.

No. Our family left Madagascar, and the tides of Malagasy life closed over our memory, leaving no trace.

England is not, and never will be, home for me, although Tante Leni and I maintain a dutiful correspondence. She wrote a strangely incoherent letter when my mother died, and even offered to come out to Australia if I needed her. Perhaps she was suddenly aware of the role her big sister had played in her life.

I think the only time she and my mother met after their respective marriages was at my graduation from the University of Manchester. Somehow my mother defied all my father's strictures about vainglory and worldly success, and turned up, flanked by both Tante Leni and Uncle Raoul, to witness my moment in the sun. I thought at the time my uncle had paid for her trip, but now I wonder if she used her secret cache of shares.

She brought me a tiny set of red and green woven baskets that made nostalgia well up and almost overwhelm me, and an umbrella with a carved handle in the shape of a lemur's head 'for the English rain'. I was so pleased to see her I thought my heart would burst. I hope she knew.

I want my mother. My mother who is both vividly alive in my memory and forever fixed as a broken, frozen, bloated travesty of herself, surrounded by dirty melting ice. In Madagascar, I would have been able to make things right by performing *famadihana*. Why don't Western societies have ways of looking after our dead? I don't even have her body. I can't even visit her. I feel a horrible sense of guilt, of having let her down.

The occasional church visitors who would arrive unexpectedly, looking uncomfortable and out of place, by *camion-brousse*, zebu-cart or, on the most desperate occasions, by clapped-out bicycle, were horrified by *famadihana*. They saw it as primitive and savage. I don't agree.

If I could take my mother's bones, handle them reverently, wrap them in clean linen, and tell her all my news, I'm sure I'd feel less terrible about her death. 'Civilisation' can often mean denial. Civilisation is leaving your parents' bodies and their possessions to be dealt with by officials, by strangers. No Malagasy would let their parents down like that.

The mother who came to my graduation was very much alive. 'You have a special *friend*?' She said it in the Dutch way and it took me a moment to realise she meant a boyfriend.

'Sort of.'

'I'd like to meet him.' She said this tentatively, as if it might be asking too much, but there was determination underneath. I explained that Jonathan was studying law, so we weren't graduating on the same day. Not being fond of formal occasions, he had gone on an expedition with the rock-climbing club.

'You met him there?' I nodded. 'Not at church?'

I was dumbfounded. 'No.'

To my amazement, my mother began to laugh. '*Goed.* Good!'

I guess after losing first her old life and then her son to the church, she was not eager to lose her daughter as well. Perhaps that was why I, unlike Abel, made an effort to visit whenever I could afford to, no matter how far afield my father's crazy evangelism took her.

This time, however, she was visiting me and while my uncle and aunt were with us and the formal proceedings were going on I was reminded of why I could never feel at home in England, and why Jonathan had chosen not to share in my special day.

I had learned at school the complete disdain the English superior classes held for anyone they considered inferior to them. I don't know whether it was my funny accent, my Dutch nationality, or the fact that my family lived in Madagascar ('*Where?*') but this deeply institutionalised snobbery still seems to me to epitomise the English. No matter how nice an English person may seem, even those in a lower place in the hierarchy are able to pinpoint any given person's class status within seconds.

At the slightly less snobbish University of Manchester I was almost acceptable. Jonathan, as an Australian exchange student, a 'colonial', for some reason was not. (Perhaps it was more due to his transparent scorn of the 'ponciness' of the English students.) Through climbing, and an informal Australian network, we formed our own society, rarely mixing with the English at all, to everyone's satisfaction.

But when Uncle Raoul turned up at my graduation all the sycophants came out of the woodwork. You would not believe the number of friends I suddenly acquired. It was good in one way because my mother must have thought I was highly popular, but it made me determine that never, ever could I live in a country so dominated by caste.

I think if I had stayed on in England to do my higher degree, they would have tried to befriend me, for the sake of the connection. Even weeks after, people who had never spoken to me before would stop me in the corridor. 'How's Sir Raoul' they'd ask, as if he was a familiar mutual friend. 'Are you going home for the summer break?' Perhaps they were hoping for an invitation. Fortunately I didn't stay around long enough to find out.

And Nederland? I have no memory of it, no sense of connection, but it was always regarded, especially by my mother, as Home. Is your nationality a product of where you live, or of the culture you grow up with?

One thing the missionaries had left us was a set of ancient encyclopaedias. These were dated in the 1920s, so they pictured a world long gone, but I found them comforting, with their pages of maps of all nations, potted (and sanitised) histories, and quaint views about the non-English world. Madagascar, for example, seemed to have no people in it at all, judging by the pictures, but lots of animals. There were pages of lemurs, sifaka and aye-ayes, not to mention orchids and exotic birds, none of which I had ever seen.

It was in these pages that I first discovered the world view of Dutchness – plump rosy-cheeked flaxen-haired people wearing funny clothes and wooden clogs on their feet. When they weren't skating on the Zuider Zee, or tiptoeing through fields of tulips, they seemed to spend all their time making cheese.

My parents were tall, dark-haired people who wore ordinary clothes. Abel resembled them in build and features though lighter in hair and complexion, but I was totally unlike any of them. Almost everything about me was medium and undistinguished – complexion, height, weight, hazel eyes – except for my hair. Jonathan, in an unusually romantic moment, said it made me look like a Boticelli angel. It was lighter than that, though, a sort of mid-brown streaked with red, but it was definitely my best feature.

My mother's memories of Home, the ones she shared with Abel and me, were of bicycling tours, eating *Rijsttafel* at an Indonesian restaurant on very special occasions, spending holidays with Vader's family on the island of Terschelling. The only familiar images in the encyclopaedias were the cheeses. My mother's family had been cheesemakers and she sometimes told us funny stories of the various mishaps attendant on the dairy business – cheese failing to set or setting too hard; the efforts of mice and rats to get to the ripening cheeses; rainy market days when all the cheese sellers had to compete for customers. There was a photograph of the market in the encyclopaedia. I wondered if Moe had worn a white hat with flipped side wings and coloured ribbons. I couldn't picture it.

What little else I know of Dutch culture has come from the occasional homesick remark from my mother or, even more rarely, from Vader. One thing he did miss was the Dutch religious observance. '*They* go to be with God,' he'd thunder, throwing off his hat as we returned from the tiny church, when only a sparse congregation turned up to hear his fire and brimstone because there was a festival on in the neighbouring village, 'Not for entertainment. This is a Godless land. Godless!'

I wonder if the modern Dutch population is equally devout. I wonder also if I'll ever go there to find out.

Jonathan always thought of me as Dutch. His final words as he saw me off on the plane to Western Australia were: 'There's a lot of Dutch people in Perth. Maybe you'll fit in there.' I was stunned. I hadn't known I didn't fit in.

I think of a piece of graffiti I read on a wall in the Northern Territory that brought a sudden chill of recognition – 'I was born in a taxi. I'm never going home.'

CHAPTER EIGHT

Temperatures in the sea vary far less than air
temperatures, due to the buffering effect of
the huge ocean-water mass. Sea temperature
changes characteristically lag behind changes in air
temperature. The sea is at its warmest one to two
months after air temperatures are highest, and the
same principle applies in reverse.

Atkinson's Guide

FIELD DIARY - Friday 20 April

I woke to the alarm at 5 a.m. and then waited until
the first light began to show through the cave roof.
I'd had plenty of time to mull over and modify my
daring survival plan and now the hour had come to
implement it. I have only two days' worth of food
rations left, and once that runs out it will be too late
to take action. Ignoring the muddy debris left after
the floods, I gathered my scattered clothes and
searched out what I needed. No time for a clean-up.
I'd leave that for when I came back. *If* I came back.

Emerging into the half-light is so much easier than in the full glare of the sun that I think I'll follow this procedure from now on, though perhaps setting the alarm a little bit later, for half past five. My plan was this: to climb down the stone stairway to the beach, swim around the point to where the rocks dipped into the sandy beach on the other side, and leave Kathryn's red rain slicker and my backpack tangled in the rocks and cut by what I hoped would look like toothmarks. As if I had tried to swim for it and been taken by a shark. Simple really.

This plan, however, had a few minor drawbacks. I could see by the colour and the way the rocks sheered into it that the water around this end of the island was extremely deep. I am a reasonable swimmer, but I was not fully convinced that I had the stamina to make the distance, knowing there would be little possibility of touching land en route, and even less possibility of touching bottom. In addition, I had no real idea of how far it was and I knew that the basis of my plan was not so very farfetched. The area was probably infested by sharks, and I might well be inviting the fate I was trying to fabricate. I had to will myself to not think about the ferry. Or those other sharks. Or my parents.

I listened carefully at the door of the cave for several minutes and heard nothing. So I set off. I couldn't swim in shoes, nor could I leave them neatly waiting for me on the shore, so I started off barefoot down the rough sandy path, dragging my disguise branch behind me, and dumping it in a scraggly leptospermum bush for use on my return journey. *If I made it back again.* I had decided to wear the dirty light blue T-shirt I'd used to mop up the floor last night. I hoped that it would blend in with the colour of the water and not make me seem in any way like a prey animal, and also that it might get cleaned in the process. I don't know much about sharks, but I remembered vague stories of surfers being popular targets because their black wetsuits made them look like seals. I also seemed to remember that sharks didn't see very well. Hard to know if that was a good thing or a bad thing in the circumstances. My backpack was also blue, with yellow piping, and I hoped in a way this would make me resemble a sea snake, an unlikely creature to be a shark's food of choice.

When I got to the rockiest part of the path I put on the pair of thick socks I had been saving for this purpose. I would have to leave them buried in the sand, which was perhaps risky, but the last thing I wanted before going into possibly shark-infested waters was scratched and bleeding feet.

The climb was not difficult. I did not need rope, although I proceeded very cautiously just to be sure. *Festina lente*, as my father would say. Hasten slowly. Always the showman, he loved to pepper his Sabbath readings with impressive Latin phrases. When I got to the beach I could see lots of fruits still clinging to the karkalla stems. These would be my reward if I came back. *When I come back. Think positive, Alix. You've survived this far.*

But when it came time to actually get into that blue-black water, when I had buried my socks in among the karkalla (along with my knife), shrugged my backpack over my shoulders, tied my hair back with two rubber bands, when there was no more excuse for delay, I didn't think I'd be able to do it. I seemed to see black shadows moving ominously in the depths, and though I knew they were probably clumps of kelp, swimming through clumps of kelp suddenly did not seem a particularly appealing idea, even forgetting the sharks, and the cramps, and the lonely drowning. But I was here now and I could not come up with a better plan so I clambered with difficulty until I reached the jutting rock, said a quick prayer to my parents' God, *Lord, please don't let me die*, dived in, and swam as strongly as I could out beyond the breaking waves.

I had expected the water to be cold. Not freezing, Arctic, dead-in-two-minutes cold, but miserable, clutch-at-your-heart, numb fingers cold. It was not warm, but it was surprisingly comfortable, the aquatic equivalent of room temperature. I swam out further to get clear of the rocks, then struck out towards the point. From the moment I first ventured outside I had known I had to do this today because there was no wind and the sea was as flat as an ice-rink. If it hadn't been, I'd never have made it. As it was, I'm very lucky to be alive. If it had been even a little further, or a little colder, I don't think I'd have been able to go the distance, and the steep cliffs of the point offered no possible landing place. I would have drowned, *alone, alone, all, all alone, alone on a wide, wide sea.* One thing that had defeated both Moe and me was a set of the works of the best English poets, most of which we could only read with great difficulty, finding the language beyond anything our English lessons had prepared us for. The one poem we had both loved was *The Rime of the Ancient Mariner*, both the language and the rhythm, and now I found the poet's words droning round and round in my head, all the time I was swimming, almost driving me crazy, although I took comfort in remembering that whatever happened to the Ancient Mariner, he didn't drown.

I swam and swam, in a kind of dogged delirium, until I was far round the point and the rocks began to fragment and lower and form inlets and rock pools and, finally, a sandy beach, the same beach that I had swum on only days ago, that terminated in front of the cabin.

I didn't go up onto the sand at first. I was too afraid of being seen. I pulled myself into the last inlet, hidden from the beach by a pile of seaweed-covered rocks, and coughed and gasped and shook for what seemed like a very long time. Time was what I did not have. With great difficulty, because it was wet and salty and firmly stuck to my T-shirt by now, I eventually managed to get the backpack off. It was time to get to work. I needed to leave it somewhere where it would not float away, but somewhere where it would be seen. I needed not to be seen doing the leaving. Nervously, I peered over the rocks. It was quite a long beach. And totally empty. I couldn't see the cabin and I didn't think anyone walking along the beach would be able to see me – at least not before I saw them. Clutching my backpack firmly, I climbed over to where the beach proper began.

And here I had a stroke of luck. Instead of an abrupt division between rock and sand, there were several little inlets with remnant rocky walls reaching like fingers onto the beach, where the rocks had been weathered into holes and crevices filled with brackish pools and broken rocks. I was able to move under cover of the rocks until I came to the last one and, still remaining hidden, I worked on my sacrificial offerings.

Although I had prepared as much as possible, there were some things that couldn't be done in advance. I had counted on finding a sharp rock to help in my task, but found in this little cove something even better, a scattering of shells of all shapes and sizes. It didn't take long to find a broken one with a sharp edge, and I used this to completely sever the left strap of my backpack, which I had partially severed with my knife before leaving the cave. In the pack was Kathryn's slicker, which I had calculated I would not need, and which had the major advantage of being red like the anorak I had worn on leaving the cabin. I was hoping Dave would remember a red jacket, but not notice that this was a different one.

Now that I had everything ready, I had to risk a brief exposure to anchor them on the other side of the rocks, high enough so they wouldn't be likely to wash away, and visible enough for the jacket to act like a beacon. Taking a deep breath, I peered over the edge of the rocks. Nothing. Heart thumping, I climbed over, trying not to hurry too much. I didn't want to risk cutting myself. Just beyond the tideline there was a dried-out rock pool and beyond that a scatter of rocks varying in size from tennis ball to basketball. I snagged the backpack around a jutting rock overhanging the rock pool, and then spent precious minutes finding a method of anchoring the slicker with stones so that it looked natural but was secure enough not to fly or float away. Glancing nervously at the other end of the beach and scuffing out any stray footprints slowed me down a little, but eventually I decided that it was as good as it was going to get, and that I should be out of there before any more time passed.

Without giving myself time to think, I climbed back to my landing place. I knew I was rested as much as I was going to be, and at least this was almost like a beach, and not quite so daunting as my original launching place. I wasn't going to think about how I'd get back onto the rocks. I had enough to worry about.

The swim back was worse than the swim out because I was tired and worried about the time. What if someone came while I was in the water? I'd be a perfect, visible target. It was still early, but the sun was already climbing in the sky. The swim had taken longer than I'd expected, and I had to stop myself from looking at my watch every few minutes, and force myself to keep on swimming. On the one hand, the lack of wind and smooth glassy surface of the water was a lifesaver, but on the other hand it made anything in the water much more visible. However, there was nothing I could do but keep going.

Just as I had rounded the last of the point and could see my goal in the distance, my leg hit something and my heart was gripped by icy

terror. *Shark*. In defiance of all common sense, I
immediately panicked and began losing my rhythm,
splashing and flailing around. If there had been a
shark, I was turning myself into a shark magnet. I was
so desperate to know what was in the water that I
took a deep breath and looked at the underwater
world, something I had deliberately avoided doing
for the entire journey up until now. There was no
sign of a shark or fish of any description. I had swum
into an area of submerged rocks and my leg had
brushed against one. It was bleeding, not profusely,
but steadily. Now I was doubly attractive to sharks,
and my panic swelled. I think I was almost ready to
give up and let myself drown or be taken. But then
that streak of stubbornness came through, and I took
a few deep breaths to calm myself down, closed my
mind to all these possibilities and swam steadily to
the rocks. I don't know how I got up onto the beach.
I think fear drove me. I tried to keep hidden and
looked all around and as far as I could see up the
rocky pathway. No sign of movement or anything
untoward.

I was exhausted. All I wanted to do was lie on
the sand and eat the karkalla fruits I could see
gleaming temptingly among the dark leaves. In fact
I had a vague memory that the leaves were used by
Aboriginal people as an antiseptic. I began to make
my way over to the plant when I saw something

that made my heart contract for the second time. Footprints. Boot prints. They were definitely not there before. If Dave was up there somewhere I was hopelessly trapped. There was no shelter down here. The only possibility was to climb up to the cave and hope he wouldn't see me. Quickly, I unearthed my socks and put them on, dug out my knife, and cut two karkalla stalks, winding them around my waist. The salt water had stemmed the bleeding temporarily, but blood was now beginning to ooze from the shallow wound on my leg. I didn't want to leave a trail, so even though every part of me wanted to get away from there and hide, I took the time to break off one of the karkalla leaves and apply it to the area. It hurt. *Boy, it hurt.* But it was sticky and looked as though it might be effective in stopping the drips.

If I had come down the steps carefully, I fairly flew up them. *As if the Devil was at my heels.* Except that the Devil was somewhere above me. When I got to the top the boot prints were right there. They turned left and followed the path, past my cave and into the boobialla scrub. Was Dave standing in that scrub now, watching my every move? Somehow I didn't think so. He would be more likely to be up there taunting me, knowing I had nowhere to run. *Unless.* What if he had found my cave? He could be waiting in there, ready to pounce. The thought of being caught in that claustrophobic space was more terrifying than being caught out here. At least in the open I'd have some chance to fight, and he probably wouldn't expect me to have a weapon.

I stood for a minute, undecided. Then I followed the boot prints all the way to where the path dips towards the cabin side of the island. I kept to the right of the prints, so that when I returned I could scuff out my own prints, leaving the other ones there. And when I got back to the cave, I could see the tree hadn't been moved, so I just pulled it aside, went in, pulled it back behind me, and crawled into the cave. No-one jumped me. No-one had even been there. I almost fell into a sitting position, ignoring my wet clothes and bleeding leg, and found myself, to my great surprise, sobbing with relief. I cried for a good half hour. If Dave had come back, he probably would have heard me. But somehow I knew he wouldn't come back. He'd come early, trying to catch me out, and with any luck he'd find my jacket and decide he could finally stop looking. Would he be pleased or disappointed? Pleased that I was out of his hair, or disappointed that he didn't get the opportunity for his revenge?

When I'd finished crying, I poured out my water ration for the morning and, using a clean handkerchief, wiped first my eyes, and then my leg. I didn't have any bandages with me, but I'd removed all the spare straps from the backpack before I set off this morning, so I wound one of those around the handkerchief and buckled it. Then I peeled off the almost-dry blue T-shirt, now clean of gunge but encrusted with salt, and my knickers (likewise), and hung them on protruding fingers of rock. Despite the salt, I felt much cleaner, except for my hair, which was itchy, and felt dirtier than when it actually was dirty. Dressed in the familiar Amnesty T-shirt and reasonably clean socks, I was ready to start my day.

8.00 a.m.: Housekeeping.

After giving the cave as much of a clean-up as was possible with my limited resources, I spent some time planning how to manage both stores and sleeping arrangements without my backpack. I also needed to dispose of the sheoak branches, which were clogged with mud, and replace them with new ones, not to mention collect more water, pick some fruit to supplement my almost-exhausted food supply, and find a cure for cancer. Since Dave had been here this morning, I hoped that he'd check the rest of the island just as thoroughly, and would come upon my backpack and slicker before they could be washed away by the tide. I figured he would not be back on this side until at least tomorrow, so I should be safe going out tonight. Not that I had much choice.

I decided to take inventory of what I had left besides the food. I didn't need to take inventory of that. I knew exactly what was left, to the last nut and sultana.

Without my backpack, however, I needed to work out ways of carrying everything I needed and, eventually, if Dave left on Monday as I so fervently hoped, a way of transferring all my belongings to the cabin.

I had already moved the food into one of the kitchen tidy bags and hung the bag from the cave roof. My hammer has now become my second weapon, to be kept by my side, along with the knife, but I began sorting out the things I don't currently need but can't leave behind and putting them in a kitchen tidy bag on the low rock shelf, so that if I need to move out in a hurry I can just grab the bag and run. Into this bag I placed my torch, compass, matches and pencils. In another bag I gathered the things I'll need when I go out – specimen bags, rubber bands, pen and diary, half-full water bottle. Later I can store all this in my anorak, but until I collect more sheoak branches I'll need the anorak to sit on. Many of my dirty clothes are hung from various protuberances around the cave, but the remainder I gathered into the last remaining kitchen tidy bag, which I left open to at least let in some air.

That's everything. I have folded my anorak into a seat and now I'll sit and dream of the smell of freshly laundered clothes as I wait until it's time for breakfast.

Sunset: Prepare for sleep. Finish diary.
Most of the rest of today proceeded just as planned. I ate my morning rations and took a tiny sip of water at the right time, did my exercises diligently, and ate the few remaining boobialla fruits at midday. As predicted, I heard nothing from Dave and, knowing I had no choice, I pulled on my jeans and boots, filled my anorak with necessities and went out.

I had gathered the soiled sheoak branches into a tight bundle, which made it difficult to wipe out my footprints but I managed as best I could, while keeping my eyes and ears open for any sign or sound of human presence. It was a relief to reach the little grove of sheoaks and be able to dispose of them as naturally as possible, and then to select a new pile of branchlets. I sucked on a coast banksia flower, and got a taste of honey, but no liquid at all. I'll have to come out at dawn tomorrow. I did find some more boobialla trees a little further on, however, and managed to pick half a bagful. Heartened by this, I returned to the cave with my spoils, dropped them inside and then stood outside to take off my jeans and boots. The jeans are now almost falling off me by themselves and I'll have to devise some kind of belt to keep them up.

Again, I didn't need to make a toilet visit, and so here I am, safe in my cave. I have been on this island for eight days now, living to write another day. The time is 5.50 p.m. on Friday the 20th of April.

* * *

But as soon as darkness falls this strange sense of security vanishes and I am visited by a succession of horrific dreams. Each time I wake up bathed in sweat.

Sometimes I see the shark coming at me; sometimes it's my mother's body I see; at other times a sea of blood and floating babies. Eventually I reach a stage when I am too afraid to fall asleep, and in the half-dozing state that results, I find myself back in my bedroom at Tante Leni's house, surrounded by books. These are not the kind of books my mother had used to teach the Malagasy children English, the kind left behind by English missionaries, the respectable works of Elizabeth Gaskell, Austen, Thackeray and Dickens, and the slightly less reputable works of Enid Blyton and Arthur Ransome. These books belonged to Uncle Raoul and his brothers as children, and a strange and motley collection they were, with an entire shelf of medical textbooks and sensational chronicles of real-life crimes, including *Lives of the Great Poisoners*.

Although I pored over the pictures in these books and dipped with a kind of awful fascination into the crimes and medical horrors, it was the shelves of adventure books I loved, reading them over and over again. My favourites were the works of R.M. Ballantyne – Martin Rattler's adventures in the jungle, Ralph Rover's time as a castaway in *The Coral Island*. I still know whole sections of these books word for word, though I found myself skipping the parts where the author strayed off into religious meditation and homily. I'd had enough of that at home. There was a selection of Arctic and Antarctic memoirs as well, and these I also devoured, finding their matter-of-fact language and harrowing descriptions of starvation, frostbite and falls into ice chasms strangely comforting.

My mother's English lessons had prepared me well. She loved the English language with its thesaurus of words to say one thing in a multitude of different ways, and she passed on this enthusiasm to me. I'm often taunted about the formality of my English, which is probably because a lot of our family's knowledge came from reading our old-fashioned library of English 'classics'.

Although I spent my weekends at my aunt and uncle's house, I rarely saw them. Uncle Raoul's work seemed to take up all of his time and my aunt was busy with the choral society, the church, and doing good works among the ungrateful poor. I was free to do what I liked, which meant lying on my bed reading and weeping or, when misery and loneliness made me too restless, roaming the moors, with only Tante Leni's dogs for company.

At first Leni worried about me 'wandering about, all by yourself', but soon I was able to tell her I'd made a friend during my wanderings. 'Oh? That's good, Alix. What's her name?'

'Edward.' That she enquired no further is a measure of her relief to be rid of my sodden, tear-laden presence.

Edward was the best kind of friend. He listened patiently, never interrupted, and was never critical of anything I did. You might say he was my first boyfriend. There have not been many. Maybe Jonathan is right and I'm not suited to being in a relationship.

Or perhaps it's more the case that I don't know how to do it. How do people learn these things? Watching their parents? Talking to their friends? Certainly Kathryn has given me plenty of advice, but she's not so successful herself. I think of the couples I've known, and realise that there are only two: my parents and Leni and Raoul. I've never met Abel's wife. Or his children. He's still married, however. What did he learn from our parents' strange alliance that I didn't?

I think about the relationships in my life: Jonathan, the first Australian I ever met, and my first and only sexual relationship; the long-distance relationship with my parents and brother; and Edward, who died in 1864, and whose bones were in some ways better company than any of them.

CHAPTER NINE

He is chastened also with pain upon his bed, and
the multitude of his bones with strong pain.

King James Bible, *Job* **33:19**

FIELD DIARY - Saturday 21 April

It is eight o'clock. For the first time since being in the
cave I have slept past the dawn.

And I feel terrible.

Although I know I need to move urgently, get my
circulation going, I just sit, diary in hand, and write,
which is all I have the energy to do. Yesterday I was
amazed at the apparent lack of after-effects from
my swim around the island. Now I know the answer.
Delayed reaction. Every bit of me hurts, and when I
do try to get up my legs go into a series of painful
spasms and my stomach rises in waves of nausea so
severe I almost black out. All I want to do is lie down
and that is one thing I cannot do.

I try rubbing my legs and now they seize up
completely, with sharp pains shooting through my

calves. I have to try to stand – anything to reduce the pain …

… I must have passed out. It's now half past ten. I haven't eaten, but my stomach revolts at the thought of peanuts. I'm so thirsty. I know I'll have to move soon.

I must move …

It is now twelve o'clock and I'm still here, frozen in place. My brain knows that it may already be too late, that my limbs may have become immovable, but my body is beyond reason. Or is it my reason that is beyond reason? *Thirsty. So thirsty*. With a massive effort, I tip myself over so that I can just reach the water bottle. It's only about a quarter full. With the recent abundance of rainwater, I had allowed myself to drink without restriction. Now I don't know when I'll be able to collect any more. Do I drink it all and then just let myself die? Even if I wasn't so afraid, there's no chance I could go outside in this state to try to get more.

I gulp greedily, then somehow manage to stop, leaving little more than a mouthful. I screw the lid on, put the bottle as far away as possible and cover it with a dirty T-shirt. Out of sight, but not at all out of mind.

At least having a drink has helped diminish the nausea. I know I must eat, but can't face the same old food I've been eating without complaint for so long now. What's happened to me? Is this how people give up? Pushing themselves beyond hope of retrieval?

I recall that I have emergency food. There is no doubt in my mind that this is an emergency. I just have to remember where it is. For an awful moment I think I left it in the zip pocket of my abandoned backpack, then I recall moving a small plastic-wrapped package.

Retrieving it requires crawling, but somehow I manage, and scrabble through the bag of spare supplies, unbelievably excited as I pull out the small lumpy package.

Before crawling back to my sitting place I rub my legs and arms and tentatively try a few flexes. Both arms are sore but at least I can move them. My legs are still painful and almost impossible to move. I drag myself back and can now concentrate on my treat.

It takes a while to unwrap them, because the plastic has stuck on, but when I get to the core of the package, the two cough lollies are slightly soft but pretty much intact. I admire them from all sides, lick my finger and touch it to a surface. The taste is sweet and tangy, but it doesn't make me feel sick. If I had a knife I could cut a piece off and try it, but the knife is too far away.

I place one on my tongue, and tentatively begin chewing. No problems. I take my time, ruminating

145

slowly like a cow with its cud, and then just as slowly eat the second one. The flavours of sugar, wax and menthol burst through me, and I feel a thin wave of warmth and energy pervade my body. Now, while the impetus is there, I decide to attempt to crawl to my standing space. Then I will try to stand up ...

... It is now half past four, and although the pain is still excruciating, I can move all my limbs. It has taken hours of agony to get to this point, but the despair is gone and if I can find some way of topping up my water supply, I know I can survive in passable shape for at least a few more days.

I cannot allow myself to give in to despair again. Even with the fear of discovery and the occasional fear of accident or drowning, I realise that I have not actually expected to die here. Now I see how easily it could happen. The biggest threat is not outside at all.

But it is ...

Just as I was meditating on the different degrees of danger, a voice broke the silence, calling my name, 'Alix!'

'Alix!'

It's been so long since I've heard a human voice, I was momentarily confused. Then I heard heavy footsteps, and realised it was Dave. To my absolute horror he came right up to the entrance to my cave, still calling, and my newly freed body froze once more, afraid that he hadn't found my jacket. Or, worse, that he had and wasn't convinced that I was dead.

Quiet as a bush mouse, I crouched and listened. Dave went on calling. His voice gradually moved away, but not far. He seemed to be at the top of the rocky path.

Would he go down to the little beach? Had I left any evidence behind? Barely breathing, all I could do was keep quiet and wait.

Soon, too soon for him to have gone down the path, the footsteps returned. But not the calling. Then they stopped. Right outside the cave's entrance. Slowly, very carefully, I reached out for my knife and my hammer, and hid myself as well as I could behind one of the ridges in the cave's rocky wall.

Silence once again. And then a sound so terrifying, I almost ran out and attacked him, hoping to get in first, take him by surprise.

The sound of a zipper unzipping.

But I found I couldn't move. I was rooted to the spot, becoming part of the cave floor, a thing of sand and rock. A non-creature. Only the weapons in my hands had any life. I poured every ounce of energy into my hands, keeping the rest of my body perfectly still as I held the hammer high, ready to crash down on his head, and the knife poised, ready to plunge into his heart.

And then, another sound. A splash, a torrent, a cascade. And an acrid, familiar odour. A grunt, a zipping up, and the footsteps retreated and gradually faded into the distance.

If it was not so terrifying it would be funny. Of all the caves in all the world, Dave chose to relieve himself outside mine. Was he marking the territory? Did he know I was inside? If he had, I'm convinced he would have come barging in, ready to take his revenge for my imagined sins, which he must now feel is long overdue.

I sit compulsively writing my diary, as I have done all day, even through the worst of my misery and pain. My excuse is that it keeps me sane, but now I know I must stop writing and eat. Even now, well after five o'clock, I'm not hungry, but I must get out the day's food, this morning's rations still uneaten.

I could not face the peanuts, but I ate the sultanas, one by one, and managed to keep them down. Then I drank, very slowly, the remaining water. Tomorrow, no matter what happens, at some stage I will have to go out.

The thought makes me realise that I do need to go out. Urgently. But it's almost dark. It's too late. And I'm too afraid that Dave is hiding somewhere, waiting for the darkness to fall, waiting for me to come out from wherever I am hiding.

I've done what I've been dreading for days. I've used a plastic bag. It was difficult but not impossible, since I'm still dressed in the long T-shirt and socks, but I had to take my underpants off. I used them to wipe myself and then hung them up, and found some clean ones. I'm too exhausted to put them on, so I've left them on one of the rocks for the morning.

The time is 5.49 p.m. on Saturday the 21st of April. As I ready myself for sleep, a strong stench, like the whiff of a urinal, fills the cave.

* * *

As darkness falls, my body is heavy and exhausted, but once again my mind is wide awake.

I'm afraid I won't sleep, having drifted in and out of consciousness all day. I feel as if I've been drugged. At least I'm alive and capable of kicking, although it was a pretty close call. I rearrange my sheoak padding, trying to make myself comfortable, trying to ignore that all-pervasive stench, and …

Deep, deep blue water, horribly, eerily silent. I am trapped in some way, my foot clamped to the ocean floor. I look up and see a great white shark, teeth bared, swimming straight for me. The quiet only enhances the terror …

I wake and manage to stifle the cry forming in my throat. But the silence remains. In films there's always music when the shark comes. Silence is worse. Seeing that relentless, unblinking, emotionless eye approaching with no noise, no fanfare, all over in a second.

I wonder if it really is soundless under water. I realise I've never put my head fully under the surface. Even on that long swim I only ducked my face under briefly. Just that one shark-panicked time. Jonathan said I had a European relationship with the sea. Perhaps he was right.

I never went to the seaside in England. Although Manchester was not far from the coast by Australian standards, it didn't ever occur to me. I realise now that in all those years of exile in England, except for the voyage that took me there, I never even saw the sea. Moors and rocks and caves. That was my vision of England's green and pleasant land.

Jonathan went to the seaside once, on a cricket team trip to Blackpool. 'Never again!' he said. 'Bloody Poms don't know what a beach is for. Prancing around in suits and high-heeled shoes! Paying for deckchairs to sit on a pile of black grit.'

As soon as I arrived here, Jonathan introduced me to the glories of the Australian beach, particularly the joys and alarms of surfing at Bells Beach, and the freedom of nude sunbathing at Point Addis where, to my surprise, I was surrounded by the sound of languages barely remembered – German, French, and even, occasionally, Dutch – tantalisingly familiar, but now almost incomprehensible.

Never, at any of these times, did I dive under the surface, although Jonathan often did. And when, one weekend, he went skindiving with a group of cricket mates at Phillip Island, I stayed near the shore, bodysurfing the fairly inadequate waves, pottering in the rock pools. I told Jonathan I didn't want to hold him back because he was the stronger swimmer, but really I was afraid of sharks, though I would have died rather than admit it.

He would have taken this as another mark of my Europeanness. We often met English and German tourists who wouldn't venture beyond their knees in Australian waters because of the very same fear. Jonathan mocked them as he swam straight out into the deep, or paddled further and further out on his board. It amused him that people who came from countries where shark attack was not even listed on the statistics were the most fearful. But it made sense to me. Australians couldn't afford to be afraid of sharks, or snakes, or wide-open spaces. If they were, they wouldn't be able to go anywhere.

I managed to hide my fear of snakes pretty well too, particularly from the geology crews. One aspect of the Australian sense of humour I have never really understood is their definition of teasing. It didn't take me long to realise that if they knew you were afraid of something, they would endlessly torment you with the object of your fear – plastic spiders on the dunny seat, shouts of 'Shark! Shark!' as you reached the deep water, rubber snakes in your sleeping bag.

Although I can walk through the bush as noiselessly as the smallest of bush creatures, on geology trips I earned the title Bigfoot from the heavy tread I adopted as soon as I learned that snakes react to vibrations rather than sound. My crews thought I was brave and fearless because I always took the lead. But in my research I also found out that if a snake is going to strike it will usually not be at the person who disturbs it, but at the one who follows. So my reputation as a good leader was in this respect shamefully undeserved.

I tell myself that fear of snakes and sharks is sensible and logical. But why don't I fear spiders then? Or scorpions? Or crocodiles. While they are all creatures that inspire respect and careful handling, I'm never haunted by the fear of encountering them, even when it would be a perfectly realistic fear. I'm always careful not to wade into unknown waters in the Far North, or to camp close to water, but I've been out in the same waters in pathetically frail crafts without the feeling (common, I've noticed, to many Australians) that a giant crocodile was going to swim under the boat and throw us into the water.

Unlike its people, this country's menaces are sneaky. They lurk in bushes, under rocks, in deep water, in all their terrible silence, whereas the ancient, mythic perils of the north come crashing towards you face to face – wolves, bears, sabre-toothed tigers, vampires, werewolves. Why don't *they* haunt my dreams? How ironic that uber-Australian Jonathan is obsessed with zombies and vampires, while I, at least by heritage a child of the Northern Hemisphere, have nightmares of lurking sharks in dark and deep Southern waters.

Dave and Matt knew about the lurking sharks. On that chilling first night in the cabin, I heard them talking, late, after Lana must have gone to bed. It was their laughter that woke me. Then a sudden, horrible, pregnant pause before Dave spoke.

'She'll put up a fight.'

'Don't be such a pussy. There's two of us to one of her. What can she do?' Matt's voice was light, dismissive, amused.

'What about Lana?'

Another silence. 'Lana won't give us any trouble. I'll promise you that.' Matt's voice was becoming flatter and harder as Dave's became more hysterical.

'She'll talk.'

'Dead bitches can't tell tales, can they?'

Dead bitches. I remember another conversation overheard on that first night in the cabin. *'Bloody bitch made a fool of me.'* Dave's voice. The same hysterical tone.

That was when I first realised that he was talking about me.

'Mate, if she gives trouble, we'll take care of it on the boat. Leave it to the sharks. She'll never know what hit her.' They were drinking. I could hear the *slurp, slurp* as he gulped something down. 'Anyway, you made sure nobody knows she's here, didn't you? And you know what Kel said. They wash up on the other side of the Prom, miles away from here.'

They?

Whatever was going on, it was becoming clear that Matt was the controller. Both Dave and Lana jumped to his bidding, although Dave didn't seem to fully realise it.

Lana did. I wondered why she didn't try to escape, what kind of hold Matt had over her. Was it something to do with what I heard on the first night on the island?

I dream of bodies floating in hot, milky seas. Then the sharks come. Razor-teethed, razor-faced, like a frenzy of slate-grey torpedoes. The bodies are buffeted helplessly to and fro as they slash and grab. But these are not my parents' bodies.

Why am I dreaming of Jonathan and Kathryn? Is this some kind of preview? My whole life flashing before my eyes?

CHAPTER TEN

Bogong Moth (*Agrotis infusa*)

The traditional method of cooking Bogong moths is by rolling them lightly in hot ashes and sifting them gently in a string bag to separate the wings and heads from the bodies. However, you'll need a lot of moths as the result is very small; one writer described it as 'the size of a grain of wheat after cooking'. They can also be pounded to a mush and made into a form of cake that will keep for a few days. The early literature described the moths as being extremely 'nice and sweet, with a nutty flavour similar to an almond or a walnut', but I can't vouch for this as I've never been game to try one.

Atkinson's Guide

FIELD DIARY - Sunday 22 April

I was too exhausted last night to set my alarm, but I woke up anyway to the half-light before the dawn and, without giving myself time to think, gathered my underpants and jeans and stumbled to the entrance space to put them on. With the minimal amount I've been drinking again there's no need for a toilet stop.

It was a lovely time to be out. There was no problem of glare, and the world seemed somehow squeaky clean and new. I felt invisible as I made my way to the coast banksia thicket and squeezed and squeezed the flowers until there was no more nectar to be found anywhere. I took the time to tie the mouths of the bags tightly to prevent leakage, stripped the last of the boobialla fruits, then made my way back, panic beginning to set in as the sun tipped the horizon and the cloak of invisibility began to lift.

I've been especially careful with clearing my footprints today. I know Dave will be back, because tomorrow the boat comes, and if he believes I am gone, I think he may finally leave. He'll be checking every inch of the island before that, so I'll need to be well hidden by sunrise. I stood outside the cave entrance for a moment, taking deep, deep breaths, then disappeared into my shelter, pulling the camouflage tree behind me, and found that I was shaking with tension.

Today will be a day of tension. If Dave plans to leave tomorrow, I'll need to be ready for anything. I've kept my jeans and boots on, threading one of the straps retrieved from my backpack through the belt loops on my jeans to ensure they don't fall down and trip me, and changed into a short-sleeved T-shirt. If disaster does not come, this will be a long day, so I'll keep strictly to my timetable.

While waiting until it was time for breakfast, I assembled my weapons close to hand, and then looked for ways to reorganise my clothes and food. Since I haven't been eating the peanuts, I have an extra day's food, so I put that aside and laid out today's ration of nuts and the last sultanas, with the water bottle beside them. Then I watched the minutes slowly tick around my watch until the second hand finally showed eight o'clock. Time to eat. I opened the bag of peanuts, shook one out, took a bite and instantly spat it out. *Rancid.* I took a sip of water and then sampled one from the other bag. Same result. Waves of horror almost overwhelmed me as my careful plans disintegrated. All I now have left are eleven sultanas and a handful of boobialla fruits, and then I'll have no food at all and, if Dave doesn't leave, no way of obtaining any. I debated whether I should take a chance and eat the nuts anyway, but my initial instinctive reaction told me they would make me sick. The thought of suffering vomiting or diarrhoea while trapped in a cave the size of a two-man tent was enough to convince me.

I decided to eat all of the sultanas now, and have the fruit at lunchtime. Even taking them one at a time, the moment arrived when the last sultana was gone, and I was now almost completely cast away. By the end of today, I'll have no food and no water. I'm already hungry, and I know I can't risk going out.

Perhaps a family of bush mice will wander into the cave, and I can bludgeon them to death and have them for dinner. I begin to visualise all manner of creatures crawling in to meet their doom: rabbits, skinks, wombats, even snakes. Somehow in this fantasy I have a cooking pot and no fear of making a fire. I bake the delicious flesh and eat my fill, wrapping the remains in plastic bags and hanging them from the roof, my cave becoming a grisly larder decorated with the bush equivalent of sides of bacon.

When I move to the entrance space for exercise, I bring my weapons and my diary, so that I can continue to dream and write. For some reason I seem incapable of conjuring the meals I would normally regard as special: Tasmanian crayfish, Sydney rock oysters, venison steaks, soft, melting aged Brie, chocolates, wine. My visions are of what this island might offer if I was free to explore it fully: fish barbecued with crushed berries, stews of crabs and tea-tree leaves, roasted mutton bird.

Fired up by these fantasies, I have had to restrain myself from exercising too vigorously. My muscles are still sore and tender, and I have tried to think

yoga rather than workout. But the lack of food
yesterday and today and even this mild exercise are
making me aware of a gnawing hunger I know is
not going to go away. I now understand how dieters
become obsessed with food.

To distract myself, I ponder what to do about the
two bags of peanuts. I'm afraid to keep them, in case
hunger drives me to eat them. The risk of sickness
is far more serious than that of starvation. As long
as I can get water I know I can stay alive for four or
five days, even a week, without food, though in what
state doesn't bear thinking about. I need to dispose
of the nuts. But how? I haven't actually had a rubbish
problem until now. Dropping the stripped boobialla
stones has worked quite easily. Bad food is quite
another matter. I think incongruously of the four
recycling bins behind my current flat, always filled
to overflowing with boxes, cans, peelings and plastic
bags of junk. This certainly is the simple life, but
knowing that doesn't solve my problem.

I need to dispose of the peanuts outside the cave,
but not in a location where they could be seen, or
dug up by fossicking animals. Probably the best way
would be to drop them into the sea and hope they'll
sink, but I can't see any practical way of doing that.
I could leave them on the rocks for birds to feed on,
but that wouldn't be very environmentally friendly
either, and what if they didn't take them, and Dave

came along and found them? He may not know much about the bush, but he'd recognise a peanut. And he'd know where it came from.

This problem kept me occupied until noon, when I moved back and ate the little handful of boobialla fruits for lunch. The end of the crop, they were quite small and sour, but I ate them with enjoyment mixed with a terrible sinking feeling that they were the last food I would ever eat.

As I began to write up my diary, I heard what I had both expected and dreaded.

Footsteps going past the cave and out towards the headland. Then a voice.

'Alix! Can you hear me? The boat will be coming tomorrow and we'd better be on it. There'll be no-one here, Alix. You'll starve. *Alix!*'

He must have gone down to the beach because I heard his voice off in the distance. Then the footsteps passed me again and went on towards the centre of the island, the cries slowly fading away. I don't know why, but his tone of voice told me that this time he really did believe I was gone, that he was almost trying to convince himself that he was genuinely searching for me, that he was worried about my fate. I couldn't help wondering what kind of weapon he was carrying this time and what would happen if he did find me, but the very thought filled me with such abject horror that I didn't pursue it any further.

I just sat there pondering the conundrum of Dave, and as dusk fell I decided to act on my intuition and make a quick visit to the toilet rock. On a sudden impulse, I took with me the two bags of nuts, and when I'd finished I emptied them down the hole and heard them tumbling and splashing to the sea. Then back to the cave to discover that at least one of my fantasies had come true. A flock of giant moths were flying around the entrance, slow and ponderous and beautifully fat. I managed to catch six of them and, holding them tightly as they tried desperately to fly away, stuff them into one of the plastic bags left over from the nuts.

Professor A says these moths are edible, and from a bizarre lab visit by an insect fanatic from the zoo I happen to know exactly how to eat a moth. I had closed the bags tightly, and found when I carefully opened them that the moths were all well and truly dead. Then, holding the tail end, I quickly pulled the wings off. 'The body's full of nutriment,' Moth Man had said brightly, holding one up to demonstrate, 'but the wings have barbs that could snag in your throat, so it's best to pull them off.' And he proceeded to do so. 'You need to twist them quickly,' he had said, 'so they come off cleanly and don't bring any flesh away.'

I sometimes wonder if I'm just as fanatical about rocks as Moth Man is about moths. I've had moments when I've looked around my home office (and even my work office, come to think of it), and seen rows of books about rocks, walls covered with drawings of rocks in cross-section, and shelf after shelf displaying samples of rocks from all corners of the world. Does this make me a mad Rock Woman? I've always thought of myself as an enthusiast rather than a fanatic, but where do you draw the line? At least, unlike Moth Man, I don't produce photocopies of recipes for Bogong moth scones.

He would have been proud of the way I handled the de-winging. I'm sure he'd have given me ten out of ten. However, as I was unable to cook my moths, when it came to putting a dead grey object covered in pallid lichenous fur into my mouth, it didn't seem quite so easy. I was tempted to wait until morning, when I'd be hungry enough to eat them wings and all, but I feared they might begin to deteriorate. Fresh moth was unlovely enough. Decomposition was not likely to improve it.

After an initial and very unpleasant gagging session, they turned out to be not bad at all. I've met people who've eaten witchetty grubs and they say the same thing. It's just a matter of adjusting your mental boundaries. The moth meat, if you could call it that, was not as dry as I expected. Although it tasted like nothing I had ever eaten, it was OK, and I ate every bit, bodies, heads, even the eyes (though

I pulled off the tiny feet), keeping my own eyes
steadfastly shut throughout. Perhaps it was a bit like
grasshopper, which is a delicacy in many countries,
but then they do tend to cook, or at least dry, the
insects first. This meal had the advantage of being
more filling than grasshopper, but I wished I had
saved a boobialla fruit to take the taste away.

Then I turned my mind to matters of health. The
good news was that when I peeled the bandages off
the cut on my leg it was already partially healed and
showed no signs of infection.

Now for the bad news.

Since my last toilet visit I have been aware of
a nagging pain in my pelvis. With my cast-iron
constitution I've had very little of this kind of
trouble, but from female colleagues I know the
symptoms. Cystitis. I've drunk as much water as I
can in the hope of heading it off, but fear the high
sugar content of the nectar will serve to inflame it.
Probably what caused it in the first place. I keep
the water bottle with me, unable to think of any
other plan, and settle myself for sleep. The time is
5.47 p.m. on Sunday the 22nd of April.

* * *

The pain increases and I know it's going to be an uncomfortable
night with too much to think and worry about.

My mother had strong opinions on the inefficiency of the female body, and I now begin to understand why she was always so fanatical about making me drink lots of boiled water. I'd been delighted to find the nectar from the coast banksia flowers, but I realise that, coupled with the sultanas and fruit that have recently been my only food, I have been regularly delivering my body a concentrated sugar hit, just what all those nasty little bugs love most.

Living in exile, we were dependent on my mother's treatments and remedies. Her own mother, as well as helping with the cheesemaking, was the local midwife, and my mother had acquired from her a solid grounding in hygiene, basic diagnosis and the use of herbal as well as conventional medicines. Of course the remedies available in Madagascar (mostly of the herbal variety) were unfamiliar, but we did remain remarkably healthy throughout our time there, and I have no doubt this was largely due to the careful regimen she made us follow.

Both of my mother's parents died while we were in Madagascar, her father first, then, a few years later, her mother, my unknown grandmother. The news, like everything else in Madagascar, took a long time to reach us. Some visiting missionaries brought the news of her father's death. Although Moe went very quiet for a while, it didn't seem to my child's eyes to affect her very much. An old-fashioned yellow telegram, arriving by packhorse, announced her mother's death, and a letter from Tante

Leni, who had gone Home to look after the funeral, quickly followed. My mother cried for her mother. I'd never seen her cry before. Even weeks later, I would come upon her in one of the back rooms, wiping her eyes as she held some object from Home. She behaved as if nothing was happening, didn't mention the tears, didn't apologise, so I behaved in the same way, sitting silently with her while she wept for her lost life.

I didn't know then just how much she had lost. It was only through persistent questions to Leni when I occasionally found myself helping her around the house that I began to piece together my family history.

'Did I ever live in Nederland?'

Leni had to stop buffing a silver candlestick to answer. 'Your mother went to Nederland to have both you and your brother so that you would have Dutch nationality. Then she took you back to Denmark.'

'Denmark?'

'Don't you remember? Your name is Danish. Alix.'

Before Madagascar all I can remember is the boat trip going over, when everyone was sick but me and, somewhere in the backblocks of my memory, a place with sheep and hills and pine trees.

I have one very clear memory of playing in a field of cold whiteness with Abel, who was dressed like a clown in a bright red snowsuit. On my hands were shiny round blue covers that must have been mittens. I can still remember the feel of them and how the shiny fabric slid off the cold white stuff. Because my family has talked about it, I know that what I'm remembering is snow, and I know it's a true memory because only I remember the mittens. I wonder where they are now. Did Moe keep them tucked into one of her boxes of mementos, now packed up and sent off to Abel in Canada?

Leni also told me the story of how my parents met. My father, then a journalist, and my mother, a photographer, were sent on an assignment to interview Dutch artists in Scandinavia. They met for the first time the day they set off in my father's Volkswagen. One of the artists lived in a self-sufficient religious community. My parents, who were at that time still individuals and not yet my parents, filed the story, then severed their connection with the journal that had sent them, and joined the community.

I wonder what my father must have been like then, to have persuaded my mother to abandon her hard-won career, and her conservative Protestant background, not to mention home, family and friends, and to follow him into a life of poverty and religious fanaticism.

The father I remember was an angry man. Was he always like that? Is that what drove him to try to improve the world and its people, make them fit into the mould he wanted to prescribe for them? Or was it his failure to change people that made him angry? I wonder if Abel could answer that. It seems the kind of question that wouldn't engage his attention, but how would I know? We never discussed our parents. Or any personal matters at all.

I wish I could phone him. I don't want to die with all my questions unanswered, but even if I went to visit Abel, or Leni, would they be interested after all this time?

And what could they tell me? Like me, they liked to skim along the surface of life, ignoring the dangerous undercurrents. I wonder what my mother thought about it all.

Did she ever keep a diary?

So many questions.

She kept a plan for each week on a blackboard in the schoolroom where she took the English lessons. The left-hand side of the board was sectioned off with a chalk line and then divided in half. On the top half she neatly listed the lesson plan for the week. The bottom half was a kind of weekly personal organiser. The classes took place in the afternoon. The mornings had their own regular pattern: Monday – washing; Tuesday – mah jong; Wednesday – market day; Thursday – choir practice; Friday – house-cleaning; Saturday – games; Sunday – Bible class.

Saturday was Abel's favourite day. No English classes, and the local children (usually boys) were invited to come along and play with the balls, bats and hoops we'd found in the lean-to storeroom when we first arrived. My favourite was mah jong day, sitting on the floor listening to the comforting sound of bamboo tiles sliding and clicking, and the gentle murmur of women's voices, broken periodically by triumphant shouts of 'Pung!', 'Kong!' or 'Mah jong!'

Occasionally there would be a variation of the plan. Someone would invite us to celebrate *famadihana* with them (the attendance of strangers was believed to bring good luck), or we would need to go into Tana to buy medicines or clothes. Normally we lived on a barter system. We had a steady supply of food, provided in exchange for English lessons, and Moe's witch-doctor skills were also paid for in kind; she rarely needed to clean the house or launder our clothes.

But some things had to be paid for – toiletries, postage, journeys by zebu-cart – and for these the Money Box was ceremonially opened. I wonder now where the money came from. Certainly not from the villagers. Did the church in Denmark pay a stipend? My father used to send them regular reports of his activities, so perhaps they did. Or did it come from Moe's family?

Superstitiously, I reach for my anorak and search for the secret pocket near the hem. Neatly folded inside it is a one hundred dollar note, which I hid there before I left for the Easter break, even before Dave came to pick me up. My traditional emergency plan. I begin to see that I am very much my mother's daughter, my life proceeding through a series of such plans.

As soon as I realised, on that first night, that I had to get away from the cabin, I began to devise a plan of action. Then, as dawn broke, very quietly and carefully I put the first part of the plan into operation. I had brought with me a backpack and a small duffel bag and fortunately, not knowing what to expect of this holiday, I had left in the backpack many of the things I usually take on a short field trip. The duffel held towels, swimwear, mask and snorkel, spare clothes and nightwear.

I had to make sure I had all the things with me that would help me survive, while leaving enough behind to look as though I expected to come back. For this to be convincing I needed to leave my purse and keyring, sponge bag and at least some of the spare clothes. Not having my car, or expecting any high expenses, I hadn't brought my driver's licence or credit cards, so the purse only contained cash and my medical insurance card. I didn't think they could do much with that, so I left it there. My keyring had car keys, house key and lab keys. I took the house key off and secured it in one of the little zip pockets in the anorak, hoping the lab keys would be mistaken for house keys. The car keys worried me a bit, but they were large and jangly and difficult to conceal, and since they didn't carry any identifying information, they'd only be useful to someone who was able to recognise my car.

My plan was to go for an early morning walk around the island, preferably on my own, and case out possible hiding places, then return and eat a large lunch (since food was going to be my main problem) and, having lulled them into a false sense of security by returning the first time, take a late afternoon stroll from which I would fail to return.

Assuming Matt would search my things while I was out on the morning walk, I spent the sleepless part of the night preparing, switching everything I would need into the backpack, and leaving spare clothes, purse and sponge bag lying around as if awaiting my return. I also cased the galley kitchen, on the pretext of getting myself a drink, in search of an extra vessel for storing water, or any food I could steal undetected. No luck there (and I quickly closed a drawer containing two pairs of handcuffs, two black balaclavas, some nasty-looking whips and a terrifying object like an oversized pistol).

The pantry was seriously padlocked, which made me suspect it contained something I'd very much rather not see, but I did manage to remove a handy supply of plastic kitchen tidy bags from a pile in another kitchen drawer, which I stuffed into my backpack when I got back into the bunk room.

And all the planning paid off. It worked perfectly. I hope my plan for tomorrow will work as well.

CHAPTER ELEVEN

White's Skink *(Liopholis whitii)*

This is a common and widely distributed small reptile. It prefers dry areas with grassy vegetation and logs that provide both shelter and insects for food. Skinks are cold-blooded so they also like basking on rocky outcrops and paths. They grow to about 20 to 25 cm, and are usually black or brown in colour with a pattern of stripes or spots, making them difficult to see. The tail is longer than the body, and can be shed in a threatening situation and later regenerated. Skinks and other lizards can be roasted on a fire on sticks, like marshmallows.

Atkinson's Guide

FIELD DIARY - Monday 23 April

I woke, weak and exhausted, after a night wracked by cramps and pain, and realised immediately that something was wrong. My alarm hadn't performed its usual vibratory dance. I looked at my watch, then looked again, unable to believe what I was seeing. Its silvery numbers showed 3.47 a.m. I knew that couldn't be right. Light was coming into the cave and I feared it was already too late to go out in search of nectar. Today my need for water is more desperate than usual. Even full of sugar, it's the only remedy available to deal with the cystitis. I looked at the watch again. No change. My heart lurched and a lump came to my throat. My watch, my companion, timekeeper and friend, had stopped. I tried everything, rewinding, resetting, moving every tiny pin and button, removing and replacing the battery. *Niets.* Nothing.

I knew I'd have to go out, both to use the toilet rock and to check the time as well as I could by the position of the sun, something I'm not particularly expert at. Though terrified of hearing Dave approach, I managed the first task with some pain, though less acute than I feared. But the sun was fully up and I knew I couldn't risk going to collect nectar in case he made another search before the boat arrived.

At least I'm confident the boat will come today. The sky is blue and clear, the sea like glass. Perfect weather for a day on the water. Since I'm now stuck without food or water, I concentrate on preparing for the dangerous task ahead. Although the hide I used on previous boat days is well hidden and relatively safe to access, today I am determined to see exactly who gets on and off the boat. For this I will have to find a hiding place above the cleared area that

bisects the island and runs between the landing
stage and the cabin.

The island is shaped like a flattened figure eight,
and my cave is on the north-west side of the highest
point. The southern end is lower and less rocky,
and from what I have seen, covered for the most
part by grassy tussocks. Probably because of the
congenial vegetation and relatively sandy soil, this is
the favoured area for mutton-bird burrows. It is also,
for the same reason, Snake Country, so I have not
explored it in detail, but from what I remember the
tussocks seem to give way to a narrow strip of pebbly
beach leading to tumbled, weed-covered low rocks.

The waist of the eight runs between the landing
stage and the cabin, and looks like a combination of
natural sandblow and human clearing. My guess is
that the cabin was once a mutton-birder's hut and
the flattest and clearest area was chosen as the best
landing and building site. Now the Duffy brothers
probably run a small bobcat or Dingo digger over it
every couple of years or so by way of maintenance.
It's unlikely that the number of visitors would provide
enough foot traffic to keep it clear. Possibly because
of this natural separation line, the northern end
is quite different from the south, and much more
diverse. The cabin is on the eastern extremity of the
sandblow, facing the beginning of a long, sheltered
beach that stretches almost to the northern point,

the point where I left my decoy slicker and backpack only a few days ago. I'm sure the rocks that tower above it are the same formation that houses my cave. If I'd had my climbing equipment, I could probably have got across in a quarter of the time and with much less danger, but it hadn't occurred to me to bring climbing gear to a beach, and even if I had, I couldn't have taken it with me without arousing suspicion. It's one thing to go for an afternoon stroll with your anorak and a small backpack. Setting off laden with ropes, harness and climbing shoes would be likely to set off alarm bells.

When I left that first afternoon I timed my departure carefully. Matt had programmed for us to go swimming after lunch and, after making sure of eating a well-balanced and nutritious lunch, I pretended to join in the drinking that continued after the food was finished. Fortunately, sand is a very accommodating medium for hiding unwanted gin and tonic.

By swim time, everyone but me was pretty relaxed and sleepy. We all went into the water and splashed around, the cold serving to wake the others up a bit. After what I hoped was a convincing amount of time, I started slapping my arms and legs.

'Something's biting me!'

Matt swam over and had a look at my arm. 'I can't see anything.' He looked at me narrowly, so to allay any suspicions I ducked under again and gave my arms a few good pinches, then surfaced and displayed the blotchy result.

'Ugh. It's all red and itchy. I think I'd better have a shower.' I quickly got out and went into the cabin, grabbed my water bottle and filled it to the top, organised a final pack and got out the clothes I was going to wear, all the time glancing out of the window to make sure nobody came back. Then I had as thorough a shower as I dared, paying particular attention to my hair. No matter what the future held, I knew this would be the last wash in fresh water for some time.

Skin soaped from top to toe, hair squeaky clean, I sat on the beach and waited, heart almost stopping with anxiety, wondering how I would find the opportunity to carry out my plan. I had to make a real effort not to stare too obviously at my watch. It was almost four o'clock when they finally straggled out of the water and into the cabin. I didn't want anyone looking into my backpack so I followed immediately in their wake. Lana made for the shower, and Matt and Dave grabbed beers from the gas fridge and threw themselves into armchairs, ignoring the spreading wet patches left by their board shorts.

It was now or never.

I went into the bunk room, put on the anorak, threw the backpack casually over my shoulder, and bounced out, putting on my sunniest voice. 'Anyone want to go for a walk? I thought I might see where the beach goes to, see if there are any interesting rocks.'

'Rocks?' Oh God. Matt was suspicious. Surprisingly, Dave came to my rescue. 'She's a gee-ologist, mate. Gets off on rocks.' After a good day's drinking, he thought this was pretty funny. He muttered something to Matt that sounded like 'get her rocks off', but I ignored him.

'How about you, Matt? Feel like a bit of rock-pooling?'

He just looked at me. 'Don't be long. Lana'll need help with dinner.' What a gentleman, looking after his lady-love's interests.

'Won't be. Just to the end of the rocks.' I was afraid I was overdoing the cheeriness, but they didn't appear to notice.

At first I thought I'd missed the path from the beach to the rocky headland, but after a few false starts I found the crossed sticks I'd left to mark the spot. Quickly, hoping nobody was watching, I took off the beacon-like red anorak and the backpack, so that in pale-blue shirt and jeans I wouldn't stand out in the rapidly dimming light. Then I pulled a switch of tea-tree and retraced my steps to the high-tide mark, scuffing out my prints as I went. Treading heavily, I left a clear trail along the water's edge to the rocks at the north end of the beach. Then I climbed up through the rocks, picked my way up into the scrubby heathland and made my way back, stepping from tussock to tussock, to collect my anorak and backpack.

From there it was a slow and careful climb through the heathland on a rough path that must have been man-made at some time but was now so overgrown it had almost disappeared, all the time scuffing out my tracks behind me. Then across the ridge into a small valley filled with stunted sheoaks and coast banksias where the path pointed westwards and I searched again for the set of crossed sticks that marked the narrow path I had found that morning that led to the headland. And the cave.

Today I must take that trail again but this time I'll have to leave the path and find a way to penetrate the sheoak thickets that overlook the sandblow. I tried this on that first day and was defeated. Now I have no choice. I must be sure of Dave's whereabouts, whether he goes or stays. I have to find a vantage point that overlooks the area between the cabin and the landing stage.

Sunset.
Dave has gone, I know he has, but I still can't bring myself to believe that it's safe to go down to the

cabin. Even the lure of fresh water couldn't bring me to overcome my fear that his leaving was a trick, that if I trustingly made myself at home in the cabin he'd return, with the others, under cover of darkness.

At least now I have another hiding place. I got to the top of the path without incident then, guessing as well as I could from memory where the midpoint of the sandblow would fall, I just kept trying to get through the densely packed scrub until I found a course of rocks running between a stand of sheoaks. With a lot of twisting and turning I was able to follow the seam of rock through the tree trunks until I finally found myself, panting, scratched and exhausted, within sight of the cleared area near the landing stage. The soil was also fairly sandy, so I kept away from the edge in case it crumbled under me, and searched for a hiding place.

And I found one, even better than the one on the headland because it was off the ground. An old but solid sheoak had fallen across an outcrop of rock, forming a climbing platform that reached the understorey of a dense stand of sheoaks and coast banksias that leant right out over the path from the cabin.

Very slowly and carefully, I made my way from branch to branch until I reached a hollow I had spied from the ground, formed around a kind of nest. Working even more slowly, I removed the nest, piece by piece, hoping it was as abandoned as it looked, and insinuated myself into the space.

It wasn't comfortable, and I knew that by the time I'd perched there for several hours it would probably be agony, but it was extremely well hidden – I don't think someone standing directly underneath would have seen anything at all – and it was relatively safe.

I could have done with some food, or something to read. I wished I'd brought my diary, but there was really nothing to do but sit and wait. And this time I didn't have to wait long. I didn't hear the boat come, either because they had deliberately come in without power, or because the dense bush all round me muffled the noise, so when I heard Dave shout, I got such a shock I almost fell out of the tree.

'She's gone. Found her stuff on the rocks.' This was followed by sounds of muttering, no doubt the Duffy brothers expressing their doubts, then from opposite directions the three of them appeared in my range of vision. I had been away from human presence for so long now that they somehow didn't seem real. I watched them with the feeling I was an airline passenger watching a cartoon on my own little private screen. Even though they were close enough that now I could hear every word, I wasn't afraid. But I was listening so intently that I almost stopped breathing.

They didn't spend long on idle chitchat.

'I've searched every inch of this bloody island. You can check if you like.'

'Not our job, mate.'

'Believe me, she's tried to swim for it and drowned.'

I heard Mick's mirthless serial-killer laugh. 'Maybe we'll see her in the water. Do some game fishing.'

'Good thing we got the spearguns.' This was Kel.

But Dave had had enough. 'Let's go.'

'Whoa! Hold on, mate. Just gotta get the stuff.'

The brothers were back in minutes, with Kel pushing the cart, laden with white boxes. This time I did hear the boat start up. I waited a good hour in case anyone doubled back, then slid down from my hiding place and made my way to the viewing point that overlooked the cabin. Again, there was no sign of life, but I didn't go down there, even though this time I really did believe Dave was gone.

Now my biggest priority was to find food. I suspected that Matt would send the Duffy brothers back at some stage to check for signs of activity around the cabin, so I took my time and continued to erase my footprints. I checked every copse and stand of vegetation for seeds, berries, sap, anything at all that might be edible. All I found were the last remnants of the boobialla crop, twelve small and sour fruits, half of which I ate immediately. Nothing else. I searched the ground for fungi without success, although if I had found something I'd have had no way of knowing whether it was safe to eat or not. The lecture series had failed to include a fungi fanatic.

I felt better after eating the fruit, but it didn't really make a dent in my hunger. I decided to continue early morning squeezing of the coast banksia blossoms for nectar, which is in some ways both food and drink, although the cystitis was making itself felt again, exacerbated by lack of fluid, and sugar water is not exactly the treatment of choice.

But now I can put bags on the leaves to obtain clear water, which needs full sunshine to be effective, so I'll have to risk Dave finding the bags if he comes back.

Almost back at the cave, I saw a skink sunning itself on a rock. Without even taking time to think, I launched myself onto it, grabbed it behind the head, and bashed it against the rock. I took out my knife, cut it in half, skinned and gutted it as if it was a lab specimen, then ate it warm, throwing the refuse into a clump of tea-tree. If I'd had time to slice it and a better knife, I could have called it sashimi and it would have been gourmet food. Then, feeling considerably better for a bit of protein and blood, I searched the area minutely in case it had a mate. No luck that time, but it does give me some hope for the future.

Then an expedition down the rocks added seven karkalla fruits to the total food tally. It was becoming dark by the time I took every specimen bag I had and tied them around the banksia leaves. I had hoped that dew might already be forming, but no luck there, so I will have to wait until morning.

By the time I have unloaded my weapons, eaten my fruit and prepared for sleep it is dark, on the night of Monday the 23rd of April.

* * *

The continuing lack of food is making me feel very strange and light-headed.

I now know what people mean by 'lighter than thistledown'. The only time I've felt as weightless as this is when I got food poisoning when I visited my parents in Laos. This is different because I feel remarkably well, like a shell thoroughly scoured by the sea, but also terribly, achingly empty. Although the pelvic pain is less I suspect I won't sleep as I drift into dream and memory.

My first impression of Laos was of dust. I'd flown into Vientiane on a high-wind, almost forty-degree day, and dust was swirling through the flimsy airport buildings and across the tarmac into my face. It was so thick at first I couldn't see my mother, and for a fleeting moment I feared she wasn't coming and I realised I had no idea how to find her.

When she emerged from the crowd she looked so familiar I could feel a silly smile forming. We rushed to meet each other, then stopped abruptly. We have never been a hugging, kissing family. Why not? Was it against the Lord's word, or was it some kind of genetic inhibition? Why hadn't I hugged her in spite of it, the last chance I would ever have to do so? Why hadn't she hugged me?

She had it all planned, of course. Two days in a hostel in Vientiane, then a slow, eccentric and, I realise now, highly dangerous road trip north to Luang Prabang. If we had been more open, less inhibited, it would have been a chance to really get to know each other, but since we weren't, all we could manage were hints and gestures, usually unstated, always covered by embarrassment and reserve.

In Vientiane we did the low-budget tourist things – temples, a trip across the Thai–Lao Friendship Bridge, a visit to the museum and culture hall, evenings eating stir-fry and drinking beer in rickety makeshift bars overhanging the Mekong – all ways to avoid actually having to talk. Our accommodation was in the Ministry of Information and Culture Guest House, where I found we were sharing a three-bed room with an elderly American woman who had already almost filled the space with her luggage by the time we arrived.

My mother had made it clear that this was her treat, so I made no complaint, even though I would have been perfectly happy to book us a room at the Novotel to give her a rare taste of luxury. I wondered uneasily how we were going to get from Vientiane to Luang Prabang, but here she managed to surprise me.

'Da-DAH!' When we had checked out and dragged our small amount of luggage outside, Moe directed me triumphantly to a snappy late-model white Jeep. Grace, our American roommate, was standing next to it, surrounded by cases, bags and boxes.

'You didn't hire this?' I knew enough about local prices to guess how much a vehicle like this would cost.

Moe grinned broadly. 'The owner had to fly back. I can have it for the price of the petrol. As long as we take Grace with us as far as Vang Vieng.'

It turned out Grace was some kind of UN adviser looking into new small business ventures in Laos and Myanmar, and Moe had cunningly devised an itinerary that would accommodate both her requirements and our own special interests. The first stop was the Nam Ngum Lake, where Grace met a representative of several village groups who were engaged in making furniture from teak retrieved from the flooding of the artificial lake. After arranging a suitable meeting time and place, Moe proceeded to carry out her own plan.

First we secured a table for lunch at one of the floating fish restaurants next to the boat jetty. Then we joined a tour boat, already booked for a package tour, but with two extra places just for us. 'How did you manage this?'

She touched the side of her nose. 'One of our boys comes from round here. His uncle owns the boat.' Of course.

The lake, studded with heavily forested islands, was absolutely beautiful. Evidently there were still tigers in the forests beyond, and I was not surprised. Laos, although bombed almost to oblivion in parts, is one of the least populated areas in the world. Despite poachers and subsistence farming, most of the forest area is still wilderness.

The fish restaurant was also owned by the uncle, and the meal was wonderful. I try to remember it now, but although the view from the open decks is clear and immediate, the food remains difficult to conjure. Probably just as well.

Grace was looking quite narrow-mouthed and tense when she rejoined us, so perhaps her day had not gone quite so well as ours.

The next destination was Vang Vieng, a world-famous area of limestone karst that Moe knew I wanted to visit. This time the accommodation was a little more comfortable and we didn't have to share. Grace's destination was an organic food-growing cooperative a little out of town, where we left her and her luggage looking somewhat out of place in a ten-bed bunk room.

The limestone caves were beautiful, and I was surprised to find that Moe enjoyed them at least as much as I did, possibly more. We had both, of course, come equipped with tough waterproof footwear and flashlights, and I had brought a handy bag for valuables that I could sit on my head like a hat when swimming through caves, which meant we could go anywhere. It also meant that less well-prepared tourists tended to turn back when faced with rivers or rope bridges to cross, so we spent two days on our own private un-guided tour.

On the last night, instead of eating at the street cafes where you crouched on tiny low wooden stools and watched your food being cooked in front of you, we decided to go a bit more upmarket and have the banquet at the tourist restaurant two doors away from our guesthouse.

The food was disappointing – it tasted as if it had been sitting around for hours – and the service was slow and surly. But we didn't mind because, oddly, this freed us to talk in a way we hadn't been able to do on the rest of the trip.

After a few bottles of Beerlao, Moe finally got down to the personal. 'Alix, I don't think your father and I have been fair to you and Abel. Picking you up and moving you around whenever we felt the need.'

I was taken aback. 'I'm all right, Moe.'

'But living in Australia …'

'I like Australia.'

'You are happy there?'

Was I? 'Yes, Moe. I am.'

Silence.

'But what about you? Are you happy here?'

And she laughed. Not exactly bitterly, more a kind of self-deprecation. 'I would like to go back to Denmark,' she said. Not Nederland, I noted, which was interesting. Then she brightened. 'But there are so many things that need doing here. And I've joined the International Mission Committee, so I am busy on the internet.'

'You should start taking photographs again.'

She shook her head. 'Oh Alix, you know your father wouldn't like that. And the people here … It would be an intrusion.'

I'm so glad to have the memory of this time with my mother, talking as woman to woman about our lives, our work, and our dreams. Even the two days spent recovering from the food poisoning that delayed our return to my father had their lighter moments as we battled primitive plumbing and the impossibility of finding Western medicines.

Then we got to Luang Prabang, where I was to meet my father. Would he finally recognise that I had achieved a successful career, and forged a worthwhile path in life? I had such hopes.

CHAPTER TWELVE

Variegated Limpet *(Cellana tramoserica)*
Found on intertidal rock surfaces on the shoreline,
where they feed on algae. The large ribbed conical
shell may grow to about four centimetres across.
Limpets are firmly attached to rocks by a strong
muscular foot, which is the edible part, and they will
attach even more firmly if threatened. This means
that you need to make your first strike with a knife
or stone count if you want to collect sufficient
limpets to make a meal. The easiest method is to
grill them in the shell over a hot flame, then remove
the guts after cooking and eat the fleshy foot. They
can also be eaten raw, but are greatly improved by
cooking in garlic and butter.

Atkinson's Guide

FIELD DIARY - Tuesday 24 April

I slept late and again I woke up feeling weak and
dehydrated. The sun was already high in the sky.
The pelvic cramps were getting worse, so I dragged
on jeans, boots and anorak and made straight for

the coast banksias where I had bagged the leaves
the night before, to be rewarded with the sight of
small pools of pure water weighing down each of
the bags. I drank about two-thirds of them straight
down, ignoring the faintly leafy taste, then carefully
decanted the rest into the water bottle, licking every
drop from the bags before stowing them in the front
pocket of my anorak.

There was no point going down the stone steps
because I had stripped the karkalla plants yesterday,
so I stayed in my jeans and began to pack for the day's
exploration, enjoying the freedom to take sips of water
whenever I felt like it. I had good reason to believe
that the boat wouldn't come back before Thursday.
I'd heard the Duffy brothers describe their other work
commitments, including 'distribution', which seems
to be another job they do for Matt, and I'd formed a
pretty good idea what it is they were distributing. I
knew I could get water from the tank, even if I couldn't
get into the cabin. Then a new fear gripped me. What
if they had emptied the tank as a parting gesture?
I had to remind myself that I could continue to bag
branches to get water. That won't be my problem.

I knew that unless I could get into the cabin, my
problem would be to find food. The fruiting season
appears to be just about over, and most other
vegetation needs to be cooked to be edible. There
must be shellfish on the rocks, but finding them

could be difficult and again there may be no means of cooking them.

The only way to find out was to go to the cabin and have a look. Even though I fully believed that Dave had gone, I delayed my departure, moving and re-moving my possessions, tidying and re-tidying, until hunger got the better of me and I knew it was time to go.

I planned to travel light. Into my anorak, along with weapons, matches, field diary, specimen bags and water bottle, I stowed hat, socks, underpants and the Amnesty T-shirt, folded as small as I could make it, into the various pockets. If all went well, my priorities were clear. First, water. Second, food. Third, washday. I didn't think I could risk moving in even if I found the cabin open, so I left all non-essentials in the cave, awaiting my return. I decided not to brush out my footprints on the way there, which should speed up my progress enormously, but to do it on the way back. *Just in case.*

The journey felt different, once I knew I was alone on the island. Oddly, I no longer felt like whistling or singing. I enjoyed the quiet, with nothing to break it but the sound of birdsong and the faint distant background noise of the sea. If I had two weeks with plenty of food, some wine, and my climbing gear, I think I could get to like it here. That is, if there was no Dave, or Matt.

It must have been late morning by the time I arrived at the viewing point above the cabin. As expected, there was no sign of life. I knew in my head that it was safe to go down and explore, but anxiety still gnawed at my stomach. I began to picture traps – snares, nets, even mines.

I shouted words of encouragement to myself (Kop op, *Alix. Get a grip!*) but still I could not move. The pain in my pelvis had diminished as a result of a good flushing out, but now those lovely gulps of water began to make themselves felt in another way. I couldn't remember if the dunny door had a lock on it, but the thought got me moving in a way that even hunger couldn't do.

Slowly, carefully, almost creeping in my effort not to be seen, I approached the cabin, and tiptoed right round it. I discovered something I hadn't noticed before, a series of spyholes in the wall on the sandblow side, and filed them away for future speculation. I peered through the first holes and saw a bedroom, the one shared by Matt and Lana. It was stripped bare. The next one showed the bunk room, also stripped bare. No sign of my things. I wondered with a shiver where they were now. There was no spyhole for the other bedroom, Dave's room, but through a natural gap in the boards I could see that all his things were gone too. So far so good.

Gathering all my courage, I tried the door. Locked. Very locked. I'd been harbouring fantasies of picking the lock with my penknife, but of course there was no way I could do that without damage so I knew I couldn't risk it. Peering through the cracks in the door, I could see the kitchen, so tantalisingly close yet so out of reach. The dunny, however, was not locked, and I enjoyed the luxury of sitting comfortably after all the balancing and squatting.

Next, water. Heart in mouth, I turned the tap on the tank and water gushed out. I washed my hands, then drank what was left in my bottle and refilled it. I checked the tank's level and looked to see if anyone had marked it, but could see no signs. After the heavy rainfall last Thursday, it was almost full. I searched the area around the cabin and the barbecue, looking for any sign of food, and some kind of vessel to cook things in. All I found were a few straggly herbs in rusted-out baked bean tins along the back wall.

Priority one, water, was going to be OK. Priority two, food, has acquired a new extension. I desperately needed a cooking pot. If the herb pots hadn't been so badly rusted, I could have scrubbed one out in the sea and used it to boil leaves and any shellfish I might find. But no amount of searching revealed anything remotely fire or waterproof. Perhaps part of the Dodgy brothers' job is to remove the rubbish. I can't imagine Matt or Dave leaving everything so perfectly clean. Of course it's possible that Lana's dainty little hands went round and collected cans, bottles and all the other refuse, but somehow I find that even more difficult to imagine.

I peered through the door cracks and could see saucepans, a kettle and a frying pan sitting frustratingly out of reach. I tried the door again and then walked round and checked the windows, but they were all securely shuttered. I guess they need to keep the place as vandal-proof as possible. I found a thin strong stick and tried pushing on the catch of the door lock but it didn't budge. Deadlocked.

I knew I was wasting time. The hunger that was making me desperate was also making me weak. I had to give up any idea of breaking into the cabin and do a serious food search. It was becoming quite hot, and I was not used to being out in the open in the heat of the day, so I pulled out my hat, wet it under the tap and then, slightly refreshed, set off.

I was hoping to find enough food at least for today on the beach area northwards of the cabin, so I worked through it systematically. I started at the vegetation line, where I was most likely to find fruit or seeds that I could eat on the spot, leaving the shoreline to cover on the way back. This way I could wipe out my footprints on the way out, and then hug the shoreline on the way back, so the tide would wipe out any prints my bare feet made on the return journey.

I found a karkalla patch not far into the search and picked about ten fruits, which I ate as I walked. There seemed to be a few new fruits forming, so I took that as a hopeful sign and continued my search, the sweet/salt taste of the fruits improving my spirits enormously, and also giving my body a tiny spurt of energy. I noted several stands of grey saltbush. If I could find some kind of utensil, saltbush leaves could be cooked along with the karkalla leaves, but neither are edible in their raw state so I left them for the moment, taking careful note of their position.

As I walked I also scanned the rising areas above leading to the headland and spied a copse of what looked like boobialla trees about halfway up one of the slopes. If necessary, I can go there tomorrow in search of fruit, but the access doesn't look easy and I'm not tempted to try it until I'm sure there's no other source of food.

I found a few more karkalla fruits and again ate them straight away. I am now so malnourished that I must eat everything I find to try to build up some strength and energy, but fruit alone is not going to achieve much. It was time to check out the rock pools. They seemed a lot further away than they did when I walked to them on the first day, and when I got there I had to sit on a rock and catch my breath, which really frightened me. I had to keep searching for food and I needed to make the journey back to the cave to sleep. Where would I find the energy?

I was almost dragging myself along as I reached the rocks, but immediately caught a small crab that tried to scuttle out of my way. This cheered me enough to start exploring more thoroughly and, to my relief, the pools were full of limpets, sea anemones and some kind of greenish small shellfish that I couldn't identify. The anemones and green things I left until I was really desperate, but I started filling my bags with limpets, striking them quickly with my knife to knock them off the rocks, as Professor A advised. I had to force myself to stop because there were more there than I could eat.

I wondered if you could eat them raw, like oysters, then realised I could probably cook them on the barbecue using the shells as tiny baking dishes. With this in mind, I made a detour to pick some saltbush branches on the way back to give some flavour and perhaps even add some vitamins. I felt so good that I laid out the fruits of my hunter-gathering carefully on some rocks, stripped off all my clothes and went for a short but thorough dip in the sea. My clothes were so disgusting by now I didn't want to put them on again, so I gathered food, clothes and anorak into one big bundle and walked back through the shallows, every so often putting my burden down and immersing myself again.

When I got back it was time for priority three. I turned on the water tap and wastefully and recklessly washed first my hair then every inch of my body. No five-star mega-spa could have felt better. Then it was time for the clothes. I rinsed every garment, squeezed them out, and hung them from the posts of the water tank while I allowed the sun to dry me and my hair.

Then I set about lighting the barbecue. I hadn't taken much notice of it before, so was very pleased to discover it was a PortaGas one and the cylinder, while not full, was far from empty. I lifted the cover and was delighted to see a thin film of grease still on the surface. I arranged the limpets and crab carefully on the greasiest spots and laid a small branchlet of saltbush leaves and a crumble of herbs on each one. Then I got out my matches, lit the barbecue, and waited for the sizzle.

Just when I thought it was not going to work I heard a faint sound, and in no time the limpets were bubbling away. I didn't know how long they would take to cook, and had to guess when to turn the heat off, but they looked cooked and I gave them a minute to cool down to handling temperature since I had no plate. Then I got stuck into them.

They were still too hot to handle, but I
remembered my knife and used the point, with some
difficulty, to prise the first limpet out of its shell. It
was not delicious but it was food, and the remnant
taste of fat from barbecues past was probably the
best part. By the time I cracked the shell of the crab
it was pretty dried out, but there was a memory of
sweetness there, and I was glad I kept it until last.
Then I scraped up all the little fatty bits of leaf and
ate them too, following my repast with a draught
of tank water. I felt better than I had for some days.
Then it was time to cover my tracks.

I used one of the leftover branches of saltbush
to scrape the barbecue down, put the lid back on,
then took the branch into the sea to wash it before
dumping it in the scrub behind the tank. The limpet
shells I tossed randomly into the sea. Then I checked
my clothes. The Amnesty T-shirt was dry, so I put
that on, not worrying about underwear but putting
on my boots as well. I wanted to try to find some
fruit for the evening meal. I think it must have been
about two or three o'clock in the afternoon, and I
had just eaten a whole pile of limpets, so a small
evening snack would suffice.

This time I headed to the other side of the cabin,
picking up the long stick I'd left leaning against the
side wall on my way. I'd noticed a little splash of
pink and green on the rocks edging the southern

side of the beach. For fear of serpents, I was not
keen to go onto that side of the sandblow, but this
area did seem fairly open, and I'd come prepared,
so I approached it tentatively but bravely. There was
indeed a good crop of karkalla growing there. Before
I ventured into it I hit the ground heavily many times
with my stick and screamed loudly, the unfamiliar
sound frightening even me. Then I stamped my feet
with each footstep and, heart pounding, quickly
gathered as many fruits as I could before panic
forced me to retreat.

Nothing was in sight except karkalla, rock and
sand, but my heart was hammering and I couldn't
bring myself to go back in there. I was proud to have
gone so far, and carried my small bag of fruits like a
trophy. I put the stick away, stored the fruit for later,
and checked my clothes again. Nearly dry, except
for the jeans. I'd need them for the walk back to the
cave, so I spread my anorak out on the sand, put my
hat back on and sat, surveying my surroundings, until
my jeans were ready to put on.

... And woke up to find that it was almost dark.
There was no way I could climb up to the cave
in that light, but the evening was quite warm,
the sand was soft, and I didn't think anyone was
going to come tonight. Quickly, before it got too
dark, I ate some of my fruit, then began to scoop
out a shallow sand bed, experimenting until I got

the pillow height exactly right. With my anorak
stretched out under me for a ground sheet, and a
T-shirt over a plastic bag on the sand pillow, I lay
back in my Amnesty T-shirt and looked at the stars.
This was the first time I'd been able to sleep lying
down for almost two weeks. Maybe I can bed down
here every night.

Warm and comfortable, water bottle by my side,
I settle down for sleep on the night of Tuesday the
24th of April.

* * *

I wake cold, shivering, and sick, with strange, hallucinatory
images swirling through my brain.

I know I won't make it to the dunny in the dark so
I stagger to the water's edge. Must have been the limpets.
The very thought makes me sick again. And again. Finally,
moaning softly, I find my way on hands and knees back to
my bed, now as cold and unwelcoming as a tomb.

I'm chilled and clammy, tossing and turning, my
comfortable bed of warm sand turned icy, lumpy and damp,
giving me a new appreciation of my cave. I drift in and out
of consciousness. Conversations, real and imagined, play
through my head like horror movies.

Matt and Dave leaning over the rail on the boat going
over. I was sick then too. Maybe it was an omen.

'Aw c'mon, Matt. You can spare a little bit.'

'You've had enough, mate. Got to be able to perform for our little friend.'

'Don't worry. I'll be ready.'

'You quite sure she doesn't suspect anything?'

'Nah. Stupid bitch. Expects everyone to jump. Can I carry your bag for you, Alix? Can I kiss your foot, Alix? Totally full of herself. Bitch'll get what's coming to her.'

For a moment I'm not sure if this is a memory or a bad dream. If this was real, how come I also remember Dave being so nice to me on the boat, bringing glasses of water, holding them for me to sip? Then it suddenly strikes me that rather than doing me a kindness he could have put something into the glass to make me more malleable, less alert to what was going on. My stomach heaves again at the thought.

This time I haven't got the strength to reach the sea. I crawl as far as possible before being sick again. All I can do when finished is cover the evidence with sand and crawl slowly back, the words 'Bitch'll get what's coming to her' reverberating through my mind.

I've heard those words before. About a girl called Danielle.

We used to have occasional Sunday community barbecues in the park opposite the flats, and one of Dave's favourite party pieces was about a girl who had accused him of sexually assaulting her. The way he told it she was the town bike and a lying bitch. I'd heard it a couple of times and taken it pretty much at face value. Dave was one of those people who impressed you as a nice guy at first meeting, when he turned on the charm, and it was only later that you gradually found yourself backing away, avoiding him for no identifiable reason. I was still living with Jonathan when he moved in next door and he didn't seem to show any particular interest in me then. In fact, the first sign of interest was when I returned from the Philippines, and he offered me a friendly shoulder to cry on. Now in retrospect I can see why I was suddenly attractive. Distressed, temporarily alone and seemingly needy, I had turned into potential prey.

But I didn't behave like prey. Dave asked me out once after that when Jonathan was away working in Sydney. 'I've got two free concert tickets. Why don't you come with me? Just as friends, of course.' I remember thinking how well I handled it, basically telling him the truth. 'I'm a bit freaked out still about my parents,' I said. 'I'm just not ready for big social occasions.' He seemed to take it OK, but would I have noticed if he hadn't?

Surely that was not enough to put me on Dave's list, his program of revenge. At the end of the Danielle story I remember now how he smiled when people, usually men, commiserated with him. 'Oh, it was all right. She got what was coming to her.' How could I have forgotten? How could I have accepted his story without question?

I don't know how he got his revenge on poor Danielle, but it seems he's waiting impatiently for my turn to come around. But why? I'm quite sure I never gave him any encouragement.

I wonder what the time is. My mouth is dry and painful and there's a foul taste on my tongue. I find the water bottle and take a couple of tiny sips. I don't want to be sick again. My stomach heaves, so I don't dare take any more. I try to settle to sleep, but memories keep flashing round and round in my head until I think I'll go mad. My misery forces itself out in little baby whimpers and I try to cry, thinking it might help to relieve the discomfort, but it just makes me sick again.

I crawl off into the sand, but I needn't have bothered. I'm dry-retching now. It's so painful I fear my throat will scar. I can feel ulcers forming, either from the sickness or poor nutrition. After being so careful, how could I have suddenly been so stupid? I don't think the problem was the limpets. There's nothing around here to pollute them. I think it was the leftover grease I was so excited to discover. I should have scraped it off and then burnt off any residue. Instead I ate every last tiny bit, and now it may be the death of me.

At least thinking about this hasn't made me sick again, but I can't risk drinking any more water. I lie down and try not to think of being found by the Duffy brothers in a few days' time, half-naked and surrounded by little pools of dried vomit. That would certainly give them a laugh.

Surprisingly, thinking about the worst makes me feel slightly better, and I settle down again with some hope of sleep.

I hear crying. A desperate, terrible crying like an animal in pain.

And wake up in a panic, but around me all is silence. I must have been dreaming.

On the first night I was also woken by crying and a lot of unpleasant crackling noises, but that time it was not a dream. As I listened, lying rigid in my virginal bunk, my bed must have creaked, because the sounds came to an abrupt stop, and after that nothing broke the immensity of the silence. My first thought was to wonder if there were koalas on the island, having heard their heart-wrenching cries once before, which sound just like a human baby that has lost its mother.

Then I realised that it must have been Lana who was crying so wretchedly, and that something on this island was terribly, terribly wrong.

CHAPTER THIRTEEN

These shall ye eat of all that are in the waters:
whatsoever hath fins and scales in the waters, in
the seas, and in the rivers, them shall ye eat ... And
all that have not fins and scales in the seas, and in
the rivers, of all that move in the waters, and of any
living thing which is in the waters, they shall be an
abomination to you.

King James Bible, *Leviticus* 11:9-10

FIELD DIARY - Wednesday 25 April

I woke up to find that the sun was high in the sky
and the air was warm, although the sand beneath
my anorak was still damp and cold. I sat up
carefully and realised the sickness had diminished
to a faint dull pain in my lower back and a feeling
of unease. I feared I would never eat again, no
matter how hungry I became. My throat ached
miserably, and I nervously took a sip of water. It
didn't make things either better or worse, so I had
a little more.

But when I stood up the water bubbled in my stomach and cramps rapidly followed. I stumbled to the dunny, and thanked God I hadn't been sleeping in the cave. And as I had the thought, my father's voice resounded in my ear: *Don't you know it's a sin to take the Lord's name in vain, Alix.*

Yes, Vader, I know.

Stom! *You'll die there. You should not have turned your back on the Lord your God. Your sins will betray you!*

Yes, Vader.

My father's voice has haunted me before, but now I seem to feel his presence, judging me with triumphant glee.

So this is what you've come to, when you chose to leave the straight and narrow way.

I forced my ears closed to his taunting and turned to more immediate questions. Would the smell be best dissipated by leaving the lid open on the dunny? Or would that attract flies? I decided to leave it closed, and resisted using up the diminishing roll of toilet paper, *just in case.* I flipped the lid shut, latched the door behind me and raced into the sea, throwing off my T-shirt on the way. After a thorough salt wash and a quick rinse under the tap, it was time to check out my clothes.

They were dry, but stiff. The jeans were almost rigid and I could only make them wearable by

205

spreading them out on the anorak and giving them a good pummelling, then rolling and unrolling them a few times. At least they've shrunk a bit, making them slightly less baggy, but they still need the makeshift belt to hold them up. Today is Anzac Day. This is the one day I am confident the Duffy brothers won't be around. I heard them telling Matt they'd be going to Melbourne for the veterans' parade – possibly to commemorate an ancestor or, more likely, to sell some of Matt's drug supply.

Anzac Day is also a day when most Australians are on holiday, so as soon as I felt well enough I knew I had to make a journey to the jetty side of the island. I was hoping there might be some form of yacht activity between the island and the mainland, though I knew there was little likelihood of an official regatta. The waters are too unpredictable and treacherous for racing, but a few yachts passed us on the way out here, so there is some hope of a bit of traffic.

My plan was to cross to the landward side of the island and build a bonfire on the jetty at the end of the sandblow, where there would be plenty of driftwood on the beach to use in its construction. In my current weakened state I knew that I needed to travel light. I wore my hat and knotted the anorak around my waist. In various pockets I carried my knife, the water bottle and the remaining fruits. I would not eat or drink until afternoon at the earliest, but I needed to have supplies with me, *just in case*, which seems to be becoming my mantra. I was worried that the matches might have become damp after a night on the sand, so I took them out of the anorak's inner pocket to examine them. They looked OK and the waterproof container seemed to have kept them good and dry. I put them back, carefully zipping the pocket.

Keeping to the shade of the trees, I managed to make slow but steady progress. My legs were weak and my head felt strangely empty, and after a depressingly short time my breathing became laboured and I had to stop. I folded the anorak and sat hunched on the sandy ground with my back against a rock protruding from between a tangle of tree roots. I wondered how far I had come. Distances can be deceptive and this time it seemed that the jetty was further away than I remembered. My thirst was terrible but I didn't dare risk a bout of diarrhoea so far from the sea, so I suppressed the urge to drink and after a short break forced myself onto my feet again.

I wondered why I was not worried about dying. Perhaps I'd gone beyond fear. I had no idea what effect sickness and diarrhoea might have on my chances of survival, but couldn't bring myself to care. I just kept doggedly on, putting one foot in front of the other, carrying out my plan.

I wished I could hurry. What if there were yachts passing within sight at that very minute and I had no way of signalling them? No-one would be searching for me. The only person who could possibly miss me is Kathryn and she wouldn't be worried yet.

Or would she?

I pondered the strangeness of my friendship with Kathryn. Would we be friends if we weren't both single? Despite not quite seeing eye-to-eye about men, Kathryn and I have had some good times. We work together like an old married couple, each of us working to our strengths and backing each other up to the hilt. But we've mostly avoided getting too personal.

Kathryn knows my parents are dead, but she's never asked me much about them, possibly fearing it's a delicate topic. She did ask me once what it was like living in Madagascar. 'I don't know what to tell you,' I remember saying. 'I was sent away at thirteen. To go to boarding school!' I added, seeing her shocked look, although this was, of course, not the full story. Now, with so much time for reflection, I'm coming to the conclusion that my mother sent me away before Vader could break my spirit. I couldn't have told Kathryn this, because I wasn't aware of it myself until now.

She came from a town in New South Wales and had five sisters, all married and, as she described them, 'great breeders'. 'I'm the one disappointment,' she'd say, and then laugh it off. 'But at least I've got a career and can look after myself.'

She poured us both another glass of champagne. 'To happy families! May they live far, far away!' Then she looked suddenly stricken, as if she had just realised that my family were about as far away as could be. I wish I could believe that they were in heaven with all the angels and the harps, but I can't. And I couldn't seem to talk to Kathryn either, about how much I missed my mother, about my brother in Canada who was a virtual stranger. Why not? There really must be something wrong with me.

But it was no use dreaming about Kathryn and what I should or could have said. Today I had a mission.

A few more paces and I could hear the sea. Resisting the temptation to take another break, I surged on. Nearly there. At least it was a straight flat walk.

And then I reached the end of the sandblow. At last. I stopped a few metres from the shoreline and took a sip of water. It was warm and unpalatable, but it didn't make me sick. After checking that the tide was going out, I dug a hole a little away from the water's edge, wedged the water bottle in the damp sand, then scooped a channel between it and the waves as a kind of beach fridge, hoping the water would be a bit more drinkable by the time I finished building my fire.

I decided to risk eating some fruit, starting tentatively with the smallest of the karkalla fruits. After a few minutes with no ill effects, I nibbled a few more, then put the rest away. *Softly, softly.* I didn't want to be sick again. Then I began collecting driftwood and piling it up on the concrete jetty ramp, far enough away that there was no risk of setting any of the surroundings on fire, but close enough to be visible, I hoped, from the sea.

I was not at all sure of the island's location, mainly because I realised belatedly that Dave went to great lengths to keep me in the dark about our destination, sticking to back roads with little or no signage, which he described as 'taking the scenic route', and airily chanting 'it's a surprise', when I asked him outright where we were going. I had a feeling after we'd been driving for about an hour that he was deliberately changing direction, even doubling back on occasion, and that was when I first began to wake up to myself and think something was not quite right, particularly as normally I have a very good sense of direction.

I started watching for clues, and keeping a casual eye on the odometer. From the distance travelled, my innate sense of direction, and the rural signposts we did pass, I was pretty sure we were heading towards the Wilsons Promontory area south-east of

Melbourne, and as I felt the time was approaching when we'd be getting close I slumped in my seat and pretended to doze so that Dave would drop his watchfulness. He did relax and concentrate on driving as we reached the trickier back roads and I was able to catch a glimpse through half-shut eyes of an old-fashioned black-and-white signpost that told me we had bypassed the town of Foster and headed away from the Prom in the direction of Toora. I was quite familiar with Wilsons Prom itself, but had never travelled on in this direction. However, I had a fairly good memory of the map and when Dave turned off and the sea-coast came into view I knew we were somewhere on the way to Toora and Port Welshpool.

Up until now I hadn't thought very much about the local geography; I had plenty of other things to worry about. But now that I had a rare chance of trying to attract attention while alone on the island, this lack of knowledge almost brought me to despair. Although there was quite a lot of air transport – mainly small tourist planes and helicopters – over the Prom, I had not seen or heard air traffic of any kind since landing on the island. I had also seen no sea traffic. Apart from the Dodgy brothers' boat, since I've been stranded here there has not been any sign of human movement or presence within sight of the island, making it clear to me that fire was really the only option.

Because of the storm last Thursday the job was easier than I had expected. Driftwood had piled up against every resistant surface – rocks, sandhills and vegetation lines – so all I had to do was scoop it up in armfuls and throw it onto the pile. First, though, I found a snake-scaring stick and bashed it into each pile. Even though I scanned each one carefully first, there could have been babies hidden, invisible among the twigs.

Fortunately the beach seemed to be serpent-free, perhaps because it was on the more exposed side of the island. I worked without pause – lift, stagger, throw; lift, stagger, throw – until my legs collapsed from under me and I knew I was done. The pile, when I examined it, was impressively large and would make a sizeable blaze. But when I looked out to sea, there was no sign of sail or boat. I didn't want to light the fire unless I was fairly sure it would be seen because, once lit, the evidence would be impossible to disguise.

I dragged myself to a higher rock and set up surveillance. I could see the line of the mainland faint in the distance, but I couldn't be sure that a fire this far away would be visible to the naked eye. Not willing to take such a risk without a realistic chance of success, all I could do was wait. My insides seemed to have settled so I took out the remaining fruits and ate first one, then the rest, carefully monitoring for after effects. All seemed well. This

was good news, but it raised the problem of finding
more food. Without cooking facilities, I had probably
almost exhausted the food resources of the island.

I checked the water bottle, and found that it had
cooled down nicely, so after a few experimental sips
I had a good drink. I didn't feel hungry, but I knew
I had to build up my strength to walk back across
the sandblow. I tried to think of any possible food
sources I hadn't checked. The only birds' nests I'd
seen had been abandoned, so even if I did find an
egg it would probably have gone bad by now. I don't
know when mutton birds breed, but of course that's
why the snakes are there. I'd have to be very sure
of the eggs, and very desperate, before I'd willingly
reach into a burrow.

I didn't think I could risk limpets again, in case
they were the cause of the sickness, so unless I could
catch another skink, I was left with a totally fruit
diet. I'd have to search the jetty area thoroughly
before I left, because supplies on the other side were
becoming worryingly scant.

I scanned the ocean again, but nothing broke
the endless blue. There was no wind. The sea
looked as though it had been ironed flat. Hardly
ideal sailing weather, which probably explained the
absence of sailing boats. I didn't expect working
boats on a public holiday, so at least that was one
disappointment less.

It was peaceful sitting there, though my eyes began to squint with all the looking.

But there was nothing to see. Nothing at all.

The sun began to lower and with all hope gone I knew what I had to do. *Slowly*, methodically, I reversed my earlier procedure, taking armfuls of sticks off the pile and throwing them as naturally as possible around the beach. For some reason the dismantling was even more arduous than the building and I was almost crawling by the time I reached the base of the wood pile. I'd also run out of likely spots on the right of the jetty to toss my burdens into.

To the left was the edge of the tussocky mutton-bird country. I only had a few piles left, and I judged that the edges should be pretty safe. I knew I should take all the precautions – stamping, poking, shouting – but I didn't have the energy. I just wanted to be rid of the stuff.

I spent some time tidying up the area so that the base of the fire looked less ring-like and more natural, then carried the second-last load to the edge of the tussocks. There was a deep mound of driftwood, leaf litter and seaweed near the vegetation line. I tossed my load recklessly on top of it, and grabbed a bushy branch to tidy up the edges and make them look nice and windblown.

When I walked back with the final load I heaved it
as far inside my neat edge as possible. And a metre-
long black snake came hurtling out towards me.

For a second I was paralysed, then the adrenalin
cut in, giving me an extraordinary boost of energy,
and I ran like hell, as far as I could go. I was halfway
along the other side of the beach before I dared
to look back. There was no sign of the snake and I
slumped, puffing and gasping, onto the sand. I didn't
stop surveying for a moment, but it was a long time
before I could manage to stand up.

Now that I was there, I knew I must do a food
search. The cove around the jetty was quite small so
I walked slowly to the end of it, collecting another
stout stick along the way. There were rock pools
at the end but I doubted if they'd be any more
productive than the ones on the other side, and I
knew I didn't have a lot of time. Instead I followed
the vegetation line, this time shouting and bashing
the ground with my stick whenever it looked at all
like snake habitat, although I still suspected that the
northern end of the island was relatively snake-free.

At first there was nothing, and I found myself
wondering what that snake would have tasted
like if I could have caught it and cooked it (and
if I would have been able to make myself eat it if
so). Fortunately after a while I came upon quite a
large area of karkalla, and took the time to strip

it of every fruit, enough to fill two bags. Almost
back to the sandblow there was a muddy little area
probably caused by the sea at very high tides. After
much shouting and banging, I made a circuit of
this area. Although there was not a hint of food, I
found something so wonderful I did a little dance, all
exhaustion forgotten.

It was a flat piece of thin metal, about a quarter
of a metre in diameter. I didn't have my hammer
with me, but I tried bashing one of the edges with
a rock, and it bent slightly. My heart leapt. I might
have found a cooking pot. To celebrate I collected
my water bottle, sat on a nice flat rock, and had an
afternoon tea party of karkalla fruits and water.

Then I gathered everything, checked that the beach
looked relatively untouched, knowing I could rely on
the elements to improve on the job I'd done. Less
disappointed than I would have expected, perhaps
heartened by my finds, I set off along the sandblow. If
I hadn't realised the importance of regular food before,
I certainly did now. Even the small amount of energy
from the fruit was enough to make the walk seem
shorter on the return journey, which was fortunate
because the metal disc was not easy to carry.

3.00 p.m.: Write up diary.
It's been a chaotic day and a tedious and exhausting
expedition, but now I'm back outside the cabin,

taking some rest time to sit and write up my diary, and I estimate the time to be about three o'clock. I hope I'm right because this will give me just enough time to have a quick swim, collect and cook some food, and still make it back to the cave for the night. I don't want another chilly night on the sand.

This time, thank goodness, everything went as planned. I stripped off and raced into the sea for a quick swim, followed by an even quicker rinse at the water tank, then put on my clothes and sat on a log near the barbecue with the sheet of metal and my hammer. My aim was to beat the sides into shape but leave a flat base to sit on the barbecue plate. It took longer than I had hoped, but after some trial and error, and a lot of manoeuvring, I had a semblance of a pot.

Next I assembled all of the remaining specimen bags and went on a search for ingredients. I'd brought the hammer to help with catching crabs and this proved an inspired plan. Instead of trying to grab them, I gave them a good sharp tap, and while they froze in shock, threw them into the bag. It took time, but I accumulated five small crabs in this way. Then I detoured to the vegetation line and picked whole branches of karkalla leaves, and as I neared the cabin I filled a bag with saltbush leaves.

I lit the barbecue, filled my pot with water, and placed it nervously on the plate, hoping it would be strong enough to withstand the heat. Heart in mouth, I watched as the water began to heave, then bubble, and I threw in handfuls of karkalla leaves, sprinkled in the saltbush leaves like herbs, and finally, when it looked almost ready, added the crabs.

Then I turned the barbecue off and used the T-shirt I had just taken off as a mitt to transfer the pot to the sand, where I gave it a minute to cool down. I didn't have a spoon or fork so I had to use the lid from my water bottle as a scoop for the vegetables and juices. When they were all gone I used my knife to skewer out the crabs onto a plastic bag, and pulled them apart with my fingers.

It was a feast. There was not much meat on the crabs but what there was tasted sweet and fresh. The karkalla and saltbush leaves imparted a salty tang to the dish, but it was not as heavy as I feared. The saltbush was a bit chewy, but the karkalla leaves were delicious, a bit like soft, salty cabbage stalks. I ate every bit, except the crab shells, and I even ate some of the softer parts of the carapace.

Now I needed to move fast. I threw the crab remains in the sea, knowing from previous experience that they would be gone by tomorrow, and washed first the metal pot, then the T-shirt, as thoroughly as possible. I hid the pot in the scrub behind the cabin, covered my traces as well as I could, filled my water bottle, stuffed the wet T-shirt into one of the anorak pockets, and set off. It seemed like days since I'd been along this path, and I almost became nervous as I approached the cave.

The disguise tree was now well and truly dead, so I took a few minutes to hide it and replace it with a new one. A delaying tactic. Now that I was there I found I was afraid to go in. Why, I'm not sure. Did I think my belongings would have disappeared, stolen by aliens? Or that the cave would have been colonised by wolves?

I knew it was illogical, but still I hesitated. Then, noticing that the sun was receding remarkably quickly, I took a breath and entered, pulling the replacement tree across the entrance behind me. And there was my cave, just as it was. I was home.

I returned to the entrance to remove my jeans and boots, then unpacked, dressed for bed and reassembled my sleep padding. Tomorrow I should get some more sheoak branches, but for tonight the existing ones would do.

After the freedom of movement of the day before, and the brief luxury of sleeping lying down, I find the cave cramped and uncomfortable. How could I have become used to this? I do not know the time, but it is the night of Wednesday the 25th of April.

* * *

When I wake it's pitch black and my head is swimming, and white lights are dancing in front of my eyes. Odd, obsessive trains of thought begin to swirl around in my mind.

I live in Australia. I speak English. I even dream in English. Why does everyone still regard me as Dutch? Is it my accent, my appearance, my manner? I've never lived in Nederland. How Dutch can I be? If I went there I'd be just as much of an outsider.

Perhaps that's what it is. I'm a natural outsider and people just think it's because I'm Dutch. After all, the Malagasy thought we were English, which for them was another name for outsider.

Would religion have helped me to belong? Abel seems to have found a stable life in Canada. Do they regard him as Dutch or Canadian? I wonder if becoming an Australian citizen would have made me any more acceptable. Or are Australians really just as exclusive as the English, but they manage to hide it better. I don't think so, but the thoughts roll round and round inside my head ...

I dream I am in Edward's grave on the moors. It is cold, very cold. And dark ... I wake with a start. My father is standing at the entrance of the cave. I scream out in terror. What's happening? Am I dead?

He comes towards me, looming in that tiny space. *Ja,* that's right, Alix, you are dead. You just don't know it yet. Dead. *Dood.'*

I scream at him to go away then close my eyes. When I open them he's gone, but the lights are still there. Now a shark comes swimming towards me, pushing through the air of the cave. It swims straight at me and I shrink against the rock wall, only remembering to shut my eyes at the last minute before it can snap its gaping jaws around me.

Then I hear voices calling. I have to look. Ghosts and wraiths appear with the forms of Jonathan and Pauline, dancing and weaving around the cave.

'See how happy we are, Alix!' Pauline sings. 'See how we dance!'

Jonathan weaves right up to me and his face grows larger and larger. Then it shrinks and fades away.

And Vader is back. 'You see. You took the wrong way, Alix. The God-forsaken way.'

I shut my eyes so tight my head hurts.

When I open my eyes again the hallucinations have gone. Thank God! But my mind is filled with memories, coming to me out of the past, clear as yesterday. I am back in Madagascar, in the Punishment Room. Just me and my father. I don't know what I have done, but it is a four-beatings punishment, so it must be something very bad. 'Your hand, Alix,' Vader says. I put out my right hand and he hits it, hard, with the big black Bible.

'De linkerhand.' This time he hits harder and my finger bends backwards in a funny way.

'Turn.' Now he uses his own hand and punches my right shoulder until I can feel the big purple bruise forming.

Then the other shoulder, and after that the worst part. He sits me on a chair, and sits himself facing me. 'Alix, why must you be so bad? You are such a disappointment to me. Why can't you be like Abel? He listens to God's Word and follows the path of the righteous. But you, Alix. Always trouble!'

I recall now what I'd done wrong. Something in the Bible didn't make sense to me and I asked a question, a major transgression, forgetting that the Bible is the True Word of God and cannot be doubted. I also remember the pain of the broken finger, but somehow I could never manage to stop asking questions. Sending me to England certainly cured me of that. Perhaps that was the plan.

And now the dormitory of the boarding school comes back. The eight beds lined up, four to a side, each with a cupboard in which only a crazy person would put anything of value. And at the end of every room a cubicle in which a teacher slept with one ear open for any suspicious sound. Can't have been much fun for them. No wonder they seemed angry all the time.

But why was my father so angry? When I visited Laos I thought it would be different. I should have known better.

Moe had delivered the car first on the outskirts of Luang Prabang. Then she said, 'I have a treat for you, Alixi.' We loaded ourselves and our luggage into a pedicab, and were taken on a magical mystery tour that wound up on the river's edge. Leaving everything with the driver, we boarded a small boat, so that we arrived at the centre of Luang Prabang adrift on the Mekong.

It was like arriving in paradise. Golden spires soared out of tropical rainforest, and we berthed at a set of delicate white steps that took us up onto the road. There our driver was waiting to take us home.

'Thank you,' I remember saying to Moe. 'I can't believe such a beautiful place still exists.' Perhaps the beauty made me too hopeful. Despite all of Moe's excuses about Vader being too busy to join us at Vientiane, the truth soon became brutally apparent. When we finally arrived and got ourselves settled, Moe led me into Vader's study. Although I knew he was aware of our presence, he waited some time before he looked up.

'Well,' he said. 'Alix. Have you finally accepted the Way of Truth? Or have you come to disappoint me once again?'

I was too taken aback to speak, but my silence was enough for Vader. 'You may leave now. I have work to do.'

At least he visits me now, in my cave.

CHAPTER FOURTEEN

Thou shalt fear the Lord thy God, and serve him, and shalt swear by his name. Ye shall not go after other gods, of the gods of the people which are round about you (for the Lord thy God is a jealous God), lest the anger of the Lord thy God be kindled against thee, and destroy thee from the face of the earth.

King James Bible, *Deuteronomy* 6:13-15

FIELD DIARY - Thursday 26 April

I woke up stiff, sore and disoriented, thinking: *Where am I? What am I doing here?* The next thing that hit me was thirst. I was so out of routine it hadn't occurred to me to set any bags yesterday, so I knew I would have to hike to the cabin to get water. At least I no longer felt sick. My mind was clear to plan this day carefully, and to try to re-establish a routine.

Today is Thursday, and even though it's pretty likely that the Duffy brothers will still be in Melbourne, or back home nursing Anzac Day hangovers, I wanted to keep clear of the cabin area around the middle of the day. I moved outside the cave entrance to put on my jeans and boots and tried to estimate the time, then returned to the cave to pack up my supplies.

Once that was done, I set out immediately, making a quick detour to the coast banksia thicket to try sucking the remaining flowers for nectar, but they were already dry. I'll have to be sure to go out early tomorrow. While not particularly nourishing or filling, nectar is a food, and at least it adds some sweetness to my diet. It also has quite good energy-boosting qualities and I guess, like honey, might aid digestion. Given my current strange eating patterns, it could be a valuable supplement, and one I had temporarily forgotten all about, although it would mean keeping up my water consumption. I don't want another bout of cystitis, but at least for the moment obtaining water is not a problem.

When I reached the cabin, I took a fast walk along the vegetation line, filling my bags with every karkalla fruit I could find. By very thorough searching and stripping every morsel, no matter how small, I collected enough fruit to make an adequate breakfast, with a small handful left over for lunch.

Then I filled my bottle and two extra specimen bags with water from the tank, cleaned up the area and took my trophies up to the boat viewing hide on the clifftop. I made a thorough sweep of the cliff area for food, always keeping a wary eye out to sea, and found a few last boobialla fruits, some interesting-looking sap congealed on the trunk of a sheoak tree, and a large grasshopper, which I grabbed and sealed into a plastic bag.

I shuffled my way into the hide, pulled my shielding shrubs across, and settled down to wait.

When the sun was high in the sky I ate my mixed fruits, taking my time, and then cautiously bit off a little of the sap. It tasted OK, quite resiny and fresh, so I chewed it a bit at a time like chewing gum, spitting out the waxy residue when I'd exhausted all the flavour. I thoroughly enjoyed this bizarre snack, which just goes to show how desperate I've become.

Then, for something to do, I began to compose a map of the island on the second-last page of my diary, which was an empty clean white page, just begging for something to happen to it. Ever careful, I chose to work in pencil and tried to keep it roughly to scale. Even though I'd never seen an illustration of it, I discovered I had quite a clear idea of the island's shape. I found a pencil with an eraser attached to its end and concentrated on getting an outline I was happy with, sketching, rubbing out, and starting again until I was satisfied I had the proportions as accurate as possible. Next I placed the important landmarks where I believed they should go; first my cave and its surroundings, then the jetty, followed by the sandblow and, lastly, the cabin with its surrounding accoutrements – tank, barbecue and dunny.

I spent a lot of time working on the rocky areas. The landscape around the cave I knew well and could confidently draw in the rock formations, the rough steps down to the tiny beach and the little copses of coast banksia, boobialla and sheoak trees. Even the other side of the rocky peak I could reproduce quite faithfully, having walked up towards it on that first day, and swum round it much more recently in my not-so-crazy plan to convince Dave of my demise.

The western-oriented beach with the boat-landing jetty I had also visited recently and most of it was clear in my mind, but for the snake-infested end of the island I could only rely on what could be seen from a distance, pencilling in a high granite tor at the far end and rocks, trees and low scrub as I vaguely remembered them. I also marked in the rough paths that I was sure had been made by human endeavour, and the rough hide in which I hid to watch the boat's comings and goings. This was a very satisfying activity and took an even more satisfactory amount of time.

Of course I didn't know the island's name, or even if it had a name. Perhaps it had taken Matt's family's name, but since I didn't know what that was, it didn't really help.

I find it somehow easier to estimate time when
the sun is going down and at about four o'clock I
packed up my small possessions and made a fast
march to the cabin. I knew no boat had come to this
side of the island. I also knew that the other side
was too shallow and rocky for landing. But I couldn't
completely rid myself of the fear, perhaps because
this would normally have been a boat arrival day.

I took a deep breath and ran down the path to
the cabin. As expected, no-one there, so I set off in
search of the evening's meal. The crab harvest was
pretty meagre this time. It took me a good half hour
to catch three small scuttlers. Perhaps word had
got around about a new predator on the block. I still
had the grasshopper-in-a-bag, so decided to make
do with that and collected several bags of greens to
accompany this strange stew.

I retrieved my cooking pot, filled it with water
and lit the barbecue, but this time I cooked the
vegetables first with the grasshopper, drained them
and scooped them onto a plastic bag plate before
adding the crabs separately in just a tiny amount of
water. I don't know what caused the hallucinations
last night – it could have been the crab cooking
water or eating the shell – so this time I was taking
no chances. I decanted the crabs onto a separate
plastic bag and left them to cool slightly while I
washed the pot and dipping cup in the sea. I hid the

pot in the scrub again and took my supper of boiled grasshopper and greens and braised crab down to the water's edge, where I sat in the sand, delicately picking out the meat and throwing the refuse to be pulled away by the tiny waves.

Then the usual routine: fill up water bottle, visit dunny, clean up area, cover tracks on the way back to the cave. This time, however, I made a short detour and tied every available specimen bag onto the coast banksia trees, ready for collection tomorrow. Finally, I remembered I needed some more sheoak cushioning and had a pleasant and fragrant time choosing the softest branchlets I could find. By the time I reached the cave and peeled off my jeans and boots it was almost dark.

I have used many of the quiet waiting times today to write up my diary, so now all I need to do is ready myself for sleep and pray that no sharks or ghosts visit me tonight.

* * *

I try to clear my mind, but remnants of last night's hallucinations swim around my brain.

I can't seem to prevent the flood of memories of my father. After barely thinking about him for all these years, now there seems to be no escape. His face, his voice is everywhere. 'The Lord thy God is a jealous God.' He loved the King James Bible, in all its pomp and resonance. His voice took on its own resonance when he read from it, and even the Malagasy boys enjoyed hearing him roar at them of fire and brimstone, births, rapes and beheadings. It always strikes me as odd that people who make such a fuss about chastity, purity and virtue spend so much of their time reading what is possibly the most prurient literature ever written.

Vader believed all other reading was a waste of time. 'You've spoiled her with those *stom* English books,' he'd complain as Moe and I finished reading and discussing *Emma* or *The Vicar of Wakefield*. He was particularly scornful of Shakespeare, and in fact we found the sixteenth-century language too difficult, never managing to progress beyond *Romeo and Juliet*.

He honestly believed that I was doomed to hellfire for my unbelief. I know that. Perhaps he's right. Perhaps I've ended up in this nightmare for denying a jealous God, and he's trying to tell me to repent, to save myself. This exile has certainly forced me into a state of unwonted self-examination. But it hasn't made me believe in the existence of a hell or a heaven. Even as a small child I couldn't reconcile it with what I knew of the geography of the earth and its place in the universe. Even now, in a state of extremity, I still can't. If that dooms me to eternal hellfire, so be it.

I finally fall asleep and dream a lovely dream, probably the first good dream I've had on the island. When I wake it is almost light and the sweet memory lingers as I rearrange my padding and change position to ease the stiffness in my legs and shoulders.

I dreamed that Jonathan came to rescue me. Kathryn told him I was missing and he went storming into Dave's workplace to find out where I was. Surprisingly for a dream there's a kind of logic to it. Kathryn has met Jonathan and would know how to contact him. She doesn't know Dave's name or where he works, but Jonathan possibly does since we were neighbours for so long. But of course it's not going to happen. It was my own desires manifesting themselves in dreams, though I feel oddly comforted. Certainly an improvement on the night before.

I'm tempted to go back to sleep to see if I can keep the dream going, but instead I find myself going back over my relationship with Jonathan.

We did have a lot of good times together, and not always related to rock-climbing. Although neither of us much liked run-of-the-mill cooking, we both loved trying out exotic recipes and often if we were home on a Saturday we'd spend the morning at the market buying all sorts of weird ingredients and then spend the night sipping wine and working together to produce the most extraordinary dishes possible. We'd play music and dance while we were chopping vegetables, then set a formal table and dine in style.

We also both had a passion for visiting houses for sale that were open for inspection. This started in England when we were impecunious undergrads looking for things to do that didn't eat into our meagre student allowances. It was a time when vendors were urged to make their offerings seem 'special' so there was often an added bonus of free coffee or muffins, or even both.

We discovered that we were both frustrated interior decorators and would come back and plan miraculous makeovers, usually from chintzy pink-and-cream frowziness to state-of-the-art modernity. And when we were living in our bare-bones little flat in Melbourne we kept up going to house inspections, although by this time we had stepped it up a little. We would each come home and do a total renovation plan, often including a garden makeover as well. Then we'd compare our offerings and the one judged the winner would have dinner cooked for them.

Oddly enough, while coming home to wax lyrical about floorboards, paint colours and raised vegetable gardens, we never talked in terms of actually buying a house.

Jonathan and Pauline bought a house. They got married too, as soon as our divorce came through. And thanks to my 'desertion' to Western Australia, this happened in the shortest possible time because we fulfilled all the criteria for an easy painless split: I had been living elsewhere for eighteen months; we owned no property; we had no children. Jonathan did visit me in Perth once early on, when I showed him the sights and we spent a seemingly happy day on Rottnest Island, but I never made the trip the other way. Why didn't I? I must have been so caught up in my job – and it *was* very demanding. Or maybe I was less caught up in Jonathan the property lawyer than I had been when we were both students together.

When we were in England we had discussed the topic of marriage in tones of scorn. It was outdated, restrictive, unnecessary in this secular age. So why had Jonathan been so keen for me to come to Australia? And why had he suddenly been so keen to get married? It can't have been to please his mother. She didn't like me much. But then, she also didn't like to see her son 'living in sin'.

I do feel the absence of that special intimacy when I think of Jonathan's long and gentle courtship, and the way he allowed my erotic education to proceed like a comic strip, where each unfolding takes you further on your journey of discovery. I realise that Kathryn is right about my fear of meeting 'a new man'. Things seem to move so quickly now. You click online and have sex before you even know each other's full name. Then you decide after one 'date' whether to see one another again or move on. I don't think I could do that.

I'm surprised to be thinking so much about Jonathan. Does he still think about me? Would he jump into action if Kathryn contacted him?

Not if Pauline had anything to do with it.

I shouldn't resent Pauline. I left the field open for her and she took it. Even when Jonathan refused to go with me to the west, I still in my naivety expected him to be there when I returned. An eighteen-month contract seemed no time at all to me, and the thought that he might not wait hadn't entered my head. I must have had an inkling at the back of my mind, though, because when I was invited to apply for a senior position back in Melbourne I jumped at it, but it was already too late. The only person who didn't know about Jonathan and Pauline by then was me.

It took him three weeks to pluck up the courage to tell me. I moved right back into what I thought was our home, began to pick up what I thought was my life, until one night after dinner when we were sitting on the deck watching the bats fly over, Jonathan suddenly said: 'I'm moving out.' I was still a bit slow on the uptake.

'Where are you going?' I thought he'd got a job somewhere where he had to stay until the work was finished.

'For the moment I'll stay at Mum's place. We'll need to find you a new place.'

Just as it hadn't occurred to me that Jonathan wouldn't follow me interstate, it hadn't occurred to him that I'd be upset. Once he realised that I was more than upset, I was devastated, it took him even longer to tell me about Pauline. Jonathan hates trouble.

Would it have made a difference if I'd tried to win him back? I don't think I saw it as an option. In my mind Pauline held all the cards. She'd been there for him, as I was not, while he settled into the dog-eat-dog legal world, and being a paralegal, was a lot more interested in the whole legal system than I was. She was also in a hurry to marry and have children. She was older than me, older than Jonathan too, and I guess, as Kathryn would say, she felt the clock ticking. The pressure she put on him was relentless, and I was so miserable I think I just gave up.

You got what you deserve, Alix. A woman should stay by her husband, not parade around the country like a hoer. Thanks, Vader. Good to see you back again. Now all I need is a shark and my night will be perfect.

I shut my eyes to banish the unwanted intrusion, but all that brings is a succession of long-suppressed memories. Deirdre, Jonathan's mother, the first time we met, saying: 'Well, I suppose we'll have to try to get along, but I had hoped he would do a lot better than this.'

Abel, pulling me along behind him as we scramble to hide in the shed. 'You mustn't provoke him, Alix. Why do you always provoke him?'

Tante Leni when she didn't know I was listening: 'She's not like her mother. Berthe was always such a lovely person.'

And, finally, Dave: 'Bitch'll get what's coming to her'.

Although it's not cold in the cave, I'm shivering, the memories stirring up all kinds of horrible emotions. Why did Jonathan's mother dislike me so much? Does she approve of Pauline? I always thought she wanted him to find someone with a classier background like her own, but perhaps she just wanted someone more biddable than me. Not that Pauline struck me as particularly biddable, but I suspect she and Deirdre would have pretty similar ideas about wifely behaviour.

Both of them would have wanted children. I wonder if Jonathan did? We never talked about it, which is strange when you think about it. I crossed the world because he begged me to come with him and we didn't really discuss the future at all.

I think now it was because he was a romantic, and in the romantic story the handsome prince rescues the damsel in distress, and makes her his princess. But damsels in distress don't take jobs on the other side of the country.

It's funny how when I'm working I'm told I have 'good people skills'. I don't know anything about people. Look at the mess I've made not only of my life, but of the lives of people around me. What they mean is I make a good boss, which probably requires not-so-good people skills. You need to be fairly insensitive to get the most out of people without getting bogged down in their personal lives.

All Jonathan ever knew about me was that I came from Madagascar, missed my mother and brother, and hated school. I didn't know much about him either. When you meet on neutral ground those things don't seem to matter. No wonder everything fell apart when I came to Australia. He was in his own milieu, and I was too alien to fit into it.

Even with Kathryn, who would have been delighted to listen, I didn't confide very much about my life. Except for the breakup. One thing Kathryn knows all about is breakups. They are her speciality in fact, so as soon as word got around that I was officially dumped she swept me off to her flat, where she poured us strong gin and tonics, and sat me down to watch *Anna Karenina*, followed by *Casablanca*, which, as she explained, is what girlfriends do. I didn't weep, I still hadn't regained the ability to cry, but it was remarkably cathartic all the same. I'd never had a girlfriend before, so it was something of a cultural shock for me. But I did feel better.

Kathryn, where are you now? Can you hear me calling? I'm not on love island. I'm on the island of bad dreams. Please find me.

I try to conjure her, but the face that comes to haunt me is Dave's. What with him and my father, not to mention the shark, the cave is becoming quite crowded. No boy-next-door charm this time, his face is ugly with anger, taunting me. 'Stupid Alix. Thought I was pleased to see her. Thought I was her *friend*.'

How did it come to this? What was it about me that spurred him on to seek revenge and punishment? I remember always making an effort to be nice, particularly because he lived in the next flat, so bad blood would have been very uncomfortable. What a strange phrase, 'bad blood'. Is that what's wrong with Dave? And me? In Dutch it would be *slecht bloed*, not surprisingly an accusation my father never threw at me. He certainly didn't blame himself for my wrongness. I wonder if anyone feels guilt about Dave's wrongness. What on earth happened to a nice-looking, well-educated young country boy to make him turn out like that?

Was it, as my father would have it, original sin? I still feel an ache when I think about my father. I didn't feel sinful, and I don't think I ever set out to upset him, but I managed it just the same. Am I naturally bad, or were his expectations unreasonable? After all, he turned on Abel in the same way once he knew he'd lost control of him. Was that it? Abel tried to toe the line, but I never got the knack for that. I didn't mean to provoke him. And neither did Moe. We just didn't seem to be able to keep our heads down low enough.

Well, I'm low enough now. If Dave could see my present discomfort he'd revel in it. So would Vader. So would Matt, for that matter, and probably the Duffy brothers as well.

But none of them will see it unless they come searching. And unless they do that I'll probably die here in my well-hidden cave and my bones will never be found. And if the men do come back I'll very possibly end up dead anyway. These are not happy thoughts.

I take refuge in sleep, but the dream of Jonathan is gone. Instead, my mother is here, she has collected my bones and is washing them and wrapping them in clean linen. *Dank u, Moe. Dank u wel.*

CHAPTER FIFTEEN

And the nations were angry and Thy wrath is
come, and the time of the dead that they should
be judged and that thou shouldest give reward
unto thy servants and prophets, and to the saints
and them that fear thy name, small and great; and
shouldest destroy them which destroy the earth.

King James Bible, *Revelations* 11:18

FIELD DIARY - Friday 27 April

Thirst woke me again, with daylight piercing the cave
as I took my jeans to the entrance to put them on,
pulling the strap belt another notch tighter. Then I
returned to the sitting position to put on my boots.
Everything took so long, and I felt so weak, that
it was almost more than I could manage to dress
myself and gather my knife and water bottle for the
short trip to the coast banksia trees to collect the
nectar, and immediately feel the familiar wash of
energy coursing through my body. After that I made
a detour to the nearby copse of boobialla trees, but

all that remained were three lone fruits, so wizened
and dried out they were hardly worth harvesting.

So that was breakfast. All I could hope was that
there would be some remaining fruit on the other
side of the island, as I made my way back to the
cave to pack a few necessities for a trip to the cabin.
I crammed my hat, water bottle and the last of the
specimen bags into every available pocket and then
sat for a while to catch my breath and write up my
diary. Then I set off once more, and as I walked I
made a plan to cook a large lunch and then try to
collect enough fruit for a light supper back at the
cave.

Although my thoughts were dominated by
the hopeless conviction that I am trapped on this
island without any possibility of escape, I had
to concentrate on my day-to-day survival. I felt
less panicky now that I was getting into a routine
again, and decided to try to get up early tomorrow
and make it washday at the water tank. I was so
absorbed with planning that it was a moment before
I registered a noise coming from the far side of the
island.

The noise of a boat.

I was almost to the viewing point above the
cabin, and was immediately and horribly aware of
the fact that I hadn't been brushing my footprints
away, saving that ritual for the return journey. How

long would it take whoever it was to get across the sandblow? At least there was no other access on that side, so I could be sure that if they were coming to the island, they'd come that way.

Without giving myself time to think, I tore off two small branches of grey saltbush and, trying not to rush, retraced my steps, rubbing out every trace of my footprints as I went. I got back to the cave in record time, but didn't go in. I had to know who it was and what they were up to. I couldn't risk going all the way to the tree overhanging the sandblow. Instead I made for the hide on the clifftop. So terrified I could barely breathe, I forced myself to keep going, always slowed down by brushing out my footprints, until at last I arrived, panting and heart pounding, at the hide.

Then I waited. Not knowing what was going on was terrible, but I was able to hear the boat's engine stop, so at least I should be able to hear when it started up again.

After what seemed like hours, I heard voices. For a dreadful moment I thought they were coming up the cliff path, but the footsteps stopped, and then I heard the unmistakable tones of Mick and Kel Duffy.

'Maybe that fuckwit Dave was right. She's karked it.'

'Shouldn't we go up the top, Mick?'

'Nah. Looks like no-one's been up there for months.'

I heard the crunch of footsteps going back towards the cabin. After a few minutes, I crawled out of my hide and cautiously raised my head. Nothing. Slowly and carefully, staying in the brush at the side of the path, I followed the two sets of boot prints until I reached the rocky course that led to my spying tree. I didn't dare go any further, and anyway there was no adequate cover near the cabin, so I made my way as quickly and quietly as possible to the edge of the sandblow, knowing that eventually they must come past my hiding-place.

Again I waited, hearing nothing, except one excited shout that echoed down the sandblow, and filled me with foreboding. What had they found? Soon after that I heard the crunch of boots on sand, followed by snatches of conversation.

'Might not be hers.'

'Yeah? Who else d'ya think's been here? Robinson Crusoe?'

'Might've washed up.'

'Then why was it right up there? These dints look new. But how the hell she could've done them I don't know. We didn't leave no tools.' Then Mick's nasty laugh. 'Tell you what, kid. You're gonna get your wish. I think we should make ourselves a little search up that cliff path. See if we can scare the rabbit out of the hole.'

I heard their boots scrunching as they hurried back along the sandblow towards the cabin and, heart sinking, I heard them turn off along the cliff path. *Towards the cave.* Abandoning all caution, desperate to know what was happening, I again wriggled out of my hidey-hole and, darting from tree to tree, I pushed through copses and shrubs until I could hear voices again. By this time, they were nearly at the cave's entrance. I hung back, hardly daring to breathe, then I heard Mick give a shout. 'Hey, Kel, look at this! This tree's not in the ground! There's something behind it.'

Then shouts and whoops of triumph. 'It's a fuckin' cave! Now let's see if the little bunny is inside it! Go on, Kel. You're skinnier than me. Go in and see what you can find.'

I moved as silently as possible behind the trees until I found a spot where I could see what was happening. There was silence for a while, apart from Mick's shuffling feet, and then Kel emerged, dusty and dishevelled, carrying an assortment of objects: spare clothes, plastic bags and my heavy-duty, waterproof, completely useless watch.

'She's not there. I went right in,' says Kel.

'That's her stuff though. I recognise that fancy watch. You think she's still alive?'

'I dunno. Maybe. There's no food.'

'No signs of life?'

'Nah. Not really. Maybe she did drown?'

'Well, if she *is* alive she's not goin' nowhere.' Then something that chilled me right to the bone. 'Tell you what, Kel. We'll come back Monday. Bring the dogs.'

'Or tomorrow.'

'Nah. Tomorrow's B&S night. She can wait.'

'What if she swims for it?'

'Then she'll drown.' Another unpleasant laugh. 'If the sharks don't get her first. And this time we're not leavin' nothin', not even the time of day. If she is here, she's in for a nice surprise.'

They appeared in my line of sight, Kel awkwardly carrying my cooking pot, Mick clutching something that I couldn't quite see, and then gradually their footsteps faded away. I was about to climb down from my perch when I heard footsteps again and voices almost directly underneath.

'Here'll do. We can sit on that rock.'

Then there was a shuffling noise and Kel said anxiously, 'I can't find it. I had it, Mick. I'm sure I did.'

'Ya probably shoved it in a pocket somewhere.'

More shuffling. 'Got it!'

I wondered what they were searching for. Then some muffled sounds, followed by the striking of a flint and a scent reminiscent of my university days. They'd sat down for a smoko. I wondered, as I'd often wondered before, why two such unpleasant people would go to so much trouble for Matt. Did they take part in whatever dubious practices went on in the cabin? Was there some kind of long-standing feudal connection from when his family lived on the island? Or was it just about money?

I'd debated these questions over and over in my head on those long nights in the cave, but without answers.

This time I got some answers, but they left me more puzzled than ever.

'Mick.'

'Yeah.'

'What if the dogs find her, and she is dead.'

'Then she's dead.'

'But won't there be, ya know, trouble?'

'Who's gonna tell them? You?'

'No, Mick. Not me.'

A short silence. Then Kel piped up again. 'But what if she's alive? She'll tell.'

'Tell what? No-one's done nothin' to her. She ran away.'

'I dunno. How much does she know?'

'She can't prove nothin', mate, no matter what she says. Anyway, what if she did? You know how good Matt comes over in court.'

'Yeah.' Kel's voice brightened. 'And she's a foreigner.'

'Right.'

More silence, then: 'I thought she'd be different. More ... exotic.'

'Yeah. Too mouthy. I like 'em when they don't understand a word.' More silence. 'And when they're blonde.'

'Yeah.'

All this time I remained immobile until I heard the sound of the boat, and my limbs were beginning to seize up. Even when I heard the motor start and the sounds of the boat slowly taking off, I didn't move, almost paralysed by one word of their conversation reverberating through my mind.

Dogs. They'd find me. They'd sniff me out. I wouldn't stand a chance. Even if I could find an underwater cave and submerge myself, like the children in my well-thumbed adventure books, they'd track me there. I've seen the Duffy brothers' dogs and they terrified me even from a distance. The thought of having them *seek me out* filled me with horror.

I'd seen what happened on an animal hunt once when Jonathan and I were on a walking tour of the Pennines. The packs of hounds, baying for blood; the packs of humans on horseback, voices harsh with the excitement of the chase, baying in disharmony with the dogs. Male and female voices, raised in the clamour of the desire to see the prey torn apart. It was one of the most terrifying moments of my life. Until now.

Tante Leni and Uncle Raoul had dogs. I always got on well with them and often took them with me on my rambles over the moors. But the Dodgy brothers' Rottweilers aren't companion dogs like Pippin and Sherlock. They're hunting dogs like the baying pack, and would only be held back by the brothers from tearing me limb from limb. Or would they let them, give them free rein, and then throw the mangled pieces into the wine-dark sea to confound the authorities later?

My mouth was dry, my rapid breathing had parched my throat and there was no water left in the bottle. I knew they'd gone and that I was safe for the time being, but I also knew that the safety had a time limit on it, so I'd need to make the best of the time in between.

I stumbled down to the cabin and discovered the nice surprise Mick had left for me. A shiny new padlock on the dunny door. Shocked, I turned to the water tank and opened the tap. But, what relief, there was water flowing and the level hadn't changed. I topped up my bottle and drank my fill, but had a nagging feeling something else was different. I patrolled the whole area twice before I saw it.

They'd taken the gas bottle. That must have been what Mick was carrying so awkwardly.

No cooking pot. No stove.

I don't know how long I'd have sat slumped in the sand, too full of despair to move, but I felt the sun beating down on my back and knew I had to make the effort. I've got two days before they come back to think up a plan, *if I can believe what they were saying.* I think I can. Mick's smart enough to know the cooking pot wasn't there before. And unlike Dave, he's unlikely to believe I'm dead until he sees the body. The heat, and the unpleasant thoughts, were making me feel woozy, so I stripped off and had a quick swim, then rinsed myself off, dressed and spent a calming few minutes writing up my diary. But I can't stop worrying about how I can cook things now that my lovely pot has gone. And the barbecue. Mick Duffy must certainly have believed there was a chance I was alive to bother to do that. Or was it Matt's idea?

Someone bought the padlock for the dunny door.

I finally got myself moving and found that, no matter how diligently I searched, there was no fruit to be found along the vegetation line, so I climbed through rocks and sharp grasses to a few lone boobialla trees further up the slope and ate the meagre harvest as I went, but it was barely enough to provide energy for the climb. I felt as if I was working in slow motion, that I had become unreal, ghostly, half-alive. Then I saw two fat skinks sleeping on a rock and without even thinking I picked them up effortlessly and dashed their brains out. I wasn't hungry enough to eat them raw, so I

put them in a bag and scrambled back down to the
beach and the rock pools. This time the crabs were
plentiful, though small, and I collected and bagged
about half a dozen. Then back up to the vegetation
line so I didn't need to worry about footprints, a
quick clear-up of the cabin area and a top-up of my
water, and I headed back for the cave. I began to
notice dead wood along the path, and as I neared
the cave, I collected armfuls of sticks and branches.
Since I was going to be caught anyway, there was
no real point in hiding my presence. I decided to
light a fire on the rocks near the cave and grill the
food on sticks. Apart from the risk of detection, I'd
been reluctant to use up the matches, but I've still
got half a pack, and soon it won't matter, so what
the hell?

The grilled skinks were delicious. The crabs
were less successful, but there was enough edible
meat on them to make a reasonably satisfactory
meal. I cleared the remnants of the fire as best I
could, threw the bones and shells off the rocks and
into the sea, then proceeded to the coast banksia
thicket. This time I bagged flowers only to see if
the system would work for nectar, since I have no
fruits and I'd brought enough water to last until
tomorrow.

* * *

And so to sleep, as the darkness enfolds me.

But I can't sleep – all I can think about is that on Monday I'm going to be caught. Unless they don't come, and there's not much chance of that, I can't escape a dog search. So I've got to do something before Monday, but what? Most castaways seem to spend their time building rafts, but I don't think a raft would survive the seas between here and the mainland, and even if it did most of the possible landing places are rocky and treacherous. Without any means of steering it would be a doomed enterprise, which is a relief in a way. The last thing I want to do is cast myself into deep water on a frail craft of any kind. I'm frightened enough on a real boat.

So that's out. The only other option is to attract attention before they come back. *But not attract their attention.* That's the tricky part. I try to piece together what I know of the Duffy brothers' habits and as I walk and search, snippets of conversations from the boat trip over come back to me.

'You going to nail a few at the B&S night Saturday week?' Matt's voice.

'Nah.' Mick Duffy's.

'Thought you never missed it.'

'Not fuckin' on, mate. Fuckin' Easter break. School holidays.'

'That's OK. The pub's going to put one on in town instead. Could be some tasty new blood. Then why don't you come over to my place on Sunday? I'll be showing some interesting foreign movies.'

I'd forgotten all about this conversation. And the fact that when Matt mentioned foreign movies they all turned and looked at me.

I keep wondering what Lana's role is in all of this, and another conversation comes back to me, from the first night in the cabin. I was in the bunk room, drifting between sleep and semi-wakefulness, so that it was difficult for me to separate the dreams from the reality, but I remember hearing Matt say: 'She's too old, mate. And too smart. Hope she's not going to bring us trouble. You have to get them young and stupid. Train them up.' And then his voice changed as he addressed someone else. 'Don't you, darl?'

Did he get to Lana young and train her up? And then they need other girls to make the sex more interesting. (Or more saleable – I haven't forgotten Matt's camera. Or the other scary stuff they had hidden away.) Where do they find the girls? What do they offer them? A free holiday at the beach? Money? Drugs?

They didn't need to offer me anything. But Dave misled Matt about me. He presented his fantasy Alix – sad, needy and foreign. And now they are not going to let the real Alix escape. They are going to hunt her down with dogs.

A small whimper escapes me. I'm reminded of Lana's hopeless crying in the early morning before dawn. What did he do to make her cry like that? And what did he have in mind for me that has made him determined to hunt me down?

I must not think like this. I have to figure out a plan, some way to survive this new threat. But all I can think of is the slavering jaws of Mick's dogs closing on my leg, my throat …

I wake to pitch darkness and this time I recklessly light a match. I use its light to find my torch, hoping the batteries are still OK. I put new ones in before I came and have barely used it, but it was still a relief to see a thin clear beam cleaving the blackness.

I decide to relieve my sleep stiffness by taking a short walk outside the cave, and after experimentally turning the torch off, find that the moonlight gives just enough definition to paths and rocks to enable me to navigate. I climb a little way up the rocks and sit, staring at the huge black hole that is the sea.

If only I could get across it, but it's such a formidable barrier, I can't see any solution. Too far to swim, too far to sail even if I had a raft. If I had wings, I could fly across. I imagine myself winging high above the waves. I wonder where I would go. Would I head home to my flat? Or would I fly on and on, across to the west, or even further, north to Canada? I could visit Nederland, find out how Dutch I really am.

It's surprisingly pleasant sitting here. Not cold at all. I can still smell the remnants of my dinner fire, a comforting combination of smoke, fat and burnt wood. Tomorrow I'll scour the rocks for skinks, as well as doing a thorough search of all the boobialla trees for anything edible. With any luck I'll be able to have nectar for breakfast, fruit for lunch and some kind of meat for dinner. I don't really want to go over to the cabin side again, just in case they come back early, though reason tells me they won't, but if I can't catch any kind of meat on this side of the island I'll have to go crabbing again. What will happen after that? The fruit supply is pretty much dried up, and even the coast banksia flowers are almost at an end. I'll still have water, but I can't count on finding a large enough haul of skinks and crabs to keep me going for long.

And my time is running out. On Monday it will all be over, and sitting here thinking about food is not going to solve that problem. The only thing I can think of is to light another fire and hope someone sees it. Which is the more likely day for sailing boats to be out, Saturday or Sunday? I don't know. And would any boat be likely to come close enough to see a fire if I did light it? I don't know.

I stare out to sea and as I look I find I can pick out the lights on the mainland, indicating the small settlements that line the coast. And I realise what I must do. If I light a fire at night, on the edge of the clifftop, the chances of being spotted would increase enormously. People picnicking on the beach, or out night fishing, even planes flying over, would be able to see flames coming from the peak of the island, and they'd know it wasn't just a bonfire on the beach.

One thing Australians take very seriously is bushfire, and some of these islands are inhabited, so anyone who saw it would be highly likely to report it. But would they take action? And if so, who would come? What if they sent the Duffy brothers? Despite these reservations, perhaps because of them, I realise my decision has been made. It has to be Saturday night, when if all goes to plan Mick and Kel Duffy will be fully occupied with trying to nail the lucky ladies at the local pub's bachelors and spinsters night.

CHAPTER SIXTEEN

For without are dogs, and sorcerers, and
whoremongers, and murderers, and idolaters ...

King James Bible, *Revelations* 22:15

FIELD DIARY - Saturday 28 April

I sit writing my diary after a long draught of nectar.
This could be my last day on the island, so I feel I
should be trying to sum up my experience, but I
cannot find the words. I feel weak, as weak as I felt
after eating the limpets, and I hope I'll be able to
summon enough energy to carry out my plan. The
small amount of fruit and protein I managed to find
yesterday doesn't seem to have provided me with
nearly as much energy as the carbohydrate-rich diet
of the first part of my self-imposed exile.

I shiver when I think about my chances of
survival if I hadn't included the nuts and sultanas
in my pack, now that I know how limited the
island's resources really are. After harvesting nectar
from the coast banksia trees early this morning, I

combed the wooded areas and found no fruit at all. I think I have finally exhausted the crop for this season.

I'm too weak to cross the island to look for crabs. I need all the strength I can muster to build a bonfire. As I sit on a sun-warmed rock writing my diary, I feel the usual thin wash of energy course through me from the nectar. I must make the most of this and start collecting leaves and branches for the fire.

I have chosen the location for my bonfire with the greatest possible care to reduce the risk of the fire spreading and causing environmental damage to this almost pristine island. I have located it on a flat shelf surrounded by higher rocks that should block any floating embers and send them to the ground or out to sea. Fortunately there is virtually no wind, so the risk is minimal. And the island itself is, as I am only too aware, surrounded by nothing but the wide, wide sea.

I still worry but am comforted by the memory of recent heavy rains, so the trees and understorey are not bone-dry, and also by the thought that I will be utilising every single piece of dry wood and foliage up here on the clifftop, so there will be minimal or no fuel nearby.

Conscience partially satisfied; time to get to work ...

It's taken hours of leg-wearying toil, but now, finally, it's done. I purposely went as far afield as possible to build the understorey of the bonfire in case I didn't find any more food and my energy began to flag later in the day. Last week's flood had left several large drifts of branches and dried leaf debris and, after checking the area using my stick-banging technique, I gathered them and formed them into a wide circle on the rocky shelf that juts out over the ocean at the island's northern point. Then, this time feeling like a true environmental vandal, although I knew it would all be replenished soon enough, I pulled off any dead branches I could see, and even uprooted some fairly dead-looking bushes. I added the cave-screening tree to the pile with a small pang, seeing my refuge's entrance so exposed. Then I rested, gathering my resources ready to comb the ground for sticks, branches, leaves – anything that would burn.

I realised too late that if I'd thought of this earlier I could have been pulling off branches over the past few days and letting them dry to build up more fuel supply. *Stom. Stupid.* Didn't think ahead. It would have been easy to do and nobody would have noticed; the bush is full of dead waste of all kinds. How do I know that what I have gathered will be enough?

At lunchtime, since I hadn't been able to find
any fruit, I drank some of the remaining nectar.
I was beginning to feel light-headed and I was
not hungry at all, but I knew I must build up my
energy to keep on collecting. The thought of the
Duffy brothers and their dogs helped to spur me
into action.

Hands clenched, I counted to five minutes (and
ONE and TWO and THREE and FOUR and FIVE),
opening out one finger for each minute, then forced
myself to stand up. I still felt weak, so took a few
sips of water, then peered down the stone steps to
the little beach below. The karkalla stems are too
juicy to burn, but it could be worth checking for any
hidden fruits, and I thought I spied a few pieces of
wood on the little strip of rocky beach. It took me a
long time, stopping after every few steps, but I made
it to the bottom and found two last karkalla fruits,
which I popped straight into my mouth, enjoying
their chewiness, and about a dozen quite solid pieces
of driftwood, beautifully white and dry, which I
gathered together.

They were going to be a heavy load, too heavy for
one trip, but my cunning mind managed to devise a
plan. I laid out two long stems of karkalla, spread my
anorak over them, and stacked the longer pieces of
driftwood as neatly as possible on top.

Then I rolled up the anorak and tied the sleeves
to form a kind of bag, tied the karkalla stems
around this parcel, and looped the ends around my
shoulders to form a backpack. It worked surprising
well initially, but as I neared the top of the steps
I felt the weight of the timber shifting the bundle
ominously, so I slumped down, took it off and
unwrapped it, allowing the contents to tumble gently
onto the step.

Then I made three trips up the last few steps to
transport the driftwood to the bonfire site, where
I stacked it to one side. I now had no more food
and very little energy, so I found a shady spot and
sat and tried to meditate, taking sips of water
whenever I began to feel parched, but making
sure I used as little energy as possible. When I
was collecting this morning I set new bags for
tomorrow, *just in case*, but I fervently hope I won't
need to use them.

The sun was now high in the sky. I must have
dozed off. I took another small drink, filled my
pockets with specimen bags in the hope I might find
some food, and brought the anorak to use as a carry
bag. The bonfire was not yet large enough to burn for
more than a few minutes. I needed to at least double
its size and for that I would have to search the ground
thoroughly and pick up every single dry leaf, twig and

branch. I started with leaves and filled the anorak over and over, lugging it to the bonfire site and throwing its contents onto the middle of the pyre.

Then I searched for twigs and small branches and did the same. When I'd built up a good mound of small stuff, I began to arrange the larger pieces of driftwood on top so that the leaf litter would blaze up and ignite the larger sticks. Then I pushed into the boobialla thicket and collected every stick and branch I could carry. As I staggered back with the load I spied a fat skink on the path and cautiously emptied the anorak of its contents, rushed forward and dropped it on the unsuspecting reptile. After a bit of a struggle I managed to knock it on the head with the hammer and put it in a bag. Then I reassembled my cargo and lugged it onto the fire.

At least now I had dinner.

One more trip, to the coast banksia trees, and I realised I'd pretty much exhausted the resources of this side of the island. There was no question of going any further afield. I was so tired I could barely manage to stumble into the cave to retrieve a few necessities. When I woke this morning I packed all my remaining belongings, except the water bottle, plastic bags, matches, knife and torch, into kitchen tidy bags and placed them just inside the entrance of the cave. This time I refilled my water bottle from the last of the spare bags and placed my lizard-in-a-bag carefully in the shadiest spot I could find.

Then I went outside again, spread the anorak on my sitting rock, and quietly caught up with my diary, matches in one pocket, knife in the other.

But after a while I couldn't sit any longer. At least restlessness gave me a bit of energy so I walked almost briskly to the one area I hadn't fully stripped, my original toilet spot. Perhaps for hygiene reasons I'd been reluctant to collect material there, but after a little more than two weeks it could hardly matter. I entered the little copse and found several piles of brush, a good collection of sticks and branches and in a small thicket a most wonderful discovery, a largish dead tree.

Slowly, methodically, with many stops to regain my breath, I collected the brush, the sticks and the branches and dragged them onto the fire. Then I brought some lengths of karkalla stem, tied them round the tree and, like Europeans hauling home their Christmas pine, I looped the stems over my shoulders and dragged the tree, in short stages with many stops, to the edge of the fire.

There was no way I could lift it onto the top, but I realised that if I could find some way to climb up onto the higher rocks, dragging it behind me, I could drop it into the centre of my bonfire. If I succeeded in placing it correctly, it would stick up out of the pile like a candle, and continue burning when all the small fuel was used up. To give me the energy for this challenge I drank the last of the nectar, and then harnessed myself up again.

The tree was heavy and dragged my arms painfully, but the distance was not far, so I forced myself to go on. One metre, two, three and I was up on the rock ledge, but the tree was dragging me back. I stopped and rested, trying to gather enough strength for one last heave, and I finally managed it, although I felt an agonising wrench to my left shoulder and almost let the whole thing go.

But it was up and I manoeuvred it so that I could push it head first onto the pile, where it landed crookedly but well in the centre, the thickest part of the trunk with its tangle of roots pointing high into the sky. It was some time before I could move and the pain in my arm was so bad I almost fainted when I forgot and attempted to use it to balance my descent. Luckily I'm right-handed, but I wished I had strung the skink I caught onto a stick before putting my arm out of action. With one hand it was quite difficult but I managed it eventually and sat cradling the raw skink kebab on my lap, waiting for darkness. Then I realised the bonfire would be too hot for cooking, so I raked off a small pile of sticks and leaves and made a little fire for my dinner. It was not very effective, and the end result was a bit too rare, but it was food and I ate it with relish.

Now I sit on my rock, surveying my handiwork. The bonfire rises high in front of me, and I ponder the full implications of what I am planning. If I light this fire there is no going back, and no way to predict the consequences. But if I don't, by Monday I will have to face the Duffy brothers and their dogs. Fear rises through me. My throat is dry and I feel breathless. I sip water and try to empty my mind. It can't be long now until dark.

Another thought strikes me. What if rescue does come? I'll be in the cave, *just in case*, so I can defend myself if necessary. I need to leave a trail.

Like Hansel and Gretel I have gathered pebbles from along the path and formed them into an arrow leading from the perimeter of the bonfire to the cave's entrance.

I will close my diary now with this thought: *Pray for me.*

* * *

It is dark.

Shaking with nerves, because I know that once made this move will be irrevocable, I strike a match. And hover reluctantly for a moment before I plunge it into the bed of brushwood at the base of the pile. And light another match. And another until little tongues of flame are licking all around the bonfire. Then a huge *WHOOSH* and up it goes, flames leaping into the sky, and the rocks around flashing red and yellow like strobe lights in a nightclub.

Although it's really too hot for me so close to the blaze, I am transfixed. As I stare into the flames, people appear, swirling black within the raging red. Jonathan. Kathryn. Vader. Moe. All of them face me and I call out to them. 'Come and get me. Here I am.' But they swirl away.

Then Lana comes. 'Help me,' she calls. 'Help me.' But Matt appears and throws her into the fire where she burns up and disappears. Only her voice remains. 'Help me.'

Then Dave, untouched by the flames, staring out at me. 'I'll find you, Alix. I'll get you. You can't escape.'

I have to get away, into the cave, hide away in case someone comes. I duck inside, panting, then peek out to see the fire take the tree and dance up it, so that it bursts into a white-hot light, just like a candle, and I know it will be seen on the mainland, and they will know that this is not a natural fire, although it is not man-made. It is woman-made, and I wonder who will come.

The pain in my arm is excruciating. I feel faint …

I come back to consciousness, and hear, muffled by the soughing of the sea but still audible to my hyper-sensitive hearing, the sickeningly familiar sound of the Duffy brothers' boat growing louder and louder, and then, the sound I have been dreading, the barking and growling of a pack of dogs in full cry after their prey.

I can hear seagulls crying, far out over the sea. Or is it the blood pounding in my ears? I stay in my cave, where I'm safe. If anyone comes in here, I have my torch in my unsteady left hand ready to shine in their eyes, my knife in my right hand ready to plunge into their heart, until I find out whether they are friend or foe.

Flames crackling all around me, knife and torch in hand, I wait …

CHAPTER SEVENTEEN

They have sown the wind, and they shall reap the
whirlwind.

King James Bible, *Hosea* 8:7.

I woke up in a stark white room like a prison cell. It was a
relief to see machines and tubes and people in blue uniforms
with ID cards clipped to their chests, although my first,
irrational, thought was: *Oh please let this be a hospital, and not
a hidden torture chamber!*

I couldn't remember much of what happened on the
clifftop, but two SES people arrived in their orange rescue
gear to check on me, introducing themselves as Jude and
Serge. Jude seemed to be the spokesperson. 'You tried to
fight us off,' she said, and they laughed. 'We had to wait
until you passed out and could be loaded into the chopper.'
I have a vague memory of my hand brandishing a knife.
At least in my befuddled state I didn't hurt them. This time
the gods were with me.

They too remember hearing the sound of a boat, but by the time they set down on the flat area of rock it had seemed to be receding. I didn't dare ask them if they'd heard the barking of dogs. *I don't want to know.*

Coming back into the everyday world has been surprisingly like falling into a dream. Nothing seems real. There are too many people, there is too much light, too much noise. And too many nasty surprises. Like what happened with my diary.

I have learned that after following my arrows and finding me, Serge and Jude searched the cave thoroughly in case anyone else was trapped inside. They left almost everything as they found it and sealed off the cave entrance until a proper search could be made in daylight, but they did bring my field diary. 'We were hoping it would tell us who you were.'

They found my name, and as they combed through the entries in an attempt to discover more details they began to realise that I had been a virtual prisoner in the cave and that in my distraught state I must have thought they were Matt and Dave, or the Duffy brothers come with their dogs to silence me once and for all. So, like good citizens, they called in the cops. Unfortunately that turned out to be a bit of a curve ball.

It had not occurred to me that if the diary was ever found its contents would be doubted, but to my dismay that's exactly what happened. Matt's and Dave's families quickly appointed lawyers, who immediately advised them to deny everything, and describe the comments about them in the diary as simply the wild fantasies of a diseased mind. *My mind*, that is, not the truly diseased minds of Dave and Matt.

I knew only too well that everything in the diary was real, and some days elapsed before I could bear to revisit what I'd written. Once I began the slow road to recovery from the after effects of lack of food and water, and from the sheer terror of that final day, I forced myself to start at the beginning and read the entries right through. It was chilling to relive the dangers and horrors I had put down so matter-of-factly and I've spent a lot of time speculating about what was happening on that island, and why I'd been so afraid of what Dave and Matt might do. I was far more afraid of them than of starving to death, though I am not usually a fearful person.

Now that I was in a hospital I could feel some of the fear that had been weighing me down just dropping away. For a couple of days, I drifted in and out of events as tubes fed me rehydration and sustenance, and wounds were dressed. When I was finally permitted to set foot out of bed my injured shoulder was bound in bandages and placed in a sling and, at least physically, things began slowly settling back to normal.

But one fear remained. In those first days I was haunted by the idea, always in the back of my mind, that Dave would continue his relentless quest for revenge, or total control, or whatever it was that drove his sick fixation, and try to come and claim me. I was very conscious of the fact that there had been no guard set at my door, which they always seem to do in cop shows, but when I mentioned my fears to the night nurse he was able to reassure me. 'Don't worry. We had a series of drug thefts last year and now this place is like Fort Knox.'

He also pointed out to me a lovely oasis in the very centre of the building, a circular sensory garden offering plants to touch, aromas to smell, and chimes to soothe the sense of hearing. As soon as I was mobile I found my way into this safe haven and sat under a Peppermint Gum (*Eucalyptus radiata*) on one of the rugged timber benches that curved around the tree.

As I sat I found myself meditating on the enigma of Dave Grogan and his obsession with me. I didn't really understand what had brought out such a strange mixture of threats of vengeance and puppy-like adoration, neither of which were caused, as far as I could see, by anything I had done. I had never encouraged Dave, but nor had I ever treated him badly. I had behaved with distant politeness, as you do with people who don't interest you, but with whom you have no quarrel. So how had it come to this?

I was reminded of an article I once read about abusive spouses. It was entitled 'First he beats her up, and then he brings her roses', and that seemed to sum up the confusing nature of Dave's 'devotion'. But Dave was not my spouse, and although I felt safe for now in the arms of the hospital, was I going to live in fear of both his devotion and his vengeance for the rest of my days?

The police have had me go over and over again my first meeting with Matt and Dave in the St Kilda pub, and questioned me repeatedly about a prior relationship, because Matt is insisting I'd been Dave's girlfriend in the past. He probably believes it. I have no doubt that Dave is crazy enough to have invented a romantic history with me. I wouldn't be surprised if he now believes it himself.

It's a serious worry. Because of this I cannot persuade the police to take my fear of Dave seriously, although the hospital has been very good about it and is carefully monitoring all my phone calls. Just recently a call came in from a male voice who would not leave his name. They didn't put it through but it still gave me the shivers.

I didn't tell Kathryn about this when she came in to visit, despite the fact that she has proved to be a truly excellent friend (or perhaps because of it). When someone at the hospital had the good sense to google my name, it came up with my place of work. There they were directed to Kathryn, who arrived, unfamiliar without makeup, dressed in jeans and a sweatshirt like a normal person. She sat with me for the next two days, sleeping and showering at a local bed-and-breakfast, and only leaving me during the day to grab meals and takeaway coffees.

'Why aren't you at work?' I managed to ask her in one of my waking moments.

'Compassionate leave,' she said. 'I don't have anyone dependent on me, so the boss managed to stretch the rules. I hope you don't mind,' she said, suddenly nervous that she may have overstepped, knowing how much I valued privacy.

'Of course not, Kathryn. I'm really grateful.' And to my absolute shame and embarrassment I burst into tears. 'It's been – so horrible, so awful.' Kathryn put her arms around me and held me, as a mother would embrace a child, and I felt safer in this unfamiliar comfort than I'd felt for a very long time.

She stayed for a further two days after I was moved to rehab, and then had to go back to work, but she came down every weekend, and accompanied me when she could to my sessions with the doctors and the physio, because even a week later I was still having trouble remembering things.

I was very relieved to find that the rehab wing had the same security measures as the main hospital, and could only be accessed through a keypad-protected door. I could watch the TV news and read the daily newspapers, so I was able to keep up with what was happening outside.

I thought there would be something in the papers about my confinement in the cave and ultimate rescue, but it was days before anything at all appeared. Even then it was just a tiny paragraph in one of the local papers, tucked away on page ten, and all it said was that a woman had been rescued from a local island and that police were investigating.

I hoped this was not the beginning of a total whitewash orchestrated by Matt's and Dave's family lawyers. I discovered that Matt belonged to the Pentecost family, who were not only rich and powerful, but who owned most of the area and were considered to be local gentry. Dave's mother and father were both on the local council, so between them the parents were in a position to put a lot of pressure on the police and the law to protect 'the boys'.

'Those two were always in trouble,' the physio, who'd gone to school with both Matt and Dave, told me. 'Small charges at first but when they left school they moved up to car theft and drug dealing. It got harder for the families to bury the charges, but they still managed it. You know how those born-to-rule people are: "Boys will be boys", "Don't want to ruin a promising future", "Those girls all lie through their teeth anyway".'

'Sexual harassment?'

'Oh, yes. We all knew to keep away from Matt and Dave when they were out on the town.'

'Didn't their parents try to pull them into line?'

'All that mattered to them was that their sons wouldn't have a criminal record,' she said. 'And it's worked. There's not an official word against either of them.'

I felt a sudden jolt as if I'd been punched in the stomach. Does that mean they might get away with it again? Surely not with some of the dreadful things they've done. To Lana. And to me. But I guess it's only my word against theirs, and mine has been well and truly compromised.

The next surprise was a visit from Lana. After completing all the protocols, including being issued with a Visitor Pass, she was escorted into my presence by two uniformed members of the hospital's security staff. 'This is

nearly as bad as the airport security to get into Australia!'
And for the first time I saw Lana smile, a little lopsided
grin that made her look younger and much, much prettier.

There was another difference too. 'Lana. Your voice.
You sounded different on the island.' Her voice was now
soft but firm, with a slight accent, but not a hint of the little-
girl voice I remembered.

Lana frowned and bit her lip. 'Matt has this obsession
with Marilyn Monroe. He wanted me to talk like her. He
even made me dye my hair to look like her.'

I felt myself go cold. 'Lana, that's really creepy.'

She nodded gravely. 'Every single thing about Matt is
creepy. He is a total creep.' Then she brightened. 'Because
of what was in your diary the police got a search warrant for
the cabin and the boat and they found all kinds of dodgy
stuff. They took Matt's laptop, and all that gear they used
when they made movies.' Lana's expression darkened for a
second, then brightened again. 'Most of the drugs were still
there, and all of the weapons he'd bought through the Dark
Web, because smart-arse Matt never thought he'd get raided.'

I was pleased to hear that the diary was now helping
to move things along, and that the police were at last
taking the matter seriously, but I was worried about Lana.
Although I can't see how I could have done anything to
help her while we were on the island, I have a sense of guilt
and a feeling of responsibility towards her.

'Where do you go from here?' I asked her. 'Will you go
home?' Then I paused. 'Where *is* home?'

'I grew up in Ukraine, but I got moved on to Estonia. I don't really have a home anywhere.'

'Family?'

'There's no-one left. All dead.' She smiled a little, twisted smile. 'Do you have family?'

'I have a brother. He lives in Canada.'

'Lucky you,' she said, so softly I could barely hear, and we both sat quietly for a moment, thinking about lost families and lost lives.

Then, an absolute bombshell: a newspaper article referring to other lost lives, discovered and reported while I'd been sequestered in my cave. The news took me completely by surprise, and made it horribly clear why what I'd seen and experienced on the island had made me so afraid.

It turned out that when the police finally interviewed Lana, they mentioned the washed-up bodies, and to their amazement she knew immediately who they were. Not surprisingly, she came to see me in a terrible state. 'I didn't know,' she said, wringing her hands. 'Matt never let me see the TV news, or the newspapers.'

She looked at me imploringly. 'I found them.' She searched for a word. 'I *recruited* them. Matt said it was for a movie about travellers from Eastern Europe, but I knew it wasn't because they didn't take me with them on the boat.' Her voice sank to a whisper. 'The girls thought they were going to get good money. And all the time ...'

THE COURIER

ISLAND OF NIGHTMARES

By Elsa Vajda and Simeon Cornish

Shockwaves are pulsing through South-east Gippsland as the son of one of the area's first families is being interviewed by police after detectives, following a tipoff in a seized diary, conducted simultaneous raids on a fishing boat and a cabin on Muttonbird Island, known locally as Pentecost Island.

After removing a number of suspicious items from the cabin, including illegal weapons and a commercial quantity of drugs, the police undertook a wide-ranging operation to investigate a possible connection with two young women's bodies that had washed up along the coast in the previous month.

The bodies have now been identified as those of two young backpackers, Hanna Lerberg, 17, from the Czech Republic and Daria Savluk, 19, from Belarus, who had been staying in a St Kilda hostel and working as waitstaff at a nearby cafe.

Matthew Pentecost, 26, the son of local billionaire Niall Pentecost, and brothers Michael and Kelvin Duffy are currently being questioned by police in relation to these offences. Another local man, David Grogan, 25, is being sought by police for questioning in relation to these crimes, but has not yet been located.

For a moment we shared an appalled silence. Then she spoke again. 'It wasn't an accident or anything like that. Matt told me to look for girls with no-one who would come searching for them. And I did, Alix. *I did.*' She was trying to hold herself together, not very successfully. 'I should have done something! I knew it wasn't right.'

Although we both knew that if she'd tried to intervene she'd probably also be dead, Lana still looked wracked with pain and guilt. If Kathryn had been here she would have comforted her with a hug. The best I could manage was to reach out and hold her hand, and so we sat together, connected but not speaking, while her breathing settled and she gradually calmed down.

After Lana left I had a sudden, fleeting vision of my parents' bodies, mixed up with the unwelcome, devastating visions of the pathetic corpses of those young girls. But this time Moe and Vader were beginning to become misty and vague and amid all the grimness it gave me hope that the spectres would fade and I would soon be able to remember the living, and not the dead.

The next time the police came they had been through the entire contents of Matt's laptop, and were now much more respectful of my experience on the island. They asked if they could show me some of the footage Matt and Dave had produced to see if I could recognise anyone. Many, and some of these involved Lana, were strictly women on women, but for the others both Matt and Dave joined in. Most consisted of variations on sex and violence, utilising the whips, handcuffs and other horrors I'd glimpsed in the kitchen drawer. The gunlike object, I discovered, was a taser, illegally imported from overseas. When I saw it being used on film I recalled with a shudder the night I heard Lana crying, and the strange crackling noise followed by instant silence. The films were amateurish, graphic and very, very nasty. I can't begin to imagine the type of person who would want to watch them.

The police had to explain to me the concept of snuff movies. 'They torture somebody to death, usually a young woman, and they film the entire process. It's the worst fucking thing I've ever seen.' The cop looked at me apologetically. 'It's pretty rare.' He paused. 'Very rare.' Then he put his head in his hands. 'I can't believe it. I've got teenage daughters. What kind of monster does things like this?'

'Those movies are worth a fortune on the Dark Web,' the other cop told me. They didn't show me any snuff movies but of the ones I looked at I was easily able to identify Matt, Dave and Lana. No sign of the Duffy brothers. Perhaps they're not photogenic enough.

My next visitor was even more of a surprise. He looked both familiar and unfamiliar, like a waxwork figure of somebody you once knew. 'Jonathan! Come in,' I heard myself say, my voice steadier than I felt, and my ex-husband, large as life, came over and plonked himself in the visitor's chair. 'Your friend Kathryn sicced the cops onto me. Did she tell you?'

'No, she certainly did not. What on earth could *you* say to them?'

'That you're the most honest person I know, so they could safely believe anything you've told them.' He grinned, to indicate no hard feelings. 'Anyway I knew you were telling the truth about not dating Dave.'

'How?' As far as I knew Jonathan had barely had a conversation with Dave.

'I never told you, but he came to see me, all strutting and self-important, and announced that you and he were in love and wanted to be together, and that I should let you go.'

I must have looked as horrified as I felt because he immediately reassured me. 'Don't worry. I knew he was talking out of his arse, and then he put the lid on it by saying he'd taken you to see Nick Cave and you'd decided he was the man for you. Even showed me the two ticket stubs as proof.'

I stared at him, aghast. 'He did ask me to go with him but I knocked him back.'

'I know, Alix. I was able to tell the coppers that we were away climbing Mount Arapiles with eight other people who could attest to your whereabouts on that date. *If* they wanted to doubt my word.' That was true. It was our last climbing trip together. I wonder if Jonathan was thinking that as well. I didn't want to talk about the past, but I needed to know more details.

'What happened with Dave?'

Jonathan's face hardened. 'I told him to rack off and if he ever bothered you again I'd fucking kill him.'

'You didn't say that to the police?'

'No, I do have some sense of self-preservation. I told them I made it very clear he wasn't welcome at our place. He never came back, did he?'

I thought about it. 'No, he didn't. I wish you'd told me though.' *You could have saved me from the risk of starving or dying horribly, mauled by sharks or dogs.*

Perhaps sensing my thoughts, Jonathan gave me an oddly sad look. 'There's quite a lot of things I should have done differently. Particularly the way I behaved when you went over to the west.'

'We both have things we could have done differently.' I paused. This was serious stuff to have to deal with out of the blue. 'I should have discussed it with you.'

He rubbed his chin and looked away from me. 'I thought you were treating me with contempt. I couldn't see that you were just being your own honest, practical self.' It definitely wasn't as simple as that, but if that was how he wanted to remember it I was willing to let it go.

'You're happy now?'

He looked me in the face this time. 'Yeah, I guess I am. You might say I've found my level.' I stood up and he did too.

'Goodbye, Jonathan. Thank you for coming.'

And he laughed. 'The way you always call me Jonathan, never Jon or Jono. You're so … formal.' He left, still laughing, and I couldn't help wondering what Pauline called him.

I'm grateful that Jonathan was willing to come to my rescue, but it makes me so mad that the cops and the legal people all believed Matt's testimony that I had been Dave's girlfriend, even though both Lana and I had told them that it was not so. It took the testimony of another man for them to fully believe our story.

However, let's hope that it's a portent for a satisfying outcome to this dreadful case, with Matt now being questioned by the police without his father's protection. When the suspicions about the young girls looked all too likely to be true, both sets of parents, as the police said, 'washed their hands of the perverted bastards'. But what is hanging over my head is the big question no-one seems able to answer: Where is Dave Grogan and what is he up to?

I'm terrified I'm going to find out only too soon …

I'm glad I chose a very secure apartment when I decided to move out of St Kilda and leave the past behind. Apart from taking great care when entering and leaving the building, I'm not too worried about Dave coming out from whatever hole he's been lurking in and trying to break in. Each apartment has an outer security door and a lockable safety mesh door. The front entry has all the bells and whistles you could possibly want: cameras, buzzers, triple locks. Even the lifts are password-protected.

My only worry is the area at the back of the building where the rubbish bins are stored. It is also protected by a securely locked gate leading out to the street, which residents like to use as a shortcut to the local supermarket, although some of the residents seem to resent having to remember to take their key. This means that now and then I've found the gate rammed open, so when I go down there I make sure I'm carrying my hammer or my knife. *Just in case.*

Tonight I have two exceptionally heavy rubbish bags to wrangle into the lift, so I almost decide to leave my weapons behind, since things have recently been so quiet. However, caution gets the better of me and I shove the knife in my right pocket as I grab an oversized bag in each hand and lock all the doors behind me.

There's no-one else down there and the gate is securely latched, so I begin to relax, when suddenly one of my neighbours, Gabi, emerges from the lift to join me, carrying a pile of empty but fragrant pizza boxes. She drops them into a bin and then, without warning, takes out her key and opens the gate. 'See you,' she says, and slips out, oblivious, as a heavily booted foot stops the gate from closing and Dave Grogan comes in very quietly, shutting the security gate behind him with a decisive click.

'Hello, Alix Verhoeven,' he says. 'I knew you'd come. I've been waiting here for you. I've been ready for this for a very long time.'

And I realise that I am also ready, and that I am absolutely furious. I feel as if I've swelled to twice my usual size, filled and expanded with righteous anger at this man who has caused me so much pain and fear. Without taking my eyes off Dave, I find the emergency pager the police recently gave me, which I keep on a chain around my neck, and press to turn it on. *How long will it take before someone registers my call for help? And how quickly will they respond?*

I look Dave over, and see that wherever he's been hiding hasn't done him any favours. He's dirty, unkempt and a great deal thinner than when I last saw him, his black jeans hanging off him as if he's picked them up from the Salvos, his T-shirt in dire need of a wash. Looking at this unprepossessing figure standing there, I ask the question that has been haunting me for so long: 'Why can't you just leave me alone?'

His voice is thick with emotion. 'We're meant to be together, Alix. All I've ever wanted was to care for you and look after you. We could be so happy. *Why won't you understand?*' His emotion sounds convincingly real, as if he's about to cry, but I'm not buying it. He may be able to fool himself with such a display of sentimentality but he's certainly not fooling me. I'm way beyond that.

'You have stalked me, you've threatened me, you've harassed me in every possible way. What on earth makes you think I'd want to go anywhere with you?'

He looks, for a moment, as if he's heard, as if he's taken it in and realised the extent of what he's done. Then he draws himself up. It was just a mirage. Crazy Dave is back. 'You're mine,' he hisses. 'We're meant to be. I knew that the moment I first saw you. Why are you making me do this?'

This only increases my anger. 'I am not *making* you do anything. I've never given you the slightest encouragement. This is your doing. *All your doing.* You have tried to ruin my life for no reason. *Fuck you!*'

His expression turns ugly and he makes a move towards me. 'You stupid bitch.'

'*Just leave me alone!*' I begin to back away and draw my knife and hold it so he can't lunge for me without risking injury. I'm shaking like a leaf, my legs feel like jelly and I'm afraid I might fall but I hang in there. 'I don't want to hurt you, Dave. But I will if I have to.'

He laughs, a very nasty laugh, like a horror-movie clown. 'I don't think so,' he says, and from behind his back he produces what looks like Matt's taser, and a wave of horror takes over my body, from my toes to the hairs on my head. My little knife has no chance against such a monstrous object. He's still laughing as he raises his arm, ready to fire.

Then, oh miracle of miracles, there's the sound of a key and Gabi comes back through the gate, so startled by the spectacle of a man in black about to taser me that she drops her plastic bag of milk and bread and screams bloody murder. For a split second Dave is paralysed, unable to process what's happening, and in that second I drop my knife, leap forward and wrench the taser from his grasp.

And then, without taking any time to think of the morality of what I'm doing, I point the weapon straight at Dave's heart. I've never fired a gun, but I manage to find the trigger and squeeze it. There's a loud crack and two wires snake onto Dave's chest, the electrical current making the horrible sound I heard not so long ago in Matt's cabin. And it's Dave's legs that collapse from under him, he can't speak, he doesn't seem to be able to see what's going on, and Gabi shrinks against the wall and stares at me, white-faced with horror.

I hear sirens, far away, and then nearer. And nearer. Finally, Dave looks around as if awakening from a trance and hears them too. He's still bewildered, lying helplessly on the ground. He tries to rally, to crawl towards the gate, but he can't move, his limbs are completely uncoordinated, and I hear a racket outside, and run to open the gate to let in the police.

To my great relief, Dave was quickly cleared of having any lasting physical damage. To my even greater relief, Gabi's statement, plus what the police already suspected about Dave, meant that he was taken immediately into custody. Seeing him being led off in handcuffs gave me the best night's sleep I'd had for quite some time.

He didn't go quietly, of course. His last words were: 'I'll get you, Alix. You *will* be mine. I'll never give up,' and regular reports appeared in the media of escape plans and threats by Dave to come back and kidnap me. Some elements of the media, mainly gossip magazines and commercial current affairs shows, tried to make it into a romantic story, calling him 'the Jailbird Casanova', but the more reputable media outlets described him as what he was, a stalker. My name was never released by the police, and I'm very grateful that so far it has not appeared in print or online.

From all the reports it quickly became clear that Dave blamed Matthew Pentecost for 'frightening off the love of my life' after Dave had lured me to the island. He seemed to believe that all his dreams of a union with me would have been realised if not for Matt's threatening behaviour, and in his rancour he gave detailed statements accusing Matt of organising the drug network, dealing in the importing and sale of prohibited weapons, and distribution of pornographic materials. But the *coup de grâce* was his description of standing 'helplessly' by as Matt tied the two young backpackers up, force-fed them lethal doses of drugs, tasered them when they screamed and filmed every moment as the two men watched them slowly die.

Even just the suspicion of his role in this was enough for Matt to end up in remand with his former partner-in-crime, where he in turn tried to put all the blame onto Dave. The police, and the media, were still trying to get to the truths hidden in this tangle of accusation and counter-accusation, when Dave took matters into his own hands.

THE COURIER

MAN SHOT BY POLICE DURING ESCAPE ATTEMPT

By Simeon Cornish

Known as one of the two main suspects in the notorious 'backpacker' killings, David Grogan, 25, was being transferred to remand when he attacked two prison guards and made a bid to escape. When police arrived and attempted to subdue him, Grogan produced a knife and threatened to stab one of the prison guards.

'It was not possible to reason with him,' a police spokesperson stated. 'In the end shots were fired and Mr Grogan died at the scene.'

Grogan, who was being sought by police on suspicion of involvement in the murders of two young girls, and a number of other crimes, was arrested two days ago after being caught in the act of attempting to 'taser' another intended victim.

Matthew Pentecost, 26, the son of local billionaire Niall Pentecost, is also in police custody in relation to this case.

I can't begin to describe the depth of my relief when I heard that Dave had been shot dead by the police. I know I should feel sorry for him, but I can't. 'Suicide by cop' the media are calling it, but I don't think so. Dave was in the grip of an obsession to get back to me, and I don't believe he would have wanted to die before that mission was fulfilled. The question that continues to haunt me is who supplied him with that knife, and I don't think I'll ever know the answer to that particular puzzle.

Now at last the whirlwind has arrived. It has already taken Dave Grogan, and I have a strong feeling that it will go on blowing until the lives of those two innocent young women have been fully avenged.

AFTERMATH

I have been a stranger in a strange land.

King James Bible, *Exodus* **2:22.**

And what about me? What about Alix? Physically, I'm back to my old level of fitness. My memory has almost completely returned, but that is definitely a mixed blessing. There are so many things that I'd be happy to forget.

Where I live now is in a very closely packed urban area. Fortunately the block is fringed by trees and greenery, but unlike our old place in St Kilda there is nowhere to walk, or even anywhere to sit outside. I work in the centre of the city, so after my time on the island surrounded by trees, shrubs and rocks, I have found the endless concrete and lack of gardens cold and uninviting. For a while I took to walking the streets in the evenings, back to my old habits, but the stunted street trees and paved gardens with their spindly potted succulents did nothing to relieve my longing for green.

Then one day I stumbled upon a local park planted entirely with native Australian trees and shrubs and I now find my feet turning automatically to walk the three blocks to enter its cast-iron gates. It's never crowded and the path that takes you in a leisurely circle through its different sections is generously dotted with old-fashioned wooden seats. I spend happy half-hours among the acacias and eucalypts, excitedly recognising old friends as I come across a stand of sheoaks or a windswept common boobialla drooping over a sculpture of strategically placed rocks. One wet day when I had the park to myself I gently squeezed a coast banksia flower and greedily sucked my fingers to taste the familiar nectar.

My lovely friend Kathryn came with me for a walk through the park and I was able to show her some of my lifesaving trees and plants. There wasn't a lot to see, certainly no fruits or berries, but I showed her the stands of coast banksias and sheoaks, and was able to tell her about the nectar and how I used sheoak branchlets as cushioning material. I think it brought home to both of us in quite a visceral way how harsh my life on the island had been.

We've had a couple of walks in local state parks as well and I think I'm having a bit of an influence. Her mother has all sorts of rules for women to live by, such as 'Never let a man see you without full makeup and high heels', so encouraging Kathryn to get out and about in sensible shoes and without worrying about appearances seems to me a good way to lighten her up and perhaps give her a chance of meeting some more down-to-earth blokes.

She's influencing me too. We've actually been out on a 'double date', with the compromise (for my sake) that it was a picnic in a park, not a night out clubbing. It was with two guys she met at a conference, not online. They were both earth scientists, and my guy, Bill, was keen on photography – had actually been to the exhibition I'd seen in St Kilda where I ran into Dave. If only I'd met Bill instead of Dave, my life would have been very different. And I have to admit it went rather well. I might even do it again.

I certainly want to break out of my hermit-like existence of working long hours and going home alone, broken up by occasional climbing holidays with virtual strangers. It's my time for a richer life, with friends, perhaps even a lover, and new horizons. Oddly enough, having seen Jonathan again has served to banish his ghost once and for all and left me ready to move on.

I know that being in the cave has left its mark on me. Although I don't have the dreams, even hallucinations, I experienced there, I feel forever changed. Stronger at my core, yet more vulnerable. It's as if a protective layer I had built up to shield me from harm, and perhaps from too much feeling, has been torn away, that I am now unarmoured in the face of life's slings and arrows.

When I was living like a castaway on the island I realised that this strange antipodean landscape has become my shelter and my friend. After years of not knowing where

I belong, I have found my true country. I didn't initially comprehend how close I came to crossing that wavering line between life and death, but what I did come to understand is that although sparse in gifts and harsh in nature, this unforgiving landscape has nurtured me and kept me alive. I have lived with this country as intimately as is humanly possible and I feel that I am part of it now and it is part of me.

Work has offered me time off whenever I need it, but I still have to wait on clearance from the police and the legal teams before I can leave the country. I won't get that until a date is finally set for Matthew Pentecost to go to trial.

When that time comes I know what I will do. I'm going to take extended leave and fly to Nederland to explore the place my parents thought of as Home. I might even visit Tante Leni in England and see if she has the answers to some of my questions about my mother.

Then I plan to visit Canada and have a long, long talk with my brother Abel, the kind of talk we have never really had.

And then I'll come home.

AUTHOR'S NOTE

The island in this book does not exist. If it did exist, it would be located in Corner Inlet off the coast of South Gippsland, Victoria, somewhere between Port Welshpool and Port Albert.

Professor Atkinson is also a figment of the author's imagination, although I think a copy of his guide should be in everyone's backpack.

READING GROUP QUESTIONS

1. What is your first impression of Alix? Does this change at all as the story progresses?
2. Does the fact that the novel is set on a remote island have any impact on how the story plays out? Would this story have worked in another setting?
3. Dave develops an unhealthy obsession with Alix, becoming her stalker. Were there any signs of Dave's obsession early on in the book, or in the beginning of Dave and Alix's relationship?
4. 'Some elements of the media, mainly gossip magazines and commercial current affairs shows, tried to make it into a romantic story, calling him "the Jailbird Casanova", but the more reputable media outlets described him as what he was, a stalker.' Does this passage about how stalking can be viewed by others ring true? Is there a fine line between romance and something more sinister?
5. 'One in five Australian women have experienced stalking in their lifetime.' Does this statistic surprise you? Given its prevalence, does the media give stalking enough attention?
6. It is clear that Alix learns a lot about survival from her time on the island. Does she learn any other lessons about her own life over the course of this journey?

7. Alix has had an unusual upbringing. How do you think her childhood experiences, such as living in Madagascar or being brought up by her puritanical father, influenced her personality and the ways in which she dealt with her ordeal on the island?

8. Alix suffers from a lot of trauma connected with her parents' death. How does this manifest throughout the book?

9. Alix has plenty of time to reflect on her relationships with the significant people in her life. Does anything change in her mental attitude to her friend Kathryn? Or her opinion regarding Lana?

10. How does this time of reflection affect Alix's attitude to her failed marriage?

11. How does this time of reflection affect Alix's feelings towards her family, in particular her brother?

12. What scene did you most enjoy in this story, and why?

13. Were there any surprises along the way?

14. Does the story reach a satisfactory conclusion?

15. Did you find the book's world believable?

16. What part, if any, do the epigraphs at the head of each chapter play in *Beware of Dogs*?

17. What feelings did this book evoke for you?

18. Are there any passages of text you found particularly appealing?

ACKNOWLEDGEMENTS

My deepest thanks are due to the people who have supported me from the moment this book came to me one night in a dream. First and most heartfelt thanks to my daughter, Christina Flann, who has been my reader, most dedicated supporter and most eagle-eyed critic throughout its gestation, and to Niels Bijl for his assistance with old and new secrets of the Dutch language.

I have also greatly appreciated the support of my writing companions, Richenda Rudman and Melanie Hayes, so huge thanks to them and also to Vikki Petraitis, who introduced us and taught us so many tricks of the trade.

I am deeply grateful to HarperCollins Publishers for making this book possible by awarding me The Banjo Prize for Australian fiction for 2019, to publisher Anna Valdinger and editor Rachel Dennis, who have done everything possible to ease the passage of *Beware of Dogs* towards publication, and to Lucy Inglis and Georgia Williams, who looked after the marketing and publicity.

Sincere thanks to all the people who helped by sharing their expertise, reading text, checking facts or just being supportive: in particular Freya Headlam, Sheila Drummond, Amanda Tokar, Meg Warren, Hilary Ash, Charles Meredith, Kay Hart and John Wallace. Thanks also to Dr Steve Sinclair, who very beautifully visualised the map Alix might have drawn in her field diary.

Elizabeth Flann worked in the publishing industry in both the UK and Australia. She then moved into academic teaching of writing and literature, completing her PhD on cultural myths in Australian film in 2001. She is a co-author of *The Australian Editing Handbook* and was a director and non-fiction writer for Sugar and Snails Press. Elizabeth lives by the sea in south-eastern Victoria.